W9-DDU-254
3 4028 07822 1240
HARRIS COUNTY PUBLIC LIBRARY

Do You Remember Me Now?

Do You Remember Me Now?

Karen Hanson Stuyck

FIVE STAR
A part of Gale, Cengage Learning

Detroit • New York • San Francisco • New Haven, Conn • Waterville, Maine • London

Set in 11 pt. Plantin.

LIBRARY OF CONGRESS CATALOGING-IN-PUBLICATION DATA

Stuyck, Karen Hanson.
Do you remember me now? / Karen Hanson Stuyck. — 1st ed.
p. cm.
ISBN-13: 978-1-59414-958-0 (hardcover)
ISBN-10: 1-59414-958-5 (hardcover)
1. Plastic surgeons—Fiction. 2. Women surgeons—Fiction. 3. Murder—Investigation—Fiction. 4. Class reunions—Fiction. 5. Identity (Psychology)—Fiction. I. Title.
PS3619.T89D6 2011
813'.6—dc22 2011004263

Published in 2011 in conjunction with Tekno Books and Ed Gorman.

Printed in Mexico
2 3 4 5 6 7 15 14 13 12 11

For my fellow Tuesday Writers: Ida, Julia, Irene, Lynne, Guida, Patsy, Vanessa, Jackie, and Louise. Many thanks for your suggestions, your editing, your support, and your friendship.

Prologue

The pain started early on the morning of her eighteenth birthday. *Happy birthday to me,* Jane thought, eyeing the line of beached whales lying in their beds. *You are now officially an adult. Old enough to vote and go to war. Or become a mother.*

Old enough to ruin your life before it's hardly begun, her father had told her, while her mother said nothing, only cried.

Jane lay there for a moment, wanting to make sure this was the real thing. Wanting too to avoid, until the last possible minute, her removal to the charity hospital maternity ward. She'd heard stories about the grim labor room, the tight-lipped nuns who ignored a girl's screams and—some of them—whisked the baby away before the new mother caught more than a glimpse of slippery skin or a tiny flailing arm.

"It may not seem like it now, but it's better for you not to make contact with the newborn," Sister Agnes had explained to her big-bellied charges at their prenatal orientation. "It's harder for you girls to resume your normal lives if you get attached to your babies." Harder for a girl to do the right thing—give away her baby to responsible married parents who would not make the child suffer for his mother's wantonness—Sister Agnes meant.

"Cali," Jane whispered to the girl sleeping next to her. "Cali, wake up." Cali was only 15, but as the oldest of nine children, she was knowledgeable about the intricacies of birth.

"What?" Cali opened one eye.

"I think I'm in labor. My water just broke!"

This time Cali sat up. "I'll go get someone."

A large crucifix hung on the wall of the labor room. Jane fixated on it, the intersecting lines blurring as the pain hit, her eyes focusing again on the burnished metal as the agony subsided.

"Let's see how dilated you are," a nurse, Sister Ignatius, said in a gentle voice. But her probing fingers made Jane gasp.

She shuddered, reminded of the pain ripping her insides when Todd entered her for the first—and only—time. Remembering the sour beer taste of his kiss, his fumbling hands, his "Oh, Jane, please—I really want you." Remembering too the silent ride afterward, Todd not meeting her eyes when she got out of the car a block from her house so her father wouldn't know that she hadn't been at the library.

"I'm afraid it will be a while, Jane," the nurse said. "First babies always take their time."

Another pain hit her. And despite vowing that she'd never think about it again, Jane envisioned the mocking note someone slipped into her locker the next day: At last! Plain Jane Gets Laid!

Lisa, the blonde Queen Bee of The Six, had made it all clear. "You don't think that Todd *wanted* to do it with you, do you, Jane? He's not *that* hard up. He just lost the bet. I made him pay up."

By the time Jane realized she was pregnant, The Six had forgotten about her, moved on to other prey. She heard whispered stories about these three all-powerful couples—stories too about their other victims: a football player whose leg was broken in a freak car accident shortly after he was slotted to take the quarterback job coveted by one of The Six; a high-strung girl who attempted suicide after the clique launched a smear campaign claiming she was a lesbian; another girl who transferred mid-year to a different school after being harassed into giving up her run for student council president.

Jane wasn't entirely sure about her own crimes against the clique. She was a candidate for class valedictorian, an honor coveted by the one brainy member of The Six. Then she and Lisa's boyfriend, a football star who Jane tutored, had smiled at each other in the hallway. *Don't Take What Is Ours:* that seemed the cardinal rule of The Six. And what they considered theirs seemed to encompass every accolade the school offered—as well as exclusive smiling rights to their boyfriends.

It was probably a testimony to Jane's invisibility, her non-entity status, that when she graduated, second in her class and six months pregnant, no one even noticed that beneath her graduation gown her belly was swelling like an inflatable beach ball.

Oh, God, oh, God, the pain was getting worse. Jane tried to focus on her baby fighting to be born. The infant she would refuse to sign over to strangers. She was eighteen; the decision was now hers.

She had planned this all out during those nights when her classmates were out partying and she sat alone in her bedroom. She and her baby would move out of state. She had enough money saved to support them until she found work and to provide a deposit for a decent apartment and good daycare. She'd already finished two college classes by correspondence and intended to keep up her studies while the baby slept. She was even thinking about legally changing her name. Plain Jane Murphy was ending her run.

"Not much longer now," the nurse said, smiling at her. "Doctor is on his way."

The baby made little mewling noises. "A girl," Sister Ignacious said, bringing her over for Jane to see.

She was so tiny, red-faced, and dark-haired. Jane reached out to touch her daughter's face, her tiny nose, and her rosebud mouth. All the suffering—everything—was worth it, payment, for this moment. "Such a pretty girl," she whispered. "Your mommy loves you, pretty girl."

Jane was only vaguely aware of the commotion at the other end of the table, the suddenly sharp voice of the doctor. "She's hemorrhaging," someone said right before a needle was jabbed into her arm. "Call her parents STAT."

She awoke in another room, feeling nauseated and dizzy, an IV connected to her arm, her mother standing beside her. "Ah, you're awake, Jane. How do you feel?"

"Awful." She tried to smile. "I thought I was supposed to feel better once the baby was born."

"You had to have an operation. You were losing too much blood. To save your life the surgeon had to remove your uterus."

Jane stared at her. "I want to see my baby." The only baby she would ever have.

Tears in her eyes, her mother leaned over and took Jane's hand. "I'm so sorry, honey. Your baby's lungs weren't developed. The doctors tried to save her, but they couldn't." She paused and swallowed. "Your father says maybe it's for the best. Now you can get back to your old plans, go to college just like you always wanted."

Jane's howl—a high, animal sound—filled the room, obliterating everything: her white-faced mother, the hospital with its totally inadequate medical capabilities, and even Jane herself. Plain Jane, Maimed Jane, Pained Jane.

Sorry. So sorry. They did not even know the meaning of the word.

One

She could see it in his eyes. The man was thrilled, thinking that he'd talked her into coming to his room.

"It's so noisy down here," he'd said in the hotel bar. "We'll have more privacy in my room. Have a chance to talk and really get to know each other"—he tried to hide his glance at her conference name badge with a big, shit-eating grin—"Juliet."

"That sounds like fun"—she peered at his nametag—"Todd. Do you think we could take a bottle of champagne upstairs with us? I'd love to sip champagne while we chat."

So here they were, sitting thigh to thigh on the faded plaid couch, sipping mediocre champagne while he launched into verbal foreplay. "I could tell the minute I spotted you at the reception you were someone I'd like to know."

He clearly didn't recognize her. "And what exactly made you suspect that?"

He laughed nervously. "Why everything about you—the way you carry yourself, the way you dress and speak, your whole aura of confidence."

Aura of confidence? Not the boobs that were spilling out of her too-tight suit? Or the long, to-die-for legs so well displayed by her mini-skirt? She studied him, noticing the rapidly receding hairline, the jowls, and the beginning of a pot gut. Maybe ten or even five years ago, this b.s. had worked for him. Or maybe he'd only thought it did.

She slid a few inches away from him. "Tell me about yourself.

Just who is Todd Lawson?"

He blinked, then grinned and gave her his spiel. He was in pharmaceutical sales, started in the company right out of school, a lucky break since he'd spent his college career majoring in the three b's: business, boozin', and babes—not necessarily in that order.

She didn't chuckle. "Are you married, Todd?" When he nodded, she added, "Kids?"

"Yeah, a six-year-old boy and a four-year-old girl."

"Have any pictures?"

He looked surprised, but pulled out a photo from his wallet. She studied it: a skinny boy with a missing front tooth and a dark-haired little girl with a shy smile sat on either side of a once-pretty woman with bleached blonde hair and desperate eyes, while Todd, smiling vacantly, stood behind them. "Cute kids," she said. "The little girl looks just like you."

"Thanks. You have any kids?"

She shook her head. "Were you and your wife high school sweethearts?

"You're a regular Barbara Walters, aren't you? Next you'll want to know what kind of tree I'd be."

He was annoyed, she saw, but tried to hide it as a joke. So the wife was a touchy topic. Maybe Mrs. Todd had heard about his behavior at sales conferences.

She picked up her champagne and stood.

"No, don't go." Todd looked alarmed. "I—I was just kidding. My wife and I started dating in college, met at a frat party."

She refilled her glass and sat down. "I guess I have high school on the brain. I just went to my ten-year reunion—*not* a fun experience. You look like you might have been a big jock, Todd, one of those guys who actually enjoyed high school."

He looked relieved. At the topic of his high school glory years or at the fact that she hadn't walked out? "I was a basketball player. And senior class president."

She whistled. "I bet I would have had a lot more fun at the reunion if I'd been senior class president."

"The only people who have fun at those things are the ones who made good after high school. My fifteen-year one is coming up, and I don't even feel like going."

He shook his head. "You know who had the best time at my ten-year reunion? It was the class valedictorian—the guy we all called 'Nerd'—who drove up in his Jaguar with a gorgeous blonde girlfriend. While all the rest of us went to Podunk U, Nerd went to Harvard, and then on to Yale Law School. Sure, some of us made his life miserable in high school, but he rubbed all our noses in it: letting us know he was pulling down a quarter million a year *and* regularly fucking the blonde. *That's* retribution, man."

The memory made him scowl. "Seeing Nerd even made me wish I'd actually opened a few books during high school. My test scores were great—I had a 1350 on my SATs—but my grades were shit. No decent college would touch me."

"So if you could go back and do it over again, you would have been a nerd too?"

"You mean would I choose to suffer then or suffer now?" He laughed bitterly. "I bet Nerd's wife doesn't whine nonstop about money. So I guess it's a choice between either being a party animal in high school and turning into a middle-aged nonentity or serving four years in solitary as a teenager and ten years later becoming a yuppie success story."

"But sometimes those four years in solitary leave scars that even making a quarter mil a year can't cure," she said.

He shrugged, clearly losing interest in the subject.

"What about the other kids at the top of your class, Todd? Did they all make good too?"

"Don't know. Most of them were the kind of people whose

names you forget the day after graduation, though a buddy of mine managed to be number three. He's a doctor in town, saw him a few nights ago. But Josh is one of those people with a photographic memory—he didn't have to work at getting great grades, not like all those geeks who did nothing but study." He grinned. "On second thought, maybe I wouldn't choose to be a nerd. It was a pretty pathetic life, man."

He leaned close enough for her to smell the alcohol on his breath. "Bet *you* weren't a nerd, Juliet. You look more like the homecoming queen or a cheerleader."

"You'd be surprised. I was kind of shy back then, not much of a joiner."

"Oh, yeah?" he said, obviously not listening.

The effect of all the liquor he'd drunk was catching up with him, she thought. She stood, holding her champagne glass.

"Hey! Where you goin'?"

"Bathroom. If that's okay with you."

"Be my guest." He snickered. "Maybe when you come back you'll want to get into something more comfortable."

"Maybe." *Maybe not.*

In the bathroom she locked the door, then pulled the baggie from her skirt pocket. Emptying the powder into the champagne, she stirred the drink with her finger, cursing under her breath when the drug didn't totally dissolve. Would he notice the residue at the bottom of the glass? Well, she'd just have to make sure he didn't.

"I've got a little surprise for you, Todd." She pulled off her jacket, then stripped out of the tight knit shell.

Yup, she'd got his attention all right. She set her champagne on the table and picked up his glass.

Slowly, provocatively, she poured the liquid over her breasts. "I thought you might be getting thirsty."

"Oh, yeah." He pulled her onto the couch and started lapping at her.

"Whoa, boy! Take it easy." She laughed and reached behind her for her champagne glass and pretended to take a drink. Then offered the glass to him.

He shook his head. "I've got everything I need, baby."

Shit. "Have a little drink for Momma," she cooed, pressing the glass to his lips.

He looked like he was going to balk, then took a tiny sip.

"I hate to waste this expensive champagne," she pouted. "I thought we'd finish the bottle before we moved to the bedroom."

He gulped the liquid, then pulled her to her feet. Unsteadily, he maneuvered them to the king-sized bed.

"Here, let me help you out of those old clothes, Toddie."

He grinned as she pulled off his shoes, then moved on to his shirt and t-shirt. She massaged his bare shoulders. "Sure you don't remember me, Todd?"

He looked confused. Then he shook his head. "I woulda remembered a babe like you."

Yeah, right. She wasn't even sure why she bothered to ask. At this point she could probably tell him she was Julia Roberts and he'd only nod idiotically.

You don't have to do this, a voice in her head advised. *You can stop right now.*

He deserves it, the other voice argued. *All of them do.*

But there are consequences to our actions. It was the gentle voice of Dr. Sanders, talking to her in the hospital. Such a kind and earnest man, Dr. Sanders. So completely out of touch with real life.

"Now let me take off *your* clothes," Todd said, the words starting to slur.

She tried to keep her voice flirtatious. "Aren't you the impatient one? Just give me a minute, big boy, and then we'll get down to business."

Heart pounding, she rummaged through her big tote bag to find what she needed.

His eyes were half closed, but he apparently managed to take in her plastic coverall, the gloves she was pulling on. And the knife. "Hey, what ya doin'?"

She could hear the fear in his voice. This time her smile was genuine. "Relax, Todd. You're only getting what you deserve."

Two

"Jane, is it really you?"

The gaunt, bald woman in the doorway looked more like the victim of a concentration camp than the woman Jane remembered—the robust, gray-haired matron with a too-tight perm.

"It's really me." Jane stepped inside and wrapped her arms around her mother, feeling as if she were embracing a skeleton. Remembering the oncologist's words during their phone conversation: "Your mother has Stage III leukemia. All we can do at this point is make her as comfortable as possible. If you were planning on seeing her, I suggest you go right away."

"I'm so glad you've finally come to visit." Her mother graciously emphasized the "glad," rather than the "finally."

"Me too," she lied. Only a life-threatening crisis had brought her back to Houston. That and a massive dose of guilt.

"I want you to see what I've done with the house," her mother said, leading her to the living room. "After your father died I decided to make some changes."

Jane left her suitcase in the hall and entered the dark, formal room she'd always hated. She gasped. Once crammed with heavy Victorian antiques, the living room had been transformed into a sunny, plant-filled space with cheerful, overstuffed furniture.

"It's wonderful, Mom." A bit too much flowered chintz for her taste, but a dramatic improvement over the oppressive room she remembered.

Her mother smiled, pleased by her reaction. "I always disliked those ornate antiques your father inherited from his grandmother. But he always used to say how privileged we were to live with the family history. After he died, though, I decided those ugly things weren't part of *my* family history, and I went out and bought furniture I liked."

"Yes, the room looks like you," Jane said, thinking of her own bare apartment in Chicago: no art on the walls, no plants, no photos, only the most essential furniture. A new neighbor who'd come over to introduce herself had looked around and said, "Oh, did you just move in too?" Jane had muttered something about being gone a lot, not wanting to admit she'd actually lived in the same place for over five years.

Her mother's plants—African violets, geraniums—had always been relegated to her domain, the kitchen. Her father had not wanted any splashes of color mixed in with the hideous family antiques. Now a white étagère held rows of flowering plants, and several larger plants sat on the floor.

Jane could feel tears well in her eyes. So much had happened since she'd last visited, and she hadn't even known it. When her father was still alive, she'd told herself that staying away was necessary for her mental health. But why hadn't she come more often after he'd died? Sure, she was busy—she was always busy—but she could have found a day or two to see her mother. Thank God when she'd phoned last week to wish her mom a happy birthday, her supremely stoical parent mentioned that she'd just got out of the hospital.

"Don't you think you should sit down, Mom? Let me go make us some tea."

To her surprise, her mother—the woman who'd always bustled about, attending to others' needs—sat. "That would be very nice, dear. I should make the tea for you, but I'm always so tired lately."

"How about a little nap?" Jane grabbed a flowered afghan and spread it over the stick-thin body on the couch.

"I'm not an invalid, I'm just a little weak. And why would I waste my time sleeping when I could be visiting with you?"

"I'm not going anywhere. When you wake up we'll have lots of time to talk."

Her mother nodded. "I'd like that, getting a chance to spend time with my girl."

My girl who's spent barely a few days with me during the last fifteen years. Somehow her mother's *not* saying it made Jane feel even guiltier.

Jane touched a bony arm. "I—I want to take care of you, Mom. Won't you let me do that?"

Her mother nodded. "I keep forgetting you're a doctor now."

Jane smiled. "And Doctor knows best." Never mind that her expertise was in a totally unrelated field. As her mother's eyes closed, Jane sneaked out of the room.

She headed for the kitchen. Comfort food, that was what the woman needed to tempt her to eat a little. Meat loaf, baked potatoes, one of those green beans, cream of mushroom soup, and onion rings casseroles her mother used to make—fortunately all recipes among Jane's very limited repertoire.

Her mom was still sleeping when Jane returned from the grocery store and threw together the meatloaf and green bean casserole.

The house suddenly seemed too quiet, like a faintly sinister mausoleum. But that was the way it had always seemed, hadn't it? Or had she only felt that way during the last, miserable year she'd lived here?

"Jane?" Her mother's voice, immediately behind her, made her jump.

"I didn't hear you coming. Did you have a good nap?"

"Fine. Oh, you didn't have to make dinner."

"But I wanted to. I want you to eat."

"That was sweet of you, dear, though I don't have much of an appetite these days."

Her mother sat at the round oak table and openly studied her daughter. "You almost look like a different person, Jane. I can see your nose is changed. What else did you do?"

Jane could feel the sudden tension in her shoulders. "I had rhinoplasty—cosmetic nose surgery—and a chin implant. And I've probably changed my hair and lost weight since you saw me."

"I thought you looked perfectly fine before," her mother said primly.

But you thought everything was perfectly fine before. That was part of the problem. "You were definitely in the minority with that opinion, I'm afraid," Jane said. Before her mother could continue the discussion, she added, "The food has been ready for a while. Let's eat."

They ate in silence for a few minutes before her mother said, "Would you mind if I turn on the news?" She motioned to a small television on the kitchen counter. "I've gotten into the habit of watching it while I eat."

"Sure." Jane got up to turn on the local news.

"The food is very good," her mother said, although she'd hardly touched it.

The weekend news anchor was listing the latest local crimes. A high school junior had just been arrested after he e-mailed a friend about his plan to shoot the jocks who'd bullied him at school. A psychologist, an animated woman about Jane's age, was interviewed about the arrest. "After several tragic school shootings, high schools have instituted zero-tolerance policies about bringing weapons on campus," the woman said. "But what disturbs me is that too many schools still ignore the behavior that makes those kids want to shoot their classmates:

the powerful students' bullying of the kids they view as weak or misfits."

"At least when you were in high school, students weren't shooting the people they disliked," her mother said.

Not that we didn't want to, Jane thought, concentrating on her meatloaf.

The anchor was describing other crimes now. A Dallas man had been killed last night at a business convention in downtown Houston. His body was discovered by a hotel maid that morning.

Her mother pointed at the screen. "Wasn't that boy in high school with you?"

Jane stared at the jowly, smiling face of Todd Lawson—some official photo, a company mug shot. She nodded. "He was president of our senior class."

"Who would do something like that—slashing that poor man's throat? That's terrible."

Jane shook her head and took another bite.

Three

Officer Sam Wolfe took a deep breath before entering the hotel room. A queasy stomach—as he was reminded at every crime scene—was a major liability for a homicide detective.

The crime scene officer photographing the body looked up as he walked in. "Hey, it's Detective Upchuck. You're going to love this case, Sam. Really bloody. Someone cut the guy's throat."

Sam steeled himself and took his first look at the victim: Caucasian, thirtyish, lying in bed wearing only his boxers—and God, yes, covered in blood. He glanced at Dr. Sandra Jones, a stocky, prematurely white-haired pathologist who was inspecting the body. "Any idea what kind of knife was used?"

"The cut's very neat and precise, almost like a scalpel."

"Wouldn't there be some defensive wounds? The guy holding up his hands to protect himself or fight off the assailant?"

Dr. Jones shook her head. "There aren't any. Maybe he was unconscious when it happened. Or maybe the killer did it while he was sleeping."

She stood. "And in answer to your next question, I'm not sure yet of the time of death. Sometime late last night, I'd guess. I can't tell you any more right now. The hotel maid found him here about nine-thirty this morning."

"Scalpel?" Sam asked. "Does that mean a homicidal surgeon on the loose? Or maybe a crazed pathologist?"

The pathologist sent him a sour smile. "Could have been any knife with a thin blade. As I said, I'll know more later."

Sam shifted his attention to the rest of the room. No signs of struggle. The man had folded his clothes—khaki pants, blue dress shirt, a tie—on the back of a chair, his shoes underneath. The coffee table was empty, the toiletries precisely arranged in the bathroom. A real neatnik.

Pulling on a pair of gloves, he gingerly picked up the man's clothes. A conference badge was still stuck on the shirt: Hello I'm TODD LAWSON. The man's wallet was in the pants pocket. Sam pulled it out. Inside were sixty-eight dollars, a Visa card, and a driver's license for Todd R. Lawson of Dallas. The guy was thirty-three, six feet tall, 198 pounds. The photo showed a jowly guy with a cocky smile and receding hairline.

"I'm going to check out that conference downstairs and talk to the hotel staff. See if anyone can tell me about Mr. Lawson's activities last night."

The photographer didn't look up. "Have fun," he said.

The maid who'd found the body was only a high school girl, red-haired and freckled, who worked at the hotel after school and weekends. She reminded Sam of his daughter Carly—a few years older but with the same coloring and aura of shy vulnerability. That and the fact she seemed so badly shaken made Sam want to pat her shoulder and cancel their interview. Instead, he tried to smile reassuringly when he asked her what she'd seen.

"I thought no one was in the room," the girl said, in a high, scared voice. "No one answered when I knocked."

Sam nodded encouragingly. "So you went inside."

"Yeah, and at first I didn't see anything. The covers were all pulled up, so I didn't know he was in the bed. But the smell—it was awful!" The girl started to sway in her chair.

Sam jumped up and pushed the girl's head between her knees. "Take slow, deep breaths. You're going to be okay."

God, he needed to find a new career. It was hard sometimes to remember that he was supposed to be the good guy.

"Just a few more questions," he said when the girl sat up again. He showed her the victim's driver's license photo. "Did you ever see this man before?" She shook her head. "You didn't see anything else unusual about the room?" *Other than a dead body, of course.*

"There *was* something kind of weird. Like I said, the covers were all pulled up on the bed, but on top of them was the Do Not Disturb sign, almost like someone was making sure I didn't look at the body. And I didn't—I ran out to find my supervisor and she called the police."

A murderer who put a Do Not Disturb sign on his victim? Either a killer with a sick sense of humor or someone sympathetic to hotel maids. "Interesting," he told the girl. "Anything else you remember?

She hesitated. "Is there some kind of murderer running around the hotel? Was anybody else attacked?"

"No, it looks like an isolated incident. I'm sure whoever did it is long gone." In fact, he wasn't sure of anything at this point, but it seemed the least he could do for the kid.

He closed his notebook. "Tell your supervisor I said you should go home now. You made your statement and you've had a big shock."

"Okay." She was still sitting, staring at her hands, when he left.

The next woman he interviewed was, thank God, older and tougher, a gaunt, middle-aged woman who said she'd worked with Todd in computer sales. She shook her head. "He was like a frat boy who never grew up."

"Was he doing a lot of drinking at the conference?"

The woman rolled her eyes. "Most people drink a lot at these things, but Todd was in a class by himself. One night a group of us went out for dinner, and Todd got so plastered that two guys had to take him up to his room and put him to bed."

"Who do you think might have wanted to kill Mr. Lawson?"

She blinked, looking startled. After a minute, she said, "A lot of people would have liked to, though I don't see any of them going through with it. Todd could be very affable and he was a good salesman, but his drinking was a big problem. He was unreliable and had a real chip on his shoulder—kind of an 'I am meant for better things' attitude. I overheard him cussing out Bill, our boss, when he told Todd to shape up. Todd may not have realized it, but it was only a matter of time before he got fired."

"Is your boss here at the conference?"

She shook her head. "He stayed home this year. His wife is expecting their first baby."

Sam jotted down the boss's name anyway. "In this argument you overheard, did Todd threaten the man?"

"Not threatened exactly. He did imply that it might be Bill who was out of a job soon—which was total bull."

"Todd have any of these fights at the conference?"

"Not that I heard of. I tried to steer clear of him as much as possible." She paused, looking suddenly tired. "I know Todd could be obnoxious, but he didn't deserve to die like that."

The next person Sam interviewed was another colleague of Todd's, just out of college and new to the company. One of the two guys who'd helped Lawson to his room.

"I understand Mr. Lawson was a big drinker," Sam said. "You see him get into any arguments at the conference?"

"No, and I was with him almost every night. Todd was a real party animal. After the first night, when he passed out in the restaurant, he gave me his extra door key so I could make sure he got back to his room."

"He give anyone else a key?"

The kid shrugged. "Don't know. But I only had to help him to bed that first night. The rest of the time he managed on his own." He grinned. "The second night I saw him in the elevator with this big blonde from the conference, Sally Somebody from Austin. She was almost as drunk as he was."

"Was he with Sally last night too?"

"Don't think so. At least I didn't see her around. Todd was flirting with some other women at our table, coming on kind of strong; one of them told him to get lost. He looked pissed, saying he was going to see if he had better luck at the hotel bar."

"You remember what time that was?"

The kid thought about it. "It was about ten o'clock. I was going clubbing with a girl I met at the conference. Todd seemed kind of envious that I was with a woman and he wasn't. I think getting old really bothered him."

Thirty-eight-year-old Sam tried not to smile.

"You know it's probably nothing," the kid said, "but Todd seemed really angry with his wife. Kept on talking about not wanting to go home—'back to jail and that money-grubbing bitch.' "

It was another angle worth pursuing: Both Todd's wife and his boss might have been very happy to get Todd out of the picture. Probably both of them, back in Dallas, had solid alibis for last night. Was one of them angry enough to have hired a hit man? Though Sam had never heard of any professional who went in for throat slashing.

He thanked the kid, who looked relieved to head back to the conference, and went to check out the hotel bar. As he expected, the bartender on duty last night was off now.

Sam ordered a soft drink and sat down at a booth to reread his notes. Todd Lawson, cheating husband, unreliable employee, mean drunk, was definitely not a prize specimen. *So who hated you enough to cut your throat, Todd? Was it someone you encountered at the conference? Maybe a former colleague you'd screwed over? Or was it someone who came to the hotel especially to get rid of you?*

It was too soon to even venture a guess about the perp's motive, but Sam knew this much: Whoever killed Todd Lawson had carefully planned this murder. He'd bet a month's pay on it.

Four

"And I go by my middle name now," Jane said, slipping in the information along with her other news: she'd found a temporary medical job that would allow her to stay in town and take care of her mother.

"You call yourself Katherine Murphy?" her mother asked. She'd been an elementary teacher until she "retired" to raise Jane, and she'd kept her old knack for uncovering half-truths.

The former Jane Katherine Murphy took a deep breath. "Katherine Dalton, actually, except everyone calls me Kate." Her disastrous marriage to Nat Dalton had barely lasted through one year of medical school, but she'd liked his name, liked ditching "Murphy" even more.

"But you haven't been married to him for years. I just assumed you went back to using your maiden name. What was wrong with Kate Murphy?"

Jane hesitated. There hadn't seemed any point in telling her parents that she was still using her married name. It would only have hurt their feelings and she couldn't have explained to them anyway why she needed to be as far removed from Plain Jane Murphy as humanly possible. But if she was going to live and work here for even a few months, she had to tell her mother *something*. If someone from the practice called asking for Dr. Kate Dalton, she didn't want her mother saying, "Sorry, you've got the wrong number."

She took a deep breath. "After everything that happened, I

wanted a new identity. I worked hard to become the kind of person I wanted to be." Not a victim anymore, not poor Plain Jane. "And Kate Dalton seems a better fit somehow."

Her mother's thin lips tightened into a long, disapproving dash. "So you changed your name and your face, and you pretended your past never existed."

"More or less." Though it hadn't been that easy. You didn't change a name, a nose, and a chin and instantly stop being the person you'd been for most of your life.

"Did it work—this transformation?"

Jane thought about it. "Sometimes." And sometimes there were disadvantages to being a self-creation.

Her mother looked tired, suddenly sapped of the energy that earlier that morning animated her pale face. Was Jane fooling herself by thinking her return could actually help her mother? Perhaps her desire to make up for all the years she'd avoided her parents' company was selfishness on her part—an atonement that only made her mother suffer more.

"Was your life as Jane Murphy really that bad?"

Oh, God, she should never have come back. "Not all of it, not my childhood." *Don't make me say it, Mom. Don't make me hurt you.*

Her mother stared at her, then said, "So what am I supposed to call you: Kate, Katherine, Jane?"

"Call me whatever you want."

Shakily her mother stood. "I'm going back to bed, Kate. I'm feeling tired."

Being a good cosmetic surgeon requires equal parts technical competence and artistic flair, and Dr. Belinda Ross obviously was using her office to impress potential patients with her sense of aesthetics. Kate liked the sleek, black and white art deco furnishings, the cool, pale-gray walls. She suspected she'd like

Dr. Ross too, if she ever met her. The framed photo of Belinda and her husband sitting on the desk showed a trim woman with a short, no-nonsense haircut and a warm smile.

Kate was seeing her patients for the four or five months Dr. Ross would be gone on maternity leave. It had seemed an ideal setup when she heard about the job: temporary, good-paying medical work she could do for the short time she was in Houston. And because the practice focused on cosmetic surgery, the hours were decent too.

So what if it wasn't the kind of practice she wanted to join or, for that matter, in the part of the country she wanted to live? For now it would serve her purpose, allowing her to be with her mother during her last months, do the work she was trained for, and also pay off some of her enormous student loans.

One of the nurses stuck her head in the door. "Your nine o'clock, Lisa Smythe, is here. A consultation for another procedure." She handed Kate the medical file.

There was something about the way she said it that made clear the woman was not a big fan of Ms. Smythe's. "She's had other surgery?" Kate asked, flipping open the chart but not really looking at the details inside.

"Oh, yeah. Boob job, wrinkle jobs, a little fat removal." The nurse rolled her eyes. "And none of it is ever as good as she thinks it should be. I'm just warning you . . ."

"I appreciate that." Kate smiled. "I guess I'm as prepared as I'll ever be. Send her in."

Two minutes later Lisa Smythe stormed into the office.

Oh, Lord! Kate tried to keep her expression pleasant. "Hello, Ms. Smythe, I'm Dr. Dalton." She offered her hand to the immaculately groomed blonde woman with the cold blue eyes. Lisa Casey? Apparently she was now Lisa Smythe—fifteen years older but not significantly changed since high school. Kate nearly choked as she forced herself to cover an involuntary gasp of recognition.

"It's *Mrs.* Smythe." The woman looked as if she wanted to ignore Kate's outstretched hand, but compromised by barely touching it. "My appointment was with Belinda Ross. Where is she?"

"Dr. Ross is on maternity leave for a few months. I'm filling in for her."

"Her due date is three months from now. She told me she'd be here."

"There were some complications, and her obstetrician prescribed bed rest. I understand she plans to come back to work eight weeks after the birth."

Mrs. Smythe shook her head in disgust. "I told her that forty is too old to have a first baby."

And I'm sure she appreciated your considered opinion, Kate thought. "Do you have children of your own?"

"Thank God, no. I have enough problems keeping my weight under control without having to deal with that. My husband has two daughters from a previous marriage so his paternal urges are taken care of."

"What can I do for you, Mrs. Smythe?"

Looking petulant, the woman moved to one of the facing black leather-and-chrome chairs and sat. "I'm not sure that you can do anything."

Kate sat on the opposite chair. "That's fine. I can understand you wanting to wait until Dr. Ross gets back. They can make an appointment for you at the front desk."

"The problem is that I can't wait that long. I have an upcoming event I want to look good for."

"Perhaps you'd prefer another doctor then."

Mrs. Smythe studied her, a head-to-toe inspection that made Kate want to lean forward and smack her on one unlined cheek. "Perhaps," she finally said. "But perhaps I'd prefer you."

Don't do me any favors, Kate thought. "What did you want to have done?"

"Right now I want liposuction on my butt. Three months from now I want to be able to fit into a tight cocktail dress that shows off my boobs and my great new ass. Then, maybe a month before the reunion, I'll get more Botox injections for my face."

"Reunion?"

"My fifteen-year high school reunion. I don't want anyone to say 'Did you see Lisa's fat ass?' "

Instead of saying, That Lisa, isn't she *an ass?* Kate squelched a snicker and said, "The recovery time for buttocks liposuction can take four to six weeks. You'll also have to wear a girdle-like support garment for the first month."

The woman waved her hand. "I know all that."

"There are also other options besides liposuction. Liposculpture, for instance, can change the shape of your buttocks. Fat is removed, often from the inner thigh, and then transplanted to the upper and outer buttock to make it higher."

Mrs. Smythe scowled. "I don't have a droopy ass. I just want fat removed. And Dr.—Dalton, is it?—I am very aware of all my surgical options." She paused. "Do I know you from somewhere? There's something familiar about you."

Kate willed herself to stay calm. "I don't think we've met. I've been in the Chicago area for the last ten years. Went to medical school and did my residency there."

"Must be mistaken then." Her eyes narrowed. "Now you have done this procedure before, haven't you? I want someone who has a lot of experience."

"Yes, I've done it several times, but as I said, you might be more comfortable with another surgeon. If you like, I can refer you to someone who does a lot of liposuction." *Please, go make another doctor miserable.*

Lisa shook her head, making the long blonde hair that was

only a shade or two lighter than it used to be, momentarily cover her face. "Since I'm here already, you might as well finish the consultation." At which time, I will determine if you are worthy, her tone said.

Kate took a deep breath before entering the examining room. Lisa now sat in an open-backed smock. She stood up when Kate came in and turned around to expose her butt. "So what do you think?" she asked over her shoulder.

Kate marveled that someone baring her buttocks to a clothed stranger could sound so arrogant. "I think you don't really need liposuction. You have a little extra localized fat, but you can probably get rid of it by exercising. You do work out?"

"Of course I work out," Lisa said testily, as if Kate had implied she didn't brush her teeth. "I exercise with a trainer for ten hours a week." Then, with less certainty, she added, "Why, do you know some special butt exercises?"

"You can use a stair stepper machine but put your weight on your heels instead of on your toes. That isolates the buttock muscles. It increases the size of the gluteus maximus and reduces the amount of fat."

"Okay, I'll start doing that."

"Great. Good luck with it." Kate turned to leave the room.

"Wait! I mean I'll do that exercise after I get the liposuction. I told you. I need fast results. And I've decided I'll let you do the procedure. You seem knowledgeable enough."

Gee thanks, Kate thought. Did this narcissistic bitch expect her to feel grateful that she'd be allowed to siphon off two or three pounds of extra fat from Lisa's ass?

"Well, when can you do it?" Lisa demanded.

It was the voice that had haunted Kate's dreams: high-pitched, smug, unapologetically ruthless.

Five

"I'm Officer Sam Wolfe," Sam told the hotel bartender, showing the man his badge.

The bartender, young and stocky with tired eyes, sighed. "It's about the man who got murdered upstairs, right?"

"Todd Lawson." Sam showed him a photo of Lawson with his family. "You remember him?"

"Oh, yeah. He was at the bar every night of that sales conference, sometimes with a group of people, sometimes by himself. The guy was a big drinker."

"You talk to him at all?"

"Not much. He was more interested in picking up chicks than in talking to me."

"He have any luck at it?"

The bartender shrugged. "He had a drink with a few of them. Don't know what happened once they left here. I saw him with a tall blonde one night and with a short redhead another—don't remember which nights."

The guy seemed nervous for someone not accused of any crime, Sam thought. Perhaps he'd had some previous negative experiences with the police? Or maybe he knew something about Todd Lawson that he didn't feel like sharing.

Sam tried to look unthreatening. "I'm just trying to get a sense of what Lawson was like. Big drinker, skirt chaser. What else can you tell me?"

"Bad temper. He came on pretty strong to the women and

really pissed off a few of them. One girl—in her twenties, pretty drunk herself—started screaming at him. Called him something like a 'pathetic old lech.' I thought Lawson was going to slug her, but this big guy from another table—looked like a former pro football player—got into the act. He pushed Lawson away from the girl and told him to get lost."

"What did Lawson do?"

"Got lost." The bartender grinned. "He was plastered, not stupid. But the next night when he came to the bar I heard him brag that he'd slashed the girl's and the big guy's tires after he left. Don't know if it's true. How'd he even know what they were driving? But he seemed like the kind of man who'd slash someone's tires and then run to hide in his room."

"You think one of them might have decided to slash Todd back?"

The wary look returned to his face. "Couldn't say. Doubt it though. I bet the drunk—Lawson?—just made up the whole tire story to save face, and I only saw that girl and the big guy that one time."

Sam still suspected that the bartender was not telling everything he knew. He shook his head, trying to look rueful. "Everything I hear about Lawson makes him sound like a real jerk."

The guy didn't take the bait. "Yeah, but if someone murdered all the jerks, who'd be left to hang out in bars?"

Under better circumstances, Sam thought, Heather Lawson would have been pretty in a blonde, aging sorority girl way, a tall, trim woman who probably spent a lot of time in the gym.

Of course no one looked her best while identifying her husband's body. These days you didn't have to see the actual corpse, but even the photos of Todd Lawson's body were hard to take. Mrs. Lawson glanced at the image on the computer screen and shuddered. "Yes, that's Todd."

Sam took her to a conference room to talk. "I only have a few questions." He noticed how pale she looked. "Can I get you a cup of coffee or a soft drink?"

"Water would be great."

When he came back with her water and coffee for himself, she looked a little better.

"It's horrible seeing Todd like that," she said. "I mean they told me what happened to him, but that still doesn't prepare you for actually seeing it."

"Everyone says that. It's a very upsetting experience."

"Have you found out who killed him?"

"Not yet. That's one of the reasons I wanted to talk to you."

"You expect *me* to know who killed him?"

He tried to look reassuring. "You probably know more than you think. For instance, did your husband have any enemies?"

Most people immediately said "no" or "no, except for . . . ," but Heather Lawson paused. Then she said, "Not enemies exactly. More like people who didn't like him. You have to understand about Todd. He was very competitive. Everything had to be his way."

"And that made a lot of people dislike him?"

"Not at first. When I met him in college, people thought he was charismatic. He was president of his fraternity, funny, and athletic. But later, after we were married and had the kids, a lot of the stuff that seemed so cool in college—the way Todd could drink everyone under the table, his clever put-downs, the practical jokes—just seemed immature and kind of pathetic."

She shook her head, tears running down her face. "I just wanted him to grow up. But now he never will."

Sam handed her his handkerchief. He gave her time to regain her composure before he asked, "Have you thought of anyone in particular who was angry with him?"

Her laugh was bitter. "*I* certainly was. We had stacks of bills, could barely pay the minimum on our credit cards, and still he'd go on spending like we were millionaires. We had terrible fights about money. Right before he left for the conference Todd told me he wanted to buy himself a new BMW. We're on the verge of bankruptcy and he wants to buy a new car to impress everyone at his high school reunion!"

Could that have been the last straw for a wife who couldn't force her spendthrift, alcoholic husband to grow up? Might Heather Lawson have decided that she'd be further ahead financially as a widow than as a divorcee—particularly if Todd had decent life insurance? She might even have been the tall blonde who the bartender saw with Todd: *Surprise, honey, I've come from Dallas to have a special night alone with you.*

Sam made a mental note to check on Mr. Lawson's life insurance policy.

"Anyone else who was especially angry with him?" he asked.

"He seemed to be having a lot of problems at work. Todd carried on about how his new boss was out to get him. Todd hated him. Said the boss, Bill Neely, was a tight-ass workaholic. I think Bill wanted to fire Todd. But Todd said it wasn't going to happen."

"Why not?"

"I asked him that, but he just got a strange look on his face. All he'd say was he intended to have Bill's job—and soon. He was going to drive up to his high school reunion in his new car and tell everyone about his big promotion."

Sam raised his eyebrows. "You have no idea how he intended to get his boss's job?"

She shook her head. "All he'd tell me was that he was a master of dirty tricks, and I should have confidence in him."

Sam wondered if the master of dirty tricks might have slashed the bar patrons' tires after all. Or if he'd pulled some stunt on his boss and the guy decided to get rid of Todd in a more permanent way than firing.

"Anyone else you can think of?"

The flinty look he'd glimpsed earlier returned to the widow's face. "Well there are a number of young women who probably won't cry at Todd's funeral. I don't know their names. Todd had this nasty habit of seducing and running. It made him think he wasn't being unfaithful—he didn't love these women, he told me, he just slept with them a few times. The way I see it, that's one hell of a lot of rejected, pissed-off women."

Sam, watching her, didn't doubt for a minute who was the most pissed-off woman of them all.

Six

Kate glanced around the table at her new colleagues, wishing she were somewhere—anywhere—else.

"Tell us about yourself, Kate," Dr. Aaron Glass, the senior partner of the group, said with a genial grin. Dr. Glass—"call me Aaron; everyone else does"—had insisted on taking her and the other doctors in the practice out for dinner so they could all get acquainted.

Never mind that Kate didn't particularly *want* to get acquainted. She had no problem with being pleasant, cooperative, collegial, but the idea of sharing personal information made her queasy. Particularly after encountering Lisa, the Bitch from the Past, that morning.

"There's really not much to tell," she said. "I just finished my residency in plastic surgery. I intended to work in the Chicago area, but then I found out that my mother, who lives here, has Stage III leukemia, and I decided to move back to be with her. I was very grateful to learn that you had a temporary opening in your practice."

It was all true—not the complete story, but a truthful incomplete one. She wanted them to know about her mother anyway, so if Mom suddenly got worse, they'd be understanding about her taking off work.

The five cosmetic surgeons sitting around the table seemed nice enough. Aaron asked about her mother's doctor and the treatment she was receiving. Dr. Emily Stone, a friendly, athletic looking woman sitting next to her, asked if her mother was at home and said she could recommend a home nurse. Kate thanked her and wrote down the name. Her mother liked Betty Sue, the LVN who now came to the house every day, but it was always a good idea to have someone as a backup.

"So are you living with your mother now?" the guy sitting on the other side of Kate asked. He'd introduced himself as Josh Edwards, a tall, sandy-haired man about her age and the newest member of the practice.

"Yes, she needs someone to stay with her at night." Kate glanced at her watch, a not-so-subtle reminder that she needed to get home to her mother.

"You're a better person than I am," Josh admitted with a boyish smile. "I'd pay somebody to be there with Mom twenty-four/seven, but I don't think I could take moving in with her again."

"It does have its challenging moments," Kate said.

Josh was studying her in a way that made her nervous—not lecherous exactly, but definitely inquisitive. She turned to Emily, seated on her right. "Do you know how Dr. Ross is doing? Since I'm in her office, with the photo of her and her husband on the desk, I almost feel as if I know her."

Emily smiled. "Belinda says she's reading her way through a pile of novels she always meant to read. I'm glad her doctor put her on bed rest. She was having an extremely difficult pregnancy and being on her feet so much didn't help at all. I know she was terrified that she'd lose the baby."

"One of the patients I saw today mentioned that Dr. Ross was forty. In fact, she said she warned Belinda not to have a baby at her age."

Josh Edwards laughed. "You must be talking about Lisa Smythe. Some of us suspect that Belinda went on early maternity leave to avoid having to do another procedure on Lisa."

"She seemed very attached to Dr. Ross," Kate said. "I suggested she wait until Dr. Ross returned, but she wanted to have the work done before that."

"To look thinner for our high school reunion," Josh said. "My wife and Lisa are good friends—that's *my* excuse for not working on her." He pulled his face into an exaggerated expression of regret. "Oh, gee, Lisa, I'd love to suction that pesky fat off your butt, but I never work on my friends."

Kate managed to laugh along with Emily. Oh, if only she could forget about dinner and walk out now! "*Our* high school reunion," he'd said. His and Lisa's—and Kate's!

The first time she'd seen Josh she thought he looked vaguely familiar. And now she knew why. Josh Edwards had been the homecoming king, a track star, and the only one of The Six in the honor society. He'd called himself J.R. Edwards then, and had a *lot* more hair. Early-onset baldness had changed him more than Kate would have imagined.

Emily glanced in Aaron's direction. Seeing that he was engaged in an animated conversation with the two other doctors, she leaned close to Kate and said in a low voice, "Too bad you couldn't talk Lisa into waiting. Belinda did some work on her a few years ago, breast implants. She made Lisa sound like the patient from hell."

Kate nodded. "I could see how she'd be pretty demanding."

"Demanding does not begin to describe her," Emily said grimly. "She expects miracles. She doesn't follow advice. And then she has the audacity to complain that she isn't happy with the results."

Josh, who'd been shamelessly eavesdropping on their conversation, snickered. "You know what Belinda calls Lisa behind her back? N.S."

Not Sane? Kate thought. Narcissistic Slimeball? But she merely smiled and said, "N.S.?"

"Never Satisfied," he said.

"So why don't you all refuse to do any more work on her? Don't you ever turn away patients?"

Emily rolled her eyes. "Don't get me started on that topic. We have way too many patients who are looking for a surgical solution to their psychological problems. I got a clinical psychologist friend of mine to come speak to our monthly staff meeting. She talked about all the people who shouldn't be getting cosmetic surgery: the scalpel slaves and cosmetic surgery junkies, women with body dysmorphia or eating disorders, the depressed person who thinks a face lift will change everything that's wrong in his life. I was hoping after that we'd get some guidelines about turning away inappropriate candidates, but that didn't happen."

Josh shook his head. "The bottom line, Kate, is that Lisa—actually Lisa's husband—has a great deal of money. And they're both more than willing to spend it on maintaining Lisa's appearance, and we're more than willing to cash their checks."

"Are you bad-mouthing Lisa again?" a female voice from behind them said.

Kate turned to look at her. For one dreadful moment she thought she was about to vomit. Instead she took deep breaths and tried hard not to look like a woman who'd just encountered an old enemy.

"Kate, this is my wife Megan," Josh was saying, gesturing to a slim, very pretty dark-haired woman with pouty lips.

She'd had a boob job since Kate had last seen her. Back then Megan Hughes had been a skinny, flat-chested cheerleader with a lethal wit. And an inclination to destroy anyone she thought was crossing her.

"Nice to meet you," Kate said, trying to smile.

"So you're Lisa's new doctor," Megan said, openly inspecting her. "She said you looked familiar to her. Are you from around here?"

Kate shook her head. "My parents moved here after I started college. I grew up in the Chicago area and only was in Houston on school breaks."

Megan shrugged. "Maybe that's why you looked familiar. Lisa has this great memory for faces. She probably saw you someplace when you were home from college. Do you have friends here?"

Kate could feel the sweat on her palms. "I was never really here long enough to make any. After my parents moved, I always spent my summer in Chicago with my friends."

"You went to college in Chicago?"

What was she, the Grand Inquisitor? "University of Chicago," Kate said. Which, in fact, was where she'd received her undergraduate degree.

Apparently Josh too was thinking that his wife was coming on a bit strong. He washed down a nacho with the rest of his margarita and stood up. "We've got to go," he told everyone.

"We can stay a little longer; I just got here," Megan said.

"No, I want to see the kids before they go to sleep." Josh took his wife's elbow and turned her toward the door.

"Nice meeting you, Kate. Thanks for the dinner, Aaron," he said before maneuvering a protesting Megan toward the exit.

Emily leaned toward Kate and whispered, "That is one very jealous woman. Steer clear of Josh or she'll attack. She got a receptionist fired last year."

"Fired for what?" Kate asked, whispering too.

"For being very flirtatious with her husband. Maybe more than flirtatious. Of course that wasn't the official reason for firing her. She was told something like they didn't feel she was a good fit with the group."

"But if the receptionist was competent, why would she be fired? Who cares if Megan didn't like her?"

Emily shrugged. "Good question. But from what I've seen, Megan usually manages to get what she wants."

Some things, Kate thought, never changed.

Seven

The funeral had already started when she slipped into a back row of the big Methodist church. Oh, if only Todd Lawson could see her there! *Do you remember me now, Todd?*

She settled in the pew and inspected her fellow mourners. A respectable crowd, mainly people she didn't recognize. The young widow, dressed in solid black, sat straight-backed in the front row with the two little kids and an older woman who was probably Todd's mother. The little girl was crying.

She felt guilty about the children. After all, it wasn't their fault that their father was a schmuck. In the long run, though, she was doing them a favor. Their mother was young and attractive and would likely remarry. Hopefully next time around she'd pick a better husband, someone who'd be a positive influence.

The minister was carrying on about what a tragedy Todd's premature death was. Probably the man had never even met Todd.

Her eyes scanned the pews, looking for—ah, there they were! Considerately sitting in a little group, just like in high school.

Lisa, the blonde bitch, sat between a gray-haired man and Megan, the cheerleader. Megan sat next to her boyfriend-turned-husband, J.R./Josh, the smart one. The couple's body language made clear that Megan and Josh weren't as close as they'd once been. Glamorous Allison, the actress, sat on the other side of Josh. The only person who seemed to be missing was Matt, the football star. Had he lost touch with his old friends, she wondered, or just been unable to make the funeral?

She'd like to know more about each of them: how they'd turned out all these years later, how they felt about each other now, what they thought about their high school behavior—if they ever thought about it. In some perverse way she'd enjoyed gathering the little information she had managed to find—perhaps because, with the exception of Josh, none of them had done all that well. Allison had shone briefly as a secondary character in a new soap opera, but after a year, the show had been cancelled, effectively ending Allison's so-called acting career. Lisa was the geezer's third wife and, according to society page photos, now had two very pretty stepdaughters only a few years younger than herself. Megan was a small-time real estate agent, and Matt was an engineer living in Oklahoma.

She'd hoped that some of them would get up to eulogize their old friend, but none of them did. After her own brief encounter with Todd, she could understand why.

Finally, the minister finished talking and a soloist began singing "Amazing Grace." Time to get out. Not that anyone was likely to recognize her with the wig and big black hat obscuring most of her face, but it paid to be cautious. As the pallbearers headed down the aisle to remove Todd's coffin, she fled from the sanctuary.

From here on, she'd have to play it by ear.

She positioned herself in a group waiting to offer their condolences to the widow and eavesdropped. Apparently some people were going on to the cemetery, but others were making the church service a solo event. The question was, Which group would The Six—now, actually, The Five—fall into?

Apparently Lisa and the geezer wanted to leave. Off in a corner of the hallway, Lisa was hugging Megan and Allison and Josh while her husband stood behind her, looking impatient.

Maybe it was time for his afternoon nap.

Pulling down the brim of her hat to make sure it covered her face, she moved nearer to the remaining three, close enough to eavesdrop.

"We could stay for a little while," Megan was telling her husband. "You'd still get home in time to get your full eight hours of beauty sleep."

He sent her a look that would have corroded metal. "Not all of us have the luxury of sleeping in every day. My morning starts about four hours earlier than yours."

"So you've told me about two billion times."

"Funny then how you keep forgetting."

Allison shook her head. "Time out, boys and girls. Does anyone know how to get to the cemetery?"

"I do," Megan said. "It's fairly close. We'll stay for half an hour, then hit the road for Houston."

Josh did not look pleased with this information, but he kept his mouth shut.

"Before we leave, I need to make a stop in the little girls' room," Allison told Megan. "Want to come with me?"

"That's okay. I'll wait here for you."

She could not believe her luck! She'd psyched herself up for long, tedious hours of surveillance. Could it possibly end up being this simple?

Don't count your chickens just yet, she warned herself as she followed Allison. The bathroom could be filled with women who'd decided to make a pit stop before they left the church.

Okay, stay calm, she told herself, as Allison walked into the ladies' room. All you're going to do now is go in and check out the situation.

Allison was already in one of the three stalls by the time she walked in. But—hallelujah!—no one else was using the facilities.

She fumbled in her purse for a tube of lipstick. When Allison emerged she was carefully applying a fresh coat of Wine with Everything.

She glanced up as Allison washed her hands at the next sink. "Why you're that actress Allison James, aren't you?" she exclaimed. "I'm so excited to actually meet you."

Allison smiled. "Thanks. I always enjoy meeting my fans."

"Any chance I'll be seeing you soon in another soap?"

Allison frowned. "I'm looking at several projects right now, but I want to branch out from soaps. That job was fine for honing my craft, but I'm ready now to tackle more challenging roles. I told my agent that what I want is a juicy part in some independent movie, something I can really sink my teeth into."

She wondered if the agent had managed not to laugh in Allison's little kewpie-doll face. But she said, "That sounds wonderful. Could you possibly sign an autograph for me? I would *so* appreciate it."

"Okay, but I'm kind of in a hurry."

"Oh, it will only take a minute." She pulled a pen and small notebook from her purse and handed them to Allison. "Inscribe it *To Juliet.*"

"Julia?"

"No, Juliet. Like Romeo's girlfriend."

"Oh, I played that part once," Allison said.

"I know. You were lousy."

"What?" Allison started to say more, but then she saw the knife. She opened her mouth to scream, but one quick slash across her jugular quieted her. Instead, she slumped, rag doll–like, to the floor.

The stupid bitch couldn't even die dramatically. She washed her hands and then pulled on the lightweight coat she'd been carrying. It hid the blood stains on her dress.

Heart pounding, she checked the church corridor before slipping out of the bathroom. No one was in sight.

As she opened the side door that led to the parking lot, she could hear Josh and Megan still arguing. She had to bite her lip to keep from laughing.

EIGHT

Reluctantly Sam Wolfe turned his attention from the television news to his sixteen-year-old daughter. Carly's normally fair face was now splotched red with rage. Hard to believe that only twelve years ago she used to run to the door deliriously shrieking, "Daddy! Daddy!" when he came home from work.

"Your nose," he said, "is fine. Not everyone has to look exactly alike."

"You *would* say that," his daughter replied. "My nose looks just like yours—gigantic."

He stifled a laugh. "It's not as if people usually point at me on the street and say, 'My God, have you seen that guy's schnoz?' "

Carly rolled her eyes. "My nose is hideous. It makes my face grotesque. I look like an anteater."

"You don't look—"

"And I could look so much better, Dad—I could even be pretty—if I got a nose job. I know a girl at school who had it done. She had this big crooked nose and now she has a cute, straight one. You wouldn't believe how much better she looks."

"You're too young, Carly. Maybe when you're older . . ."

"When I'm older? You want me to live another sixteen years with this—this *banana*—on the front of my face?"

Despite his best intentions, he glanced at the TV screen. And stared. "Shh!" He grabbed the remote and increased the volume, drowning out his daughter's protests.

Scowling, Sam listened as the announcer described the "bizarre murder" of a minor soap opera actress at a funeral in Dallas. "Holy shit!" he muttered as a photo of Todd Lawson flashed on the screen.

"I'll use my own money," his single-minded daughter said as soon as he clicked off the TV.

"What?" He was up and moving toward the kitchen phone.

His daughter glared at him as he passed.

Sam sighed. Sometimes the only thing that made him feel better during these visits was the knowledge that Carly hated his ex-wife even more.

"We'll talk some more about your nose later," he called to her. "Right now I've got to go to work. I'll drop you at your mother's on the way."

It took him a couple of hours, but eventually Sam tracked down the Dallas detective in charge of the Allison James murder. Officer Ed Watts was not the most collegial cop he'd ever met, but, once Sam cited the similarities to Todd Lawson's murder, the guy became marginally more cooperative.

So far, Watts said, they had no witnesses. The woman who'd discovered the body was a friend who'd gone to investigate when Ms. James didn't return from the bathroom. She'd seen no one else, in the bathroom or in the church hallway, and her husband, a doctor, said his wife was in the bathroom less than a minute before she ran out screaming.

Sam wrote down the couple's names. "Did either of them tell you what the connection was between Lawson and Allison James?" Why, for instance, was an actress from L.A. at a Dallas funeral?

"High school friends; they all ran in the same crowd. Didn't sound as if they had much contact in recent years, though, once Ms. James moved to California. But she was in Texas, visiting her parents, when Lawson died."

"I guess it could be a copycat murder," Sam said. "Some nut job reads about Lawson's death in the newspaper and goes to the funeral to slice someone's throat."

"And Allison James just happened to be a convenient target?" the Dallas officer asked. "A woman alone in an isolated church bathroom—easy pickings. Or maybe someone wanted to get rid of Ms. James and decided to imitate Lawson's death to divert suspicion."

Sam sighed. "Certainly is possible. What about the knife? The coroner said Lawson was killed by a right-handed perp, probably with a scalpel."

"Scalpel, huh? That information appear in the media?"

"Don't think so. Stories I read said his throat was slashed, but that was it."

"Well, I guess that's *something* to be grateful for. I'll let you know when we get the autopsy results."

Sam thanked him and they hung up.

Rubbing his aching neck, he wondered if the murderer—or murderers—was finished killing. For the first time in years, he wished he hadn't given up cigarettes.

NINE

"Dr. Dalton?" Mandy, the freckled, red-haired receptionist, was standing in the doorway to Kate's office.

"Yes?" Kate made an effort to smile at the young woman, who looked disturbingly familiar. Had she and Kate gone to the same high school? Kate shrugged; it seemed that every second person she'd met since her return looked somehow familiar.

"I just wanted to let you know that Lisa Smythe called to cancel her lipo. She'd like to reschedule for next week."

"Did she say why she's canceling?"

Mandy's green eyes widened as she moved closer to Kate's desk. "Oh, you haven't heard about the woman who was killed at that funeral in Dallas?"

Oh, yes, Kate had heard all about that. She and her mother had been watching the late news on TV when the faces of Todd Lawson and Allison James appeared on the screen. And all Kate could think was that they deserved to die.

"I saw it on the news. But what does that have to do with Mrs. Smythe?"

Mandy shrugged. "She was at the funeral. Apparently the woman who was killed was a good friend of hers, and Mrs. Smythe wants to attend her funeral tomorrow."

And then she wants to come in to have the fat suctioned off her butt: Lisa's personal style of mourning. "You rescheduled her surgery?"

The receptionist nodded. "Next week Friday." She hesitated,

then added, "Dr. Edwards was at that funeral too. His wife was the one who found the body."

"Really?" The TV reporter had only mentioned that another attendee at the funeral had made the grisly discovery. "That must have been horrible for her."

"Oh, it was! Dr. Edwards said his wife is a wreck. She's on tranquilizers and is afraid to leave her house. And even he, who's used to surgery, said he has nightmares about seeing that woman's body. There was blood everywhere, he said."

"Awful." Kate shook her head.

"I know. If *I'd* found the body, I sure wouldn't be back at work today."

Kate took a deep breath as Mandy walked out of her office. She'd intended to order a sandwich to eat at her desk while she took care of paperwork, but right now it seemed more important to get out of this airless cocoon, take care of herself for a change. She had almost two hours before her next appointment, a consultation about a facelift, and she would use the time to run some errands and have a decent, unrushed lunch.

Was she just imagining that the receptionist looked familiar? It was happening a lot lately, thinking that she'd seen people before. Last week at an office birthday party, she'd had the feeling she recognized the office manager, a woman around her age named Annette. But then when Kate talked to her, she learned Annette had moved from Boston only a year ago. Probably it was the memory of the young mother who'd stared at Kate in the grocery store a few nights ago—a total stranger who kept saying, "I'm sure I know you from somewhere"—that was making her edgy.

Don't get paranoid on me now, she told herself as she headed down the hall. In fact, her own mother had barely known her when Kate showed up at the house. Her face, her hair color, and her trimmed-down body were dramatically different from

Plain Jane Murphy's fifteen years ago. No one who knew her in high school could possibly recognize her.

Kate stopped at Mandy's desk to say she was going out for lunch. Still talking, she backed up, just as a tall man with a paper cup of coffee hurried in.

Their collision knocked her to the ground, splattering coffee.

The man stooped to her level. "God, I'm sorry. Are you okay?"

As okay as anyone could be sprawled on the floor in a waiting room full of gawking patients. She sat up gingerly. "I'd say only my pride has been damaged."

He offered her a hand. Not wanting to be rude, she let him help her to her feet. *Let's get this incident over with.* She hated—had always hated—being the center of attention.

Upright, she noticed the coffee stains on his tan sports coat and pale-blue shirt. "You weren't burned, were you?" she asked, glancing at his hands. When he shook his head, she added, "I'm sorry too. I wasn't looking where I was going."

"I was the one who slammed into you."

It was rapidly becoming one of those awkward conversations, which Kate tried to avoid at all costs. *Time to make my exit.*

"You're a plastic surgeon?" the man asked, looking at the name on her white lab coat. When she nodded, he said, "Could you spare a minute to answer a couple questions? I'd just like a professional's opinion about nose jobs for teenagers."

Great. "Do you have an appointment with one of the other doctors in the practice?" The last thing she needed was for this man to tell one of the other surgeons, "Well, that's not what Dr. Dalton told me when I talked to her in the waiting room." Though this guy seemed nice enough and was quirkily attractive, with an angular face and expressive dark eyes.

"No appointment. What I do have is a sixteen-year-old daughter who wants a new nose. Don't you think that's too young for plastic surgery?"

She wouldn't have thought he was old enough to have a sixteen-year-old. "It really depends on the individual case. Some teenagers are still growing and their faces are changing. Often bone structure doesn't mature until someone is eighteen or older. If you do cosmetic surgery too soon, the new nose could be out of proportion to the girl's adult face."

"Carly, my daughter, probably has stopped growing. Her mother grew to her adult height by the time she was twelve." He paused a beat. "My ex-wife."

Which explained why he wasn't wearing a wedding ring. "You also have to consider how emotionally mature the girl is," Kate said. "Does she realize how painful and expensive cosmetic surgery is? Does she expect a new nose will change everything that's wrong with her life?" *God, she sounded as if she was giving a lecture. What a pompous know-it-all he must think her!*

He tapped his own nose. "She says her nose looks just like mine. Gigantic and hideous, I believe, were two of the words used."

Despite herself, Kate laughed.

He searched her face with those intense brown eyes. "Do you think my nose is too big?"

She considered it. Individually his features weren't classically handsome, but the overall effect was very pleasing. "It is kind of long, but it works on your face."

He grinned. "Is that a tactful way of saying, But we wouldn't want to inflict that nose on a defenseless little girl?"

Fortunately, she was saved from having to answer that one. Josh Edwards walked into the waiting room, nodding at Kate.

"I need to get back to work," the man said, glancing at Josh's back. "Thanks for the consultation, Dr. Dalton. And sorry again about crashing into you."

Kate watched him walk to the receptionist's desk, wondering

what kind of work he did. Probably a pharmaceutical salesman, she decided, the kind of charming guy who was good at establishing instant intimacy.

A professional bull-shitter, in other words. He and Josh should hit it off, she thought, as she headed out the door.

She'd just returned from lunch when Josh appeared in her office. "You have a minute?" he asked with a genial smile.

"Sure."

He pulled one of the chrome and leather chairs closer to her desk and sat. "So how's it going?"

"Fine. Everyone's been very helpful."

"Good. I was wondering if you'd like to assist me Thursday morning. It's an interesting case, a burn victim who needs extensive work to rebuild his nose. I remember you said that reconstructive surgery is your major interest."

"I'd love to assist. What time is the surgery?"

He told her, then said, "Oh, by the way, what were you and that detective talking about? The two of you seemed to be having quite a conversation."

She stared at him. "Detective? When?"

"In the waiting room. You were talking to him when I came in. He didn't tell you he was a homicide cop?"

She shook her head. "The only thing we talked about was his daughter wanting rhinoplasty. We accidentally collided in the waiting room, and when he saw I was a doctor, he asked me about cosmetic surgery for teenagers."

"That's all he talked about?"

Kate nodded. "Then he said he had to get to work. I thought he might be in pharmaceutical sales."

Josh stood up. "Okay. I'm glad you can assist in my surgery."

"Wait!" Clearly the man was a lot better at gathering information than in sharing it. "So why was he here?"

"He came to interview me about Allison James's death a couple days ago. Megan and I were with her at the funeral for one of our high school friends, Todd Lawson. Megan was the one who discovered Allison's body."

"How horrible! Do the police have any leads?"

Josh shook his head. "Sure doesn't sound like it. Detective Wolfe—your friend from the waiting room—thinks Allison's death might be connected to Todd's."

"Why does he think that?"

"She was murdered right after Todd's funeral and they both were killed with a knife. Wolfe wanted to know if I could think of any motive for their deaths."

"Could you?"

He shrugged. "I told him to check out Allison's husband. The guy is a has-been Hollywood director who's heavily into cocaine. Allison wanted a divorce, and Ethan might have decided it would be a lot cheaper to get rid of her permanently. The man's a real sleazebag."

"But why would he kill Todd Lawson?"

"He wouldn't. Todd might have been killed by anyone—a burglar, a hooker he picked up at the bar. I'm just saying that Ethan knew how Todd died and could have tried to make it look as if the same person murdered Allison. Just a theory, though." Josh glanced at his watch. "Got to go. I have a patient."

He leaned toward her, touching her shoulder. His hand lingered longer than a collegial pat. "See you in surgery."

Feeling shaky, Kate closed the door after him. Was Josh coming on to her? She didn't believe for one minute that he'd come to her office merely to request her assistance in surgery. So why had he come—simple seduction or something else? He'd seemed unusually interested in her conversation with the man in the waiting room.

The question was why Josh would care what she'd told Detective Wolfe.

Ten

Standing in the doorway of her West University Place home, Megan Edwards looked about as happy to see Sam Wolfe as her husband had been half an hour earlier. "Josh told me you might show up," she said, making it sound like a warning of an approaching influenza epidemic. "I already told the Dallas police everything I know."

"I'm working the Houston angle of the case," Sam said, following the athletic-looking brunette to a living room with dark hardwood floors, a large fireplace, and expensive-looking furniture grouped around an Oriental rug. The house was older and smaller than Todd Lawson's had been, but whoever had furnished it had more sophisticated tastes. Megan Edwards, a real estate agent, was probably very knowledgeable about homes.

She picked a straight-backed chair and indicated that Sam should sit across from her on the sofa. He sat, thinking that the nubby beige sofa fabric reminded him of oatmeal, a food he'd despised since childhood.

She scowled. "I don't have time for this."

Sam was tempted to tell her that she had damn well better find the time. Did anyone actually buy a home from this abrasive woman? The last time he'd dealt with realtors, they'd all seemed irredeemably perky. "I need to hear your version of what happened at Todd Lawson's funeral. It might help us identify the killer."

She started to object, but he cut her off. "What happened

after the service ended?"

She told him what her husband had: just the barebones facts. Only when she got to the part about going into the restroom to discover what was taking her friend so long did her brisk, high-pitched voice break. "She was just lying there, on the floor in front of the sinks, and there was blood everywhere. Her neck . . . it was horrible. Allison had always been so gorgeous and now she was this . . . this grotesque thing on the floor."

For the first time, Sam could see what Dr. Edwards had said about his wife: Megan Edwards was on the edge. ("Traumatized by the murder," were the words Dr. Edwards had used, adding, in that condescending surgeon's voice, that he'd prefer Sam not interview Megan because "I don't want her any more upset.")

"Did you see anyone else in the area?" Sam asked in a gentler voice.

She shook her head, hands trembling.

"Not anyone in the hallway before you entered the bathroom? Or someone in one of the other stalls?"

"I told you no," she said, the steel back in her voice.

So much for her thirty seconds of vulnerability, Sam thought. "You're saying that from the time Ms. James left you to go to the restroom until you found her body, you saw no one else in the church?"

"Most people had already left for the cemetery, but I guess some could still have been there. I just didn't see them."

"Did you hear anything unusual—footsteps, any other noises?"

"No, after Allison left, Josh and I were talking. I wouldn't have heard anyone unless they were very loud."

"You and your husband were talking loudly?"

She glared at him. "I didn't hear any other noises."

"When you found Ms. James in the bathroom, did she say anything to you?"

"It's hard to say anything when you're dead."

He raised his eyebrows. "You knew immediately, just by looking at her, that she was dead?"

The woman blinked rapidly. "Why no, I went to get Josh. He's a doctor, after all. I thought he could give her first aid—do *something.* But Josh said Allison was dead."

"Did you notice anything else—anything you thought was unusual?"

She sent him a withering look. "Other than her throat being cut?"

He ignored the sarcasm. "Was her purse missing? Any jewelry gone?"

"Her purse was on the floor, but I didn't look inside. Allison was still wearing her diamond earrings and her diamond-and-ruby engagement ring."

"Can you think of any reason someone might have killed Ms. James?"

She blinked again. "I have no idea."

"Guess."

The woman's posture, good before, now would have made any drill sergeant proud. "Are you implying that *I* had something to do with Allison's death?"

Actually, he wasn't, at least not until he got more information. It was interesting, however, that she thought he was. "I just meant that as a friend of hers, you might have some theories or maybe know someone who was angry with her."

"Oh." He could see her body relax a bit, lose the military posture. "I can think of a lot of people who were angry at Allison, but I don't think they'd kill her."

"Like who?"

"Well, her husband, for one. They were going through a very messy divorce. Ethan was a real jerk, but I thought Allison said something about him being in Toronto scouting movie locations."

Sam made another note to check out Ms. James's husband. Josh Edwards had described the man as a manipulative cocaine-user with serious money problems. A clever, desperate man might have figured he had a perfect alibi—witnesses who could verify that he was in Canada at the time of Allison's death—and then hired a hit man to do the job. Because whoever had killed Allison James in a church bathroom was either very smart or very, very lucky.

"Was Ms. James afraid of her husband?"

"The only thing Allison was afraid of was that he'd manage to hide his assets from her. She was convinced he had a lot more money than he claimed."

"Who else was angry with her? You said a lot of people."

"I didn't mean I had a list of potential murderers. Allison was very selfish and determined to get whatever she wanted. Other people's feelings didn't really show up on her radar screen."

"You sound as if you didn't like her very much."

Megan Edwards's eyes widened, but she quickly recovered. "I didn't *dislike* her. We were friends in high school, but we lost touch when she moved to L.A. after graduation. She only came back to town a month ago, after her marriage broke up."

"So the only time you've seen her since high school was at Todd Lawson's funeral?"

"No, I saw her a few other times. She came to our ten-year high school reunion—the big, successful actress making an appearance. And Josh and I and Lisa Smythe and her husband went out to dinner with her a few weeks ago. Lisa was a high school friend of hers too."

Sam leaned forward. "So how'd that go—the dinner with the five of you?"

"Fine."

But clearly it hadn't been fine, if Megan Edwards's tightly pressed lips and furious eyes were any indication. He made a mental note to find out more about that dinner. "So the only times you saw her in the last month were that get-together and the funeral?"

"I have a very busy life—a husband, two children, a demanding job. That didn't change because Allison suddenly showed up after her so-called acting career tanked and her marriage imploded."

Oh, no, she didn't dislike Allison James at all. "What about Ms. Smythe? Did she see a lot of Ms. James in the last month?"

Her smile, if you could call it that, reminded him of a cartoon shark from some movie he used to watch with his daughter. "I doubt it. Lisa liked Allison even less than I did."

"Oh?" Sam noticed for the first time that Megan Edwards's breasts were very large for someone so skinny. Did plastic surgeons do implants on their own wives? Her nose too—now that Carly had got him noticing noses—was very nice. He wondered if she'd been born with it.

Which got him thinking about that little plastic surgeon he'd run into at Josh Edwards's office. Cute more than glamorous, though she'd had a good nose too and truly remarkable legs. But her attractiveness was as much about her warmth, her openness, and her sense of humor—all qualities singularly lacking in both Megan Edwards and her husband. "Why did Ms. Smythe dislike Allison James?"

He expected her to say "Oh, Lisa didn't *dislike* her," but instead she chuckled. "Lisa had lots of reasons. But I think the main one was that she always felt Allison betrayed her. In high school the two of them were very close—the two musketeers. Allison was going to be a big movie star and Lisa a super-model. And they were going to make sure that it happened for both of them: all for one and one for all. Except that the minute Allison headed for Hollywood, she forgot all about Lisa."

"And Ms. Smythe was envious of her success?"

"Sure. Allison was a real actress, even if her only big role was in a second-rate soap, and Lisa ended up as a trophy wife to a boring, demanding, but rich old coot. But it was more than simple envy. Lisa in high school did *a lot* for Allison—some not-very-nice stunts to make sure that she was the one who got the lead in all the class plays, among other things. I think she figured that Allison owed her. When Allison started getting parts on TV, Lisa expected that Allison at least would get her a walk-on part in the soap."

"But she never did?"

"Once Allison left Houston, she forgot she knew Lisa. An air-kiss at our high school reunion, and that was it. Until, of course, things fell apart and she had to come to live with Mommy and Daddy because she had nowhere else to go. Then Lisa was supposed to be Allison's long-lost best friend."

"I take it Ms. Smythe didn't feel that way."

This time there was no mistaking the malice in Megan Edwards's eyes. "You're going to have to ask Lisa herself about that."

"I'll do that," Sam said.

Lisa Smythe was a slender woman with long hair, considerably more welcoming than either of the Edwardses—or maybe simply more curious. Being a childless, jobless trophy wife might get kind of tedious, Sam thought as he followed her through her huge, silent, opulent home.

"I thought we could chat in the sunroom," she said as they walked into a plant-filled room with floor-to-ceiling windows. "Could I get you some coffee or tea?"

"No thanks." Sam glanced around the room. Clusters of

silver-framed photos were grouped on every available flat surface. He walked to a wicker table and inspected the pictures. Almost all of them seemed to have Lisa Smythe in the shot.

"You're very photogenic," he told her. Unfortunately, not quite photogenic enough to realize her early career goals. While Ms. Smythe was certainly striking—trim, blonde, and wearing a hell of a lot of makeup and big silver jewelry for someone who claimed to be just spending the afternoon at home—she didn't seem tall enough, skinny enough, or just plain memorable enough to be a successful model. Instead, she looked like one more rich, blonde Texas socialite.

Ms. Smythe seemed happy to take her compliments wherever she could get them. "Thanks. I've always thought that photos make a room feel homey."

He picked up a photo of her with Megan and Josh Edwards and Allison James. They were sitting around a restaurant table, smiling blandly at the photographer. "Was this taken recently?"

She glanced at it. "Only a few weeks ago. It was the last time I really talked to Allison. I saw her at Todd's funeral, of course, but we didn't have a chance to chat."

"So you weren't there after the service with Ms. James and the Edwardses?" he asked as they seated themselves on facing chintz-covered chairs.

She shook her head. "I think they planned to go on to the cemetery." She glanced ruefully at a large photo of herself with a stern-faced, white-haired man—presumably the boring but rich spouse. "If it had been up to me, we would have gone too, but my husband was impatient to leave."

"When you saw her at the funeral, did Ms. James seem upset about anything? Or maybe unusually nervous?"

"She seemed sad about Todd's death. We all were. But other than that, I didn't notice anything out of the ordinary."

"Ms. Edwards mentioned that you and Ms. James were very

close friends in high school."

"Did she?" There was a layer of ice beneath the words. "What else did Megan say?"

Sam shrugged. "Just that Ms. James lost touch with her old friends when she moved to Hollywood." When Lisa didn't respond, he asked, "Did you see a lot of her after she moved back?"

For some reason, the question seemed to cheer her up. "Yes, Allison and I were getting reacquainted, catching up on each other's lives. It was fun." Her expression grew sad. "Which made it all the harder when Allison was killed."

Okay. Could Megan Edwards have been wrong about the animosity between the two women? Perhaps she'd projected her own dislike for Allison onto Lisa Smythe. Or maybe—and this was probably stretching it—Lisa was merely relieved that Sam hadn't embarrassed her by bringing up the "dirty tricks" she'd done in high school for Allison's benefit.

"So you were aware of what was going on in Ms. James's life." When she nodded, he said, "Can you tell me anything she was particularly concerned about? It's helpful in a homicide investigation to know as much as possible about the victim."

Ms. Smythe cocked her head, causing long, silky hair to drape the left side of her face. "I'm sure Megan told you that Allison was going through a messy divorce. One of the reasons she moved back to Houston was to get away from Ethan Fox, her husband. She said she'd rather have their fights over the phone than in person. At least here she could hang up on him."

"Did you get the idea that she was afraid of Mr. Fox?"

"Not afraid in the sense that she thought he'd hurt her physically. Ethan wasn't violent, just a weasel. She was afraid he'd manage to hide his financial assets from her. He kept telling her lawyer that he was on the verge of bankruptcy, even though Allison was convinced he had big money stashed away in a secret bank account. She really hated the guy."

"Could Mr. Fox have decided it would be easier to get rid of his wife than to go through a protracted divorce?"

To his surprise, Lisa Smythe laughed. "Oh, no, that wouldn't have suited Ethan's purposes at all. He loved to fight; making deals—winning—was what he did best. Allison was his fourth wife. He'd been through this all before. That's probably why he insisted that Allison sign a pre-nup when they got married. It gave her half a mil for every five years they stayed married. I think Allison held on for the last year or two—turned her eyes on a lot of bad behavior—just so she could collect a million. But now Ethan was saying he didn't *have* a million, that his last movie lost a bundle, and he didn't think Allison deserved the ten-year payment anyway since they'd been separated a lot of last year."

She studied Sam's face. "Don't you see? Ethan loved to pull Allison's strings. Why kill her and end all the fun? Allison might have wanted to murder *him*, but Ethan wanted to see that Allison came out of the divorce with only the clothes on her back—or better yet, came back to him. In his own kinky way, Ethan was very attached to her."

But sometimes arrogant, powerful men who were used to getting their own way became violent when they didn't get it, Sam thought. "If you think Mr. Fox didn't kill her, who's your favorite suspect?"

"I suppose it could have been whoever killed Todd, except I can't see any motive. Todd and Allison hadn't had anything to do with each other for years. They'd dated for a while in high school but broke up our sophomore year. After that Allison pretended Todd didn't exist. He was so superficial and she hated him—hated everyone she broke up with. She always was a huge drama queen. I think she only came to the service because she liked the idea of going to her former boyfriend's funeral. It kind of sounds like a soap opera plot, don't you think?"

Actually it sounded more like Ms. Smythe had too much time on her hands. "Not much of a soap fan, I'm afraid. Can you think of anybody else Ms. James was angry with, other than her husband?"

A sly look crossed the woman's angular face. She too, Sam noticed, had a nice nose and exceptionally large breasts. Had Megan and Lisa shared the same plastic surgeon?

"Isn't a more important question, Who was angry with Allison?" When he raised his eyebrows she smiled coquettishly. "Can't you guess? It's someone you know."

Sam scowled. Apparently he was less thrilled at playing guessing games than others in her set. "Who?" he asked, fixing her with his no-nonsense cop look.

"Why Megan Edwards, of course. The way I see it, Megan had motive, means, and opportunity. She could easily have gone with Allison to the ladies' room, killed her, and then run out screaming that someone murdered her good friend and it *must* have been the same person who killed Todd because both of their throats were slashed."

"Dr. Edwards said his wife was with him when Ms. James went to the restroom. It was only when they started wondering why Ms. James hadn't returned that Ms. Edwards went looking for her. According to her husband, she rushed out of the bathroom a few seconds after she entered."

"But Josh *would* say that, wouldn't he? He's not likely to admit that Megan was in the restroom for twenty minutes before running out to get his help."

"You're saying you think that the two of them planned Allison James's murder?"

"No, I'm only offering possible scenarios. But knowing the two of them, the worst I'd see Josh do was help cover up the crime when he realized what Megan had done. After all, he'd probably feel *some* guilt."

"Why?"

"Let's just say that Josh has a wandering eye, and Allison was a very flirtatious woman. Unfortunately, Megan is insanely jealous of her husband. If she found out that more than flirting was going on—well, *I* wouldn't want to be the person who provoked Megan Edwards."

"She has a history of violence?"

"She has a history of getting what she wants. And she wants Josh Edwards as her husband—until death do them part."

She held up a hand sporting long, painted fingernails. "The only thing that bothers me, though, is the stabbing. Megan is ruthless and incredibly well organized. But she's very squeamish about blood. I can remember once in high school we were watching this gory movie on TV, where a deranged woman started slashing her rival. Megan ran out of the room; I thought she was going to puke. She still jokes that she's the only doctor's wife she knows who can't stand the sight of blood."

"This was very bloody." As someone with a similarly weak stomach, he'd had a hard time studying the crime scene photos.

"That's what I figured. So maybe Megan didn't do it."

So why had she been so vehement in proposing Megan as her favorite suspect? "What about Josh Edwards? Presumably he's not squeamish about blood, and he also had access to Ms. James. His wife could be the one who's covering up for him."

"But I don't see why he'd killed Allison. Megan is the aggressive one in the family. Even if, say, Allison and Josh had gotten involved and Josh wanted to end the affair and Allison didn't, I just don't see homicide as a Josh solution."

"What would be a Josh solution?"

"Oh, he'd probably go confess to Megan, tell her that sleeping with Allison was a terrible mistake that only made him realize how much he loved his devoted wife. And then Megan—

the bad cop—would go confront Allison."

She smiled ruefully and shook her head. "Josh and Megan have a *very* peculiar relationship—co-dependent, even kinky. They complain constantly about each other, but never once, in ten years of marriage, has either of them suggested a divorce."

Looking into Lisa Smythe's malicious blue eyes, Sam suspected there was more than one intense, kinky relationship connected to this crime.

Eleven

Kate studied her reflection in the bathroom mirror. For a moment—barely a second—she didn't recognize the face staring back at her. Was she really so . . . pretty? Surely not.

She grinned ruefully at herself. *Let's not get carried away, doctor. What you're admiring is the effect of a talented surgeon's rhinoplasty and chin implant, combined with a flattering haircut and an uncharacteristic amount of skillfully applied makeup. Your other nice features—large eyes and good skin—are merely a genetic legacy from your mother.*

She added the only expensive jewelry she owned—diamond stud earrings her ex-husband had given her as a wedding gift and a delicate necklace of tiny pearls and diamonds she'd inherited from her grandmother. With a last-minute adjustment of the V neckline of her black silk dress, she was as ready as she'd ever be for the cocktail party at Aaron Glass's home.

Kate hoped she could get in and out of the party in an hour. Introduce herself, smile, chitchat with people she had no desire to know, have a glass of wine, then thank her hosts and leave. Ninety minutes, tops.

The Glasses lived in one of the "villages" of Memorial, a wealthy suburb of sprawling homes, surrounded by even larger pine trees. Luckily, Kate thought as a hired valet offered to park her car, it looked as if this was going to be a very large party. She wouldn't be missed when she sneaked out early.

Aaron's wife, a handsome woman in her fifties, greeted her in the hallway. "I'm so happy to finally meet you, Kate. Aaron had told me such nice things about you. I hope you're getting acclimated to the practice."

Kate smiled. "I'm working on it. Everyone has been very kind in showing me the ropes." She wondered what Aaron's wife would say if she'd told the truth: she had absolutely no intention of getting "acclimated" to any practice in Houston. She'd worked too hard to get out of her hometown to ever voluntarily come back.

Mrs. Glass insisted on introducing Kate to other guests. "I particularly want you to meet our nephew. He's a law professor." She lowered her voice. "And newly single."

Kate didn't know if she wanted to laugh or groan. The nephew, a slender, nervous man with curly salt-and-pepper hair, had the depressed eyes of the recently separated.

He waited until his aunt left to ask Kate, "Did she tell you I just got a divorce and am in desperate need of female companionship?"

Kate grinned. "That wasn't exactly the way she phrased it."

He rolled his eyes. "I know she means well, but every person she's introduced me to tonight has been an extremely attractive, single female below the age of forty." He paused. "I take it you're not married?"

She nodded. Probably she should be flattered that Mrs. Glass thought she was extremely attractive.

"Ever been married?"

"Briefly, when I was in med school." It wasn't a story she felt like sharing with a stranger, not that there was anything all that interesting about her marriage or the divorce: Swept away by infatuation, two overworked medical students had married impulsively and then quickly learned they had almost nothing in common. The only good thing about their marriage was that it ended as quickly and effortlessly as it had begun. And, of course, she'd also been able, legally, to ditch her old name.

He studied her through sad gray eyes. "How long did it take you to get over it—the divorce, I mean?"

She tried to imagine how he'd react if she answered truthfully: it hadn't taken long at all. Everyone had marveled at their "civilized divorce," how she and Nat had remained so friendly. Kate always attributed it to the fact that there'd been so little real emotional connection between the two of them that neither she nor Nat felt bitter about severing it.

"It usually takes awhile." She patted his arm. "But, trust me, eventually you will feel better."

He nodded, looking a bit more hopeful. "Say, would you be interested in going out to dinner with me some night this week?"

Kate offered him what she hoped was a regretful smile. "I'd really like to, but I'm only in town to take care of my mother. She's very ill."

She tried not to feel guilty about his obvious disappointment.

"Excuse me, I see someone I need to talk to. It was very nice meeting you." Then she hurried toward the only people she recognized, a group of doctors from the practice.

Too late Kate saw who else was in the group. Talking to Emily Stone and Josh Edwards were Lisa Smythe and an older man.

But before Kate could walk in another direction, Emily was calling to her and Lisa had turned to see who was approaching.

"Just who I wanted to see," Emily said to Kate. By far the friendliest of the other doctors in the practice, Emily had twice asked Kate to lunch—an invitation she'd so far managed to turn down, with the excuse that she didn't take a lunch hour so she could leave early to get home to her mother.

Josh was eyeing her with approval. "You certainly clean up nicely, Dr. Dalton."

Lisa laughed. "Better not let Megan hear you say that, Josh, or you'll be on an even tighter leash." She nodded toward another group, where Megan Edward, Kate saw, was talking to a well-dressed older woman.

Lisa ignored Josh's glare, openly inspecting Kate's outfit. "That's an exquisite necklace. It's vintage, isn't it?"

"It was originally my great-grandmother's. I always admired it when I was a little girl, so my grandmother left it to me in her will."

"Bet your mother appreciated *that*," Lisa said.

Kate was suddenly aware that her right hand was tightening into a fist. Taking a deep breath, she unclenched it. "Actually, Mother was happy for me."

Josh smiled maliciously. "Maternal instincts are *not* Lisa's strong suit."

Before Lisa had a chance to reply, Emily interjected quickly, "Kate, have you met Jonathan Smythe, Lisa's husband?"

"No." Kate nodded and offered her hand to the gray-haired man standing next to Lisa. "Kate Dalton."

"Very pleased to meet you, Kate. Lisa didn't mention that her new surgeon was so attractive."

Was the man drunk? Kate had to practically yank her hand free.

"Jonathan," Lisa said, "don't you love that necklace? I wonder if we could have one made in a design like that. With bigger diamonds, though."

"Yes," he said, staring. "Very nice."

It wasn't her necklace he was ogling, Kate realized. And from the expression on her face, Lisa recognized it too.

With a look that could have frozen molten lava, Lisa clasped her husband's arm. "Oh, darling, the Johnsons just arrived. Didn't you say you needed to talk to him?"

Without another word to the group, the Smythes moved away.

Josh wagged his finger at Kate. "*Now* you're on Lisa's hit list."

And she doesn't even have Todd Lawson anymore to sic on me, Kate thought. What else would Lisa do to stake her claim to Her Man? Attach a sign on Jonathan Smythe's stooped back?

Exclusive Property! All Trespassers Will Be SEVERELY Punished!

Trying not to smirk, Kate ignored Josh's barb and turned to ask Emily about an upcoming medical conference.

She ended up staying two hours. Driving home, Kate told herself that, if not exactly fun, going to the party had at least been a good use of her time. She'd caught up with her colleagues, met Aaron's wife and quite a few of the Glass's wealthy friends, one of whom insisted that she wanted Kate to do her next face lift. Lisa Smythe had even coveted her jewelry.

It was what Kate had always wanted, wasn't it? To go to a party and not feel like a wallflower. To be accepted and sought after, rather than ignored.

But now that she'd achieved her goal, why did it feel so meaningless?

The minute she slid into the booth at the coffee shop, Kate saw her mistake. If she hadn't been preoccupied and hungry, she would have noticed the two of them the minute she walked in the door—and then made a hasty U-turn and headed back to her car.

But it was too late for that now. A waitress was handing her a menu and Josh Edwards—who, seconds before, had been whispering something into the ear of the cute office manager from Boston—had spotted her. He nodded, and she had to nod back.

Damn! The headache that had begun midway through the

morning's surgery seemed to ratchet up several notches. Should she order a sandwich to go or stay here and pretend that running into Josh with his latest girlfriend was no big deal? What if he asked her to join them?

"Do you know what you want? Or should I come back?" the waitress asked.

"Two scrambled eggs, bacon, whole-wheat toast, and coffee." Hopefully one of her standard headache remedies would work: mainlining caffeine or getting some food in her stomach.

Someone had left a newspaper on the table, and Kate opened it. At least this way she couldn't be accused of spying on Josh and his lunch companion.

"I never would have figured you for a baseball fan," a familiar voice said.

Kate lowered the sports page. "I have been known to read anything that's available, even the back of a cereal box," she told Josh Edwards.

He grinned down at her. "Mind if I join you?"

Actually, she did mind. "What happened to your friend?"

"She had to get back to work."

Apparently choosing to view her question as consent, he slid across from her. "So what did you think of the surgery?"

What she'd thought was he was a much better surgeon than she'd guessed. Some other time she might think about why she'd been surprised: a lingering bias against popular kids from wealthy families, the golden boys who hadn't earned their good fortune?

Instead, she told him, truthfully, that she'd found the delicate nose reconstruction fascinating. It was the kind of work she'd like to specialize in someday.

"That's what I thought too when I finished my residency. Until my wife pointed out that tummy tucks and breast augmentations were more likely to pay for the lifestyle she aspired to."

Oh, spare me, Dr. Edwards. She'd had quite enough of Little Boy Josh and his Big Bad Wife last night at the cocktail party. Did he blame Megan for *all* his less-than-admirable behavior: Hey, it's not *my* fault; my wife made me do it? Josh probably even told his girlfriends it was only because of Megan's jealous micromanaging that he pursued other women.

"And you were hoping to live in a grass hut in a third-world country, Josh?"

He laughed. "You are a hard woman, Dr. Dalton. But in answer to your unsympathetic question, no, I also wanted to live in a big house and send my kids to private schools. It just would have pleased me to be able to accomplish this through correcting birth defects, cranial deformities, and terrible burn scars. Instead, I have to make do with an occasional case like the one today."

She could feel her face getting hot. "You did good work."

"Thanks. So did you."

Fortunately, her food arrived then, giving her an excuse to keep quiet. She suspected that, with a little encouragement, Josh would be more than happy to fill the silence. Kate swallowed a mouthful of eggs, then asked, "Are you going to Allison James's funeral? I heard it's tomorrow."

He nodded. "Actually, it's a memorial service. The coroner hasn't released her body yet. I told Megan I didn't know if I could take another church service for a dead friend, but she wants to go."

Kate pictured the Allison she remembered from a school play. Back then Allison had not been a very good actress—too hammy, too obviously acting. But she'd had stage presence and she was beautiful. Among the three pretty girls in her group, Allison was without question the best-looking. "Have the police found out who killed her?"

"If they have, they haven't informed me." Josh set down the coffee cup he'd brought to the table. "Do you realize how crazy this all is? One of my oldest friends gets his throat cut in a hotel room, and then, a week later, another friend gets stabbed in a church ladies' room after his funeral. It's insane! Megan said she heard that Allison's parents have hired security guards to be at the service so no one else is murdered during or after the memorial."

Kate shook her head. What was there to say?

His eyes narrowed. "I heard that Lisa postponed her liposuction until after the memorial."

Kate nodded. She hoped he'd let the topic drop. She didn't want to think about Lisa Smythe. She'd barely slept last night, running over and over her interactions with Lisa at the party. Remembering the subarctic glare Lisa had shot at her when she'd caught her geezer husband ogling Kate's breasts. Remembering too those torturous months in high school when she'd tried to comprehend how one teenage girl could be so cruel.

But Josh was leaning toward Kate, his smile bordering on malicious. "I meant to tell you that Megan said Lisa is definitely still smoking. Tried to quit, but she can't."

Kate frowned. "I warned Lisa about that." She'd even listed all the possibly deadly complications smokers faced during plastic surgery. Lisa had assured her she'd already given up cigarettes, but there was something in her eyes that mocked Kate, that said, Rules are for other people, not me.

"Well you better warn her again," Josh said. "Give her the speech about the hundreds of people who die during liposuction."

Kate stared at him.

First, do no harm: Hadn't that been drilled into her

throughout medical school?

"I'll talk to her," Kate said and signaled the waitress for her check.

Twelve

Sam Wolfe eyed the over-the-hill rent-a-cop standing in the hallway of the Unitarian church, thinking that the only assailants this bozo might deter were either under the age of eight or over eighty. And that was only if the seniors had bad knees and the kids were cowed by men in uniform.

He found a seat at the back of the sanctuary. Coming today was probably a total waste of time. It was highly unlikely that the killer would show up for Allison James's memorial service. If nothing else, this murderer got off on doing the unexpected.

Others in the department disagreed with his assessment, but Sam didn't see the perp as a serial killer who picked victims at random. No, these crimes were personal. It was possible that Allison James's death had been a copycat murder—a second killer wanting to make her death look like the work of the psychopath who slashed Todd Lawson. But what Sam knew for sure, knew in his gut, was that someone—or two someones—had wanted Todd Lawson and Allison James dead. The question, of course, was who.

He turned his attention back to the mourners. He would have expected a bigger turnout. Allison James had been a TV actress, after all, and the circumstances of her death had drawn a lot of media coverage. Most of the people here seemed to be either Allison's extended family or her parents' friends. Only a few pews held anyone from Allison's generation. Josh and Megan Edwards sat with Lisa Smythe, this time without her spoilsport husband. Near the front of the church was Allison's estranged husband Ethan Fox, a plump, goateed man with gray hair.

Sam was glad when the service started and a motherly looking minister encouraged the group to come up to share their memories of Allison.

A young blonde woman walked to the podium and identified herself as Allison's sister Heather. She was a less-pretty version of Allison: washed-out coloring, skinny rather than fashionably slender. She tearfully told the group about her big sister. "Allie was my role model. She always told me I could do anything that I set my mind to. That was the way she lived, believing in herself and in her dreams, and that's what I'm trying to do, even without my big sister around to inspire me."

Although at the time of her death, Sam thought, Allison's dreams had not panned out. Had she been planning her second act, her comeback, when she went to Todd Lawson's funeral? He watched Allison's sister, tears streaming down her pale cheeks, hurry back to her seat with her parents. They were crying too.

Lisa Smythe, looking fragile in a long black dress, was next to speak. "Allison was my best friend," she began, describing how they met in middle school and quickly became inseparable. "My mom called Allison her second daughter. After seventh grade she went on every family vacation with us, slept over at my house at least once a week. We used to call ourselves the Two Musketeers."

And then she dumped you, Sam thought. Callously forgot that you—the other Musketeer—even existed. *Could you forgive such treatment, Lisa? Or might your feelings of abandonment, rage, and envy have simmered for years?*

"We drifted apart for a while after we graduated from high school," Lisa said. "Allison went to Hollywood to become an actress and I went away to college. But then she came back into my life a few months ago and it was as if we'd never been apart. We were the Two Musketeers again, giggling over dumb jokes and sharing confidences."

Lisa wiped tears from her eyes with a white handkerchief. "I guess I should be happy that we had these two months to get to know each other again, to reestablish our friendship. But all I can think of is what a terrible waste it is to have a luminous presence like Allison's ripped from all of our lives."

Sam watched her stagger to her seat. It sounded like a pretty intense friendship, even for teenage girls. He glanced around, trying to gauge the reaction to Lisa's eulogy.

Many of the mourners seemed to be dabbing at their eyes. But Megan Edwards wasn't. In fact, just for a second, before Lisa arrived back at her seat and Megan put a comforting arm around her sobbing friend, Sam would have sworn that he'd seen amusement in Megan's flinty eyes.

A murmur seemed to fill the church as the next speaker strode confidently to the podium. Allison's father looked furious as Ethan Fox looked around the church and then announced, "I am Allison's husband."

The man must have been twenty years older than his wife, and even as a young man, he wouldn't have been good-looking. But there was a cocky assurance about Fox, an aura of palpable power, that Sam could imagine the young Allison would have found seductive. From what he'd read, Fox had given his wife her first professional acting job and was the executive producer of the soap opera in which she'd achieved her greatest fame.

"As many of you are aware, Allison and I were going through a rough patch in our marriage. So you might be thinking, What kind of chutzpah does this guy have to come here and talk about his love for his estranged wife?"

Sam, glimpsing Allison's mother's scowl, thought that was

indeed what her family was thinking.

But Fox, a squat man in a $5,000 suit, was eager to answer his own question. "I never thought of us as estranged. We talked on the phone almost every day. We were going to work together on a new sitcom pilot." His glowering look took in the angry father, the mother who dabbed at her eyes, the audience who was either mesmerized or repulsed by his presence here. "Allison was the love of my life. I don't know how I can go on without her." He nodded and left the podium.

The service ended shortly after that. Sam took a last look at the assembled group, thinking about the fine line between love and hate. Allison James, it was clear, had been a woman who evoked strong emotions. Could one of the people who today had proclaimed their devotion to her have crossed that line?

Sam rode the glass elevator up to Ethan Fox's hotel room, wondering what kind of shape the guy would be in after his emotional eulogy.

The man who answered his knock had exchanged his dark suit for jeans and a black sweater. He appraised Sam coolly. "I saw you at the memorial, sitting in the back. Did you learn anything?"

Only that Allison wasn't the only actor in the family, Sam thought. Or maybe Fox changed emotions as easily as his clothes. "Sometimes it's helpful to find out as much as you can about a homicide victim." He sat on the couch, refusing Fox's offer of a drink. "Why don't you tell me about your relationship with Allison over the past few months."

Fox took a sip of his drink. "She was a chameleon, a different woman for every audience. Of course a lot of actresses are like that, but most of them have some core persona—someone they really are. Allison didn't, and the irony was that she wasn't even a very good actress. She was beautiful, she was ambitious, and she loved to act. But her best performances took place in her private life."

"Sounds like a difficult person to be married to."

"Never a dull moment." Fox shrugged. "You know that blonde at the memorial, Allison's old high school buddy? The last few years Allison wouldn't even take her phone calls, and today Lisa's telling us how much she misses her best friend. And I believe her! Because that was Allison. As long as you gave her what she wanted, she made you feel as if you were the center of her life. She had a gift for making people feel cherished, even though intellectually you knew she was a lying, self-centered bitch."

"And when you stopped providing what she wanted?"

Fox smiled grimly. "She cut you off at the knees and never looked back—until, of course, you promised to develop a new sitcom for her. Then *she* suggested that we consider reconciling. As long as I could get her roles, she was my loving wife."

"That was enough for you?"

"No one ever said I had good taste in women." He glanced at his watch. "But I didn't kill Allison and I didn't hire anyone to do it. And as you no doubt know, I have a lot of witnesses who can verify that I was in Toronto shooting a movie when she died."

Unfortunately, he was telling the truth about the witnesses. Sam had already checked out that angle. Though he still wasn't convinced that Fox hadn't hired a hit man. Could any husband really be so willing to reconcile with a self-absorbed woman he knew was only using him to further her career?

"Allison told her friends that she wanted a divorce, and you were hiding your financial assets so she wouldn't get a fair settlement," Sam said. Fox could have saved himself a bundle by eliminating his greedy wife. And neither Allison's friends nor her family had mentioned anything about the reconciliation Fox claimed was imminent.

Ethan Fox laughed bitterly. "Yes, she was convinced I was hiding my money from her. I wasn't; I'm broke. I sank a big chunk of my own capital in several ventures that didn't pan out. If this new movie is successful, then I might have some cash to hide. That's the way my career works: I'm either rolling in dough or dead broke. Allison never bothered to learn about our finances. As long as there was enough money for her to keep hitting the Rodeo Drive shops, she wasn't interested."

Fox glanced again at his watch. "I have a plane to catch, so if you don't have any more questions . . ."

"So who do you think killed her?" Sam asked.

Fox seemed to hesitate, then said, "There was this guy who was Allison's assistant for a while until she realized how unstable he was and fired him. He started threatening her. She was convinced he'd jump out of the bushes some day and kill her. I thought once she moved from L.A. he'd give up, but Allison told me last week that he'd started phoning her at her parents' house. He said he was coming to Houston to see her."

"You think this man was a genuine threat?"

"I never thought so. Kyle seemed crazy but not really violent." An expression of either pain or anger crossed Fox's jowly face. "If she'd been with me in Toronto—where she should have been—Allison would still be alive today. I would have protected her, the way I always did."

Sam studied the proud, aging man who'd been Allison's husband: a gambler, a power broker, a once-successful Hollywood producer who now claimed to be on the verge of bankruptcy. He wondered just who it was Ethan Fox would have protected Allison from.

Thirteen

"So how was your day?" her mother asked when Kate got home.

"Good enough. I assisted with an interesting case, reconstructing the nose of a young man who was terribly burned in a car accident."

"That's wonderful. The things you doctors can do today."

But clearly they, all the highly educated, board-certified specialists, were not able to help her mother. Day by day she seemed to be growing more frail, more tired. Dying by inches while Kate watched, helpless.

Her evenings with her mother had taken on a routine of sorts. Kate arrived from work, relieving the daytime caretaker, then she and her mother had a few minutes of conversation that seemed a charade of long-ago normalcy. Next, Kate attempted—usually not very successfully—to coax her mother into eating some dinner. And then the two of them settled down in the living room to watch television or read a book, her mother, feet propped up on an ottoman, dozing through most of it.

"Can I get you anything, Mom? You need a pain pill?"

She shook her head. "I need to tell you something—something I've wanted to tell you for a long time."

Kate sat down. "Okay."

Tears spilled from her mother's watery gray eyes, running down her gaunt face. "So hard," she whispered.

Kate leaned forward, grasped the bony hand. "You don't

have to tell me now. We'll talk later, when you're feeling better."

"No!" Spots of red dotted the ashen face. "Now. No time left." She leaned closer, her eyes boring into Kate's. "In high school, when you got pregnant, your father and I shouldn't have sent you to that place. We—we thought it would be for the best, that they'd take good care of you."

No, you thought it would be best for you and Dad, protect you from the terrible humiliation of having a knocked-up unwed daughter. Kate wanted to yank her hand from her mother's but, from sheer force of will, managed not to move.

"I'm so sorry, Jane. So, so sorry. Your father said it was the right thing to do. That if you went away to have the baby you could come back and resume your old life as if nothing had happened."

Kate could only stare at her.

"He said you could go to college like we always planned, and then, when you were older, you could get married and have other children. But I kept thinking, 'That may be fine for her future, but what about her present? We can't send her away at a time like this. We can't do that to our daughter.' But I didn't *say* that, Jane. I should have, but I didn't."

With her free hand her mother pulled a tissue from her pocket and swiped it across her cheeks. "And now I keep thinking if you'd been here with us, we would have gotten you better medical care, and the baby would have had better doctors."

Kate suddenly felt light-headed, as if she were watching this conversation happen to someone else. Finally, she managed to get out the words. "But the baby died right away." That was what Sister Agnes had told her: "There was nothing we could do, Jane. The baby's lungs weren't developed. She couldn't have survived."

Her mother looked at her hands.

"They told me—and you told me—that my baby lived for

only a few hours." When her mother didn't respond, Kate added, "She *did* die, didn't she?" Then shouting it, "Didn't she?"

Finally her mother answered. "I—I think so. She was very ill and so very tiny. I saw her when we came to get you at the hospital, after—after your operation."

Kate glared at her. "My hysterectomy, Mother. The operation that removed my uterus when I was barely eighteen years old." But then suddenly she realized what else her mother had said. "The baby was alive then? Sister Agnes told me she'd died."

"Sister Agnes thought it would be better to tell you that, to give you closure, she said. The baby wasn't expected to live, Jane. Not for more than a few days."

It was too much. All the calming techniques Kate had learned, the medical detachment she'd acquired to help her to face the most terrible of crises: none of that worked. Her baby had been alive, and everyone had lied to her. Sister Agnes, her parents—all the adults who peremptorily decided that they knew what was best for disgraced, sinful Jane Murphy.

With enormous effort, Kate managed to get out the question. "When did my baby die?" Alone in the world, without her mother to at least hold her and rock her and croon reassurances.

"I don't know," her mother whispered. "I phoned Sister Agnes a few days later, after we got you home. All she said was she'd taken care of everything, and now I needed to focus my attention on taking care of you. She'd pray for you, she said."

Her mother's face blurred, the familiar features losing focus. It took a few minutes for Kate to realize that the low moaning noise was coming from her own mouth.

"Jane?" Her mother's hand touched her shoulder. She wanted to slap it away, then go somewhere where she could be alone. Where she could cry or scream or drink herself into a stupor.

Her mother pressed a glass of water into Kate's hand. "Drink this, honey."

She would have preferred Scotch, but she took a sip anyway. Anything to stop this torture.

Her mother looked as if she were about to keel over. "You look exhausted, Mom. Why don't you get some sleep?"

"Are you sure? I know what a shock this must be for you."

"I'm fine," Kate lied. "We can talk in the morning."

As soon as she heard her mother's bedroom door close, she phoned long-distance information.

There was no longer any listing in Bider, Texas, for the Sisters of Mercy Home for Unwed Mothers. It was only when she moved the search to the Internet that she learned the nuns still had a convent in the same west Texas town. Kate jotted down the address, her hand shaking.

She left the next morning before her mother woke up, leaving a note that she'd gone to work early.

It was better that they didn't have a chance to talk. She wasn't sure if she could continue living in the same house with a woman who'd so betrayed her.

What if Kate's sickly baby hadn't died? Maybe she'd pulled through and Sister Agnes, with her rigid moral certainty, had just gone ahead with the adoption. Maybe her daughter had been alive all these years! Fourteen now, a teenager who'd never known her birth mother. Maybe she didn't even know she was adopted. Or, worse, maybe she did know and felt abandoned by the mother who hadn't wanted her enough to keep her, who'd instead just handed her over to strangers.

And even if her baby had only lived a few days, Kate should have been at her side, stroking that alabaster cheek, holding that tiny body in her arms as her daughter drew her last breath.

What was *wrong* with her mother? How could an intelligent, educated woman have been such a doormat? She knew that sending her vulnerable young daughter away to a prison for unwed mothers was wrong. So why hadn't she stood up to her husband, demanded that their daughter be treated better? And when she'd phoned Sister Agnes to check on Kate's baby and the nun had stonewalled her, why hadn't she driven to Bider to see for herself what was going on? Instead, the minute some steely eyed tyrant told Ellen Murphy to jump, her mother had complied—and then complained later that she should have objected.

There were good, valid reasons that she had avoided her mother's company for the last fifteen years. The jolt of learning about her cancer had just made Kate forget them for a few weeks.

But right now she didn't want to think about her mother. The only thing she could focus on was finding out what had happened to her baby. After that, she'd decide what she needed to do next.

At first glance Bider, Texas, was even more depressing than she remembered. Almost half of the stores on the dusty main street were boarded up. If a lone man hadn't been ambling across the street, she might very well have thought she'd driven into a ghost town.

She'd always thought her father had chosen the Sisters of Mercy home because of its desolate location. No chance that any of her parents' friends would run into the Murphys' shockingly pregnant teenage daughter out here. But what had been a thriving, if out-of-the-way, rural town fifteen years ago now seemed like a community in the throes of a terminal illness.

Had she driven all this way and called in work to cancel all of the day's appointments merely for an impulsive wild-goose chase? It was hard to believe that this dusty hellhole would offer any answers about her past.

Kate stopped at a gas station—the only one she'd seen for miles—to ask directions to the convent.

"Not many of them sisters left out there," the balding attendant told her. "The old ones are dying off and there don't seem to be any young ones coming to take their place."

"Didn't they used to run a home for unwed mothers?"

The man nodded. "But that closed. These days girls get an abortion or they keep their babies. Doesn't seem to bother 'em anymore that they're not married."

She followed his instructions to an ancient red brick building on the outskirts of town. The place looked deserted. Kate walked into a dimly lit hallway, then peeked into an empty waiting room with a large painting of the Virgin Mary on the wall. "Hello," she called, feeling idiotic.

A small white-haired woman, stooped from osteoporosis, appeared at the end of the hallway. "Can I help you?" she asked, looking surprised to have a visitor.

Kate took a deep breath. "I'd like to talk to someone who worked at your home for unwed mothers fifteen years ago."

"Sister Agnes, who was in charge of the home, has been dead for two years."

Something about the new flintiness she heard in the woman's voice made Kate step a bit closer and say in her imperious doctor's voice, "I need to see the records for one of the babies born there."

The old nun was not about to be intimidated. "Those adoption records are sealed. We couldn't release that information even if we were able to locate it."

Kate willed herself to stay calm. "The baby was mine. I never signed any papers agreeing to adoption." Which didn't mean that her father hadn't signed them. "I was told my baby died, but now my mother says perhaps she didn't."

"Wait here." The sister turned and limped down the hall.

Kate began to wonder if she planned to return when a younger nun—maybe sixty-five rather than eighty—appeared. "I'm Sister Ignatius," she said, offering Kate her hand. "Why don't we go talk in my office?"

The woman looked vaguely familiar. Kate started to ask if she'd worked at the unwed mothers' home, but then decided she didn't really want to know.

They entered a tiny room with a crucifix on the wall and a desk, computer, and two faded chairs. Sister Ignatius chose one of the chairs and motioned for Kate to sit in the other.

In a gentle voice, she said, "Now I understand that you want to find out what happened to your baby."

"Yes." Kate took a deep breath. "I was told that she'd died. But now my mother said—she just told me—that the baby was ill but alive when I left the hospital. She thought the baby died later, but she wasn't certain."

Another deep breath. All the angry words that rushed to her mind, all the recriminations—she couldn't let them out. Once that door was opened, she was afraid what might happen, afraid she might never be able to close it again.

Sister Ignatius's eyes were sympathetic, but her voice was firm. "There was a fire at the home five years ago. Fortunately, no one was hurt, but all the records were destroyed."

"Those were your only records?" Kate asked, wanting to scream.

Sister Ignatius's intense brown eyes studied her. "Have you checked the state death index?"

Kate could feel the room start to spin. The next thing she knew someone was pushing her head down between her legs.

"Take deep breaths," the kind alto voice said. "You're just feeling a little faint."

"I—I'm sorry," Kate said when the dizziness had passed.

"Perhaps there's another approach." The nun stood. "But

you'll need to drive me to the hospital."

They drove in silence down a dusty road lined with small, neglected-looking houses. "That's what's left of the residential home," Sister Ignatius said, pointing to an ugly stone building set back from the road.

Kate slowed the car to get a better look. Suddenly, she felt drenched in sweat. Images of the odious place flooded her: Sobbing as her parents drove up to the bleak-looking institution where they intended to abandon her. Gazing into Sister Agnes's hard, unsympathetic eyes, instantly knowing that all her worst fears were about to be realized.

"Miss Murphy!" A cool hand clasped her arm.

She wrenched herself from the images, instructed herself to breathe, slowly, deeply.

"Perhaps," Sister Ignatius suggested quietly, "you'd like to stop here for a minute. Or get out of the car?"

"No!" Kate slammed her foot on the accelerator. "I never want to set eyes on that place again."

"Was it that bad?"

"Worse."

They didn't talk again until they reached the county hospital.

Kate had no memory of the outside of the building. She'd been too consumed by the pain ripping her body apart to recall anything besides the tiny curtained labor room where a few feet away another woman screamed.

She followed Sister Ignatius down a set of dark hallways to a small office where a woman with a tight gray perm typed on a computer. "Why, Sister, what a nice surprise."

"Nice to see you, Linda. How's that new grandson of yours?"

Kate waited, heart pounding, as Sister Ignatius made her request. It seemed an eternity before Linda returned with a piece of paper.

Kate accepted it with shaking hands and tucked it, unread,

into her purse. The sensible thing would be to read the information, then, rationally, decide the next step. If her daughter was alive, Sister Ignatius might have some clue about what needed to be done to find her.

But she couldn't open it. Not with an audience, no matter how well meaning and sympathetic. She needed to be alone when she found out what had happened to the tiny baby she'd only glimpsed for the briefest of moments.

Silently they drove back to the convent. She thanked Sister Ignatius for her help before she sped out of town.

She didn't pull the paper from her purse until she was an hour outside Houston. In the far corner of a gas station parking lot, she took a deep breath and then read about her daughter.

The words blurred. Kate forced herself to read them again. Her baby had died of respiratory failure when she was five days old. She'd been alive for four days after hard-eyed Sister Agnes had told Kate that she'd died. Four days after her own mother, the person who'd always told Kate how much she loved her, had whispered her tearful condolences.

And as a result Kate's daughter had died, alone in her incubator, without anyone there to hold her or let their warm tears splash on her tiny, inadequate body.

She clutched the steering wheel, feeling as if all of her decisions about her life—college, med school, the change in her appearance, her new name—had been designed to run away from this moment. She'd become Dr. Kate Dalton, in control, competent, successful, attractive, to extricate herself from this searing pain, the incendiary rage.

But it wasn't working anymore. A door had been opened and she was going to have to face the monsters inside.

Fourteen

Seated in Allison's parents' large bland living room, Sam couldn't help comparing Heather James to her older, now deceased sister. An almost life-sized painting of the two sisters as children hung over the fireplace. Even at that age the girls had remarkably similar features and coloring, but only in Allison had those components translated into striking beauty. The pale young woman sitting in front of him, with her rabbity eyelashes and nervous perkiness, seemed in many ways the polar opposite of her glamorous sister.

"I appreciate your willingness to talk to me about Allison," Sam told Heather.

"I don't know how much help I can be," Heather said, playing with the gold charm bracelet on her arm. "I can't imagine anyone wanting to murder Allie, not even Ethan, the only person I can think of who had real issues with her. He'd fight with her, try to hide all his money so she wouldn't get anything in a divorce settlement, but I just don't see him as a killer."

"He told me he thought he and Allison were about to reconcile," Sam said.

"Yeah, that was his little fantasy: he and Allie would do a hit sitcom together and live happily ever after."

But what happened when an aging, once-powerful Hollywood producer had to face the fact that his fantasy was not about to materialize? Sam wondered. Could being rejected by the beautiful young wife he adored, combined perhaps with seeing his long-time television career fade, have ignited into homicidal rage? Perhaps Ethan Fox was a better actor than Sam thought. Or perhaps he was exactly the way he'd presented himself—the still-loving husband of a lethally ambitious, heartless wife.

"So what about Allison's high school friends?" Sam asked.

Heather shrugged. "What about them?"

"I'm trying to see some connection between Todd Lawson's death and hers."

"Well, they were both part of the same group in high school. You know that, right? The other kids called them The Six."

Sam nodded. "But high school was—what? Fourteen or fifteen years ago. And I got the idea that The Six didn't have much contact with each other now, except, of course, for the two who are married."

An expression that looked very much like malice crossed Heather's pale face. "Allie hadn't seen Todd in years, but, since she got back in town, she saw Lisa and the Edwardses. She had quite *a lot* of contact with Josh for a while."

"Oh?"

Heather looked as if she was trying to decide how much to tell him. "Well," she said after a minute, "Allie told me that Josh came on to her and then she slept with him."

Sam could see that she was waiting for his reaction. He didn't want to show it to her. "That's interesting. Were they having an affair when your sister died?"

Heather shook her head. "I don't think they were ever really having an affair. Allie knew from the get-go that Josh was a serial adulterer, but she was bored and he was charming and fun. And she knew it wouldn't lead to anything serious. I mean there was no emotional connection between them, and from what Allie said, the sex wasn't that great either."

"Did Megan Edwards know about this?" Sam asked.

"Probably. Allie thought she did. She said that Megan was

incredibly jealous and that kind of turned Josh on—seeing how much he could get away with. Allie said Josh felt Megan coerced him into marrying her and then wanted to micromanage his life. Sleeping around on her was Josh's way to get his revenge."

Sam considered the implications of what she'd told him. "Are you suggesting that Megan or Josh Edwards had a motive to murder your sister?" And Megan Edwards had more than that: she'd been the one who discovered Allison's body in that lonely church bathroom. And the only living person who could corroborate her story was Josh Edwards.

"I'm saying that Megan seems like the kind of person who might kill Allie if she was mad enough. Allie said she did a lot of really mean things in high school."

"Like what?"

"Like putting Ex-Lax in another girl's soda right before cheerleading tryouts to make sure that Megan got on the team. Planting drugs in the locker of a girl who was coming on to Josh and getting her expelled. Megan always wanted to make sure that she got what she wanted."

Yet there was a big difference between lacing a rival's soda with Ex-Lax and slashing her throat, Sam thought. Even though the other incidences were evidence of a ruthless cruelty that could have evolved into homicidal rage as the stakes—her husband, her marriage—got higher for Megan.

"And Megan wasn't the only one who did mean things. One night in high school Allie came home drunk and she told me about the dirty tricks that The Six did to get their way. 'The ends justify the means,' they used to say. And they all had to be the stars of the school: the head cheerleader, the class president, captain of the football team, the lead actress in the school play, the president of the Honor Society."

"Did your sister do some dirty tricks to get the lead in those plays?"

"She didn't have to. Her big buddy, Lisa, did them for her. Allie told me once that there was this new girl, who was shy and weird but a really good actress, who was probably going to get the lead in some play that Allie really wanted to do. Lisa told her not to worry about it, she'd handle things. And then suddenly there's this big rumor going around the school that this girl is gay and sleeping with the drama teacher. She left school the next week, transferred someplace else, I guess, and Allie got the lead."

"How'd Allie feel about that?" Sam asked.

"She was glad to have the part. I think she might have felt a little guilty, but she said she never told Lisa to do it, she just went out and did it on her own. Then she laughed and called Lisa and Todd 'The Enforcers.' "

"The Enforcers?"

"She said that they were the two who got off on the dirty tricks, the ones who thought them up. Todd one time fixed the brakes on the car of this guy who was the starting quarterback on the football team just so Matt, the jock who Lisa was going out with, could take his place on the team. The quarterback broke his leg when his car ran a red light. He was out for the season and Matt was in."

Sam could feel a tingle of anticipation, a rock-hard certainty that he was on to something. "Any other examples Allison mention to you?"

Heather thought about it for a minute. "Oh, I don't remember everything. But yeah, I think there was some nerdy girl who was tutoring Matt after school, and Lisa didn't like the way Matt smiled at her in the hallway."

"So what happened?"

"Lisa had Todd ask the girl out. He got her drunk and had

sex with her in the back seat of his car. Then Lisa made sure that everyone in school heard about it."

Dr. Kate Dalton didn't seem to recognize him when Sam almost knocked into her again as he opened the door to her waiting room. He smiled at her. "Hello, Dr. Dalton, I'm glad this time I wasn't carrying coffee."

She looked confused for a moment, then nodded. "No harm done."

He noticed with surprise how different she looked. The softness he remembered in her face, the attentive curiosity in her eyes were no longer there. Instead, she looked pale and withdrawn and, yes, angry. About what? he wondered.

"I told my daughter what you said about the nose job. She's trying to convince her mother to agree to let her get one as a joint birthday and Christmas present. She said high school would be a lot more enjoyable if she didn't look like an anteater."

Suddenly, her eyes seemed to focus on him. "I think your daughter might be right, and I'm speaking here as someone who didn't get her rhinoplasty until well after high school. If you don't mind coming back to my office, I have a brochure and surgery fact sheet that she might want to read."

"I know Carly would appreciate that." Sam followed her through the waiting room and down the corridor to her office. He took in the pale gray walls, the black art deco furniture.

"I like the way you decorated the place," he said, remembering Josh Edwards's coldly austere chrome-and-glass office.

"I didn't. I'm filling in for another doctor who's on maternity leave." Kate located the pamphlet she'd been searching for and handed it to him.

"Thanks. I'll give this to Carly when I see her this weekend." He hesitated. "You know I think my daughter would really like to have you as her doctor, especially when she hears that you had cosmetic work done too. How long will you be working here?"

"I'm not sure. But I'd still be happy to talk to your daughter. I can relate to a girl who hates high school."

Sam nodded. She suddenly seemed more like the warm, interested woman he remembered from his last visit. Perhaps she'd identified with his Carly's feelings of being an ugly duckling, though it was hard to imagine Dr. Kate Dalton as anything but pretty, confident, and in control.

"High school is a tough time for a lot of people," he said.

"Isn't that the truth?" The old grimness was coming back into her face. "Was it that way for you too?"

He shook his head. "No, I played football. I wasn't incredibly talented or anything, but I had buddies on the team, so I had a good enough time."

"You were lucky then." Dr. Dalton was walking toward the door.

Sam moved that way too, wondering if she had a patient scheduled or if she was just ready to get rid of him. On impulse, figuring it was definitely a long shot, he said, "Funny we should be talking about high school. I was just asking your colleague Dr. Edwards about that."

This time there was no mistaking the chill in her voice. "And what did Josh have to say about high school?"

"Not much," Sam admitted. "He seems sort of evasive, a guy who doesn't want to reveal much about himself."

"Oh, I'd say Josh was the same kind of guy in high school that you see now: as shallow as a puddle and just as shiny and real as a cubic zirconia earring. A smart, handsome, golden boy who always had someone behind the scenes doing all his dirty work."

Sam raised an eyebrow. "You sound as if you knew him pretty well in high school."

Kate opened the door. "I never met him in high school. It's just what I infer from knowing him now."

Sam studied her face as he thanked her for the information sheets. Dr. Dalton didn't strike him as someone who got this worked up for no reason. As he walked out of her office, Sam decided he wanted very much to find out what her reason was.

Fifteen

And now what? Kate thought as she woke from a fitful night's sleep. She couldn't believe she'd slept at all after her trip to Bider and her hellish day reliving her past: those lonely months at the unwed mother's home, the pain and terror of giving birth alone, and then the worst agony—the death of her perfect little baby and her dreams of ever giving birth to more children. But ten minutes after she walked in the door, and talked briefly to Betty Sue, Kate had climbed into her bed and promptly fallen asleep.

This morning she remembered Betty Sue's puzzlement at Kate's reaction—or more accurately, nonreaction—to the news that her mother had had a very bad day, a turn for the worse. She was sleeping, Betty Sue said, and had been sleeping most of the day. And all Kate could think was, how incredibly ironic. Now that she was finally ready to confront her mother, to dredge up all the banked anger from those old betrayals, Ellen Murphy had ensured that she'd be unavailable to participate.

Kate had driven into her mother's driveway, feeling like an avenging angel, returning to smite the wicked. She'd even decided on the drive back from Bider exactly what she was going to say to her mother: *Let me tell you what I learned today about my baby, your grandchild. You remember, Mom, the one who you told me had died while I was having my hysterectomy? The granddaughter Sister Agnes told you to forget about. And you, of course, being Ellen Doormat Murphy, did exactly as you were told.*

But when Kate had marched into the house, ready for confrontation, her mother wasn't there. Betty Sue, her face grim, had told Kate, "You need to prepare yourself, honey. Your mother slept all day long, and when I finally managed to get her up, to eat a little, she seemed like she was barely conscious. At first I thought she might have had a stroke; she seemed so confused. But she knows me, she can talk and move okay, and she says she's not in pain. It's just that all she wants to do is sleep."

Kate could only stare at her. Finally, she found her voice. "I'll take care of it," she told Betty Sue. "You go on home."

Her mother had always hated conflict, recoiling at the sound of raised voices, the messiness of disagreement. *It's so much easier to avoid all the unpleasantness, isn't it, Mom? How very convenient to suddenly become too sick to be held accountable.*

For Kate had known then: Now there would never be any more discussion of Kate's pregnancy and her mother's part in sending her to the prison for unwed mothers. No ugly repercussions about spreading lies to her daughter, abandoning her sickly grandbaby, or not having enough backbone to stand up to her husband or Sister Agnes.

But how could Kate live with what she'd learned in Bider? How could she go to work, coax her mom to eat a little, chat about her day, when everything was different? For the first time Kate wondered if her dogged determination to create a new self totally different from Plain Jane Murphy was more denial than an ambitious climb to success. Had she really thought that she could turn her back on all the ugliness of her past, forget it in the frenzied activity of school and work and reinvention?

Her mother was in the kitchen when she went downstairs. She glanced at Kate with no curiosity, no remnants of the tearful confessions of two nights ago. Today Ellen Murphy was too ill, too tired to deal with any of that old trauma. Who could hold such a person responsible for her past actions?

Kate forced herself to take a deep breath. "Are you hungry, Mom? I could make you some breakfast."

Her mother shook her head. "No thanks, dear. I think I just want to go back to sleep."

Work today was an ordeal. Maybe all the simmering anger she couldn't unleash on her mother was being transformed into this new impatience and irritation with her patients and coworkers. Within the course of the morning, she'd snapped at a nurse and informed a sad-eyed patient that psychotherapy seemed a more appropriate solution for her problems than another face-lift.

Then when she'd gone out to lunch, she encountered the homicide detective who'd spilled coffee on her and—stupidly—she'd revealed to him her animosity toward Josh Edwards. Officer Wolfe, she could tell, was a little taken aback by her venom. Kate wished she'd been able to find out why he was interviewing Josh for a second time, but she'd already told him too much; the very last thing she needed right now was getting Sam Wolfe suspicious about why she was so hostile to Josh.

And now, to make her day complete, she had an appointment with another high school bully. In fact, the very person who'd turned her life upside down and set everything else in motion. Kate took a very deep breath and opened her office door. "Hello, Lisa."

Sitting in one of the art deco chairs, Lisa Smythe did not look happy. Had she broken a fingernail during a session with her personal trainer? "Why did you want to see me?" she asked Kate.

"I wanted to tell you that I won't be doing your liposuction."

Lisa's heavily made-up eyes widened. "What do you mean, you refuse to do my liposuction?"

"Just that. I've heard that you're still smoking, even though I warned you against it. There are too many possible side effects when you combine cigarettes with cosmetic surgery, some of them life threatening. You run a higher risk of post-operative infection. The nicotine you've been ingesting—now and if you keep it up after the surgery—can lead to raised scars. Which you, of course, would blame entirely on the medical staff."

Lisa's pale face flushed and her eyes narrowed. "Who *said* I'm still smoking?"

"Josh Edwards."

"He's a liar."

Among other things, Kate thought. But she didn't think Josh was lying about this. And maybe, more to the point, she didn't trust herself right now to suck fat off Lisa Smythe's sedated body.

Wouldn't Lisa really be appalled if Kate told her the total story? *I'm afraid, Lisa, that I might slip up and "accidentally" kill you while I was suctioning off your extra flab.* There were way too many potentially lethal complications of liposuction—excessive bleeding, infections, problems from sedation—that could happen, even when you were trying your best to prevent them. And while Kate didn't think she could ever intentionally injure a patient, the realization that she would be able to rid the world of a sadistic and totally worthless woman might be just too much temptation.

So even if some unavoidable complication occurred during Lisa's liposuction, Kate would always wonder if her subconscious had been reminding her that the woman on the table—the person who for no reason at all had given the order to destroy poor, guileless Jane Murphy's innocence and then laughed about it—really didn't deserve to live. Kate was doing both Lisa and herself a big favor by refusing to operate on her.

And the irony was that Lisa—the person who'd irrevocably damaged her life—didn't even recognize her. Even if Kate hadn't changed her appearance so dramatically, even if her name was still Jane Murphy, Lisa probably wouldn't have remembered her. After all, if all those rumors she'd heard were accurate, Lisa had committed a lot of other "pranks" on other high school students who got in The Six's way. Who would expect this woman to keep track of her many victims?

"You can't *do* this to me, not two days before the liposuction," Lisa shouted. "I have to go to my high school reunion in less than two months. I don't have time to go find another plastic surgeon."

Kate met those hateful blue eyes and felt a definite surge of satisfaction. "Maybe you should have thought of that when you refused to stop smoking."

Lisa drew herself up in the chair across from Kate's desk. When she spoke, her high voice was exactly the same timbre, displaying the same combination of arrogance, cruelty, and contempt that Kate remembered from that last awful year of high school. "Just who do you think you are? You're just a temp here, a nobody who's filling in while Brenda is on maternity leave. I intend to go to Aaron Glass and he'll make you do it. Or fire you."

Actually she'd like nothing better than for Aaron Glass to fire her, Kate realized. It would take the decision on when to resign out of her hands.

Kate stood. "You go talk to whoever you want, Lisa. But as for who I think I am, *I'm* an ethical, conscientious surgeon."

So maybe you'll be taking your fat ass to the reunion after all, she thought as Lisa stalked out the door.

Sixteen

Carly regarded her father over the top of the rhinoplasty booklet she'd read at least six times. "I want to meet Dr. Dalton, Dad. She was really, really nice when I talked to her on the phone. And she thinks it's a great idea that I get my nose fixed this year."

Of course, Dr. Dalton would not be the one paying for the surgery, Sam thought. And she was also not the one who had to deal with his ex-wife's vocal resentment that he was taking Carly's side in this matter. "I'm not sure how much longer Dr. Dalton will be working at that office. She's only substituting for another doctor who's out on maternity leave. So she probably won't be there by your summer vacation." Which was the earliest time that Carly's mother would allow her to get the surgery.

"Yeah, she told me that. But I'd still like to meet her. She said that she can do computer imaging that will show me how I'd look with different kinds of noses. Even if another doctor had to do the surgery, I'd sort of like her input on what sort of nose to get."

It sounded a little bit too much like shoe shopping for Sam's taste, but he tried to look supportive. In fact, he'd like nothing better than to have another excuse to talk to Kate Dalton. His gut told him that she knew a lot more about Josh Edwards's high school years than she was letting on. He'd done some cursory digging. There was no Kate Dalton listed in The Six's high school yearbook, no obvious connection that explained the venom he'd heard in Dr. Dalton's voice when she discussed the kind of teenager Edwards had been. Despite his colleagues' skepticism, Sam still felt that Todd Lawson's and Allison James's deaths were somehow connected to The Six's high school lives. Finding out what Kate Dalton wasn't telling him might provide some vital information. And even if it didn't, he still liked being around the paradoxical Dr. Dalton.

Sam studied his shy, auburn-haired daughter whose largish nose still looked just fine to him. "Why don't you see if you can make a late afternoon appointment with Dr. Dalton some day this week. Thursday's my day off; that would be the best day for me, if you can manage it. I'll pick you up from school and take you to her office."

He thought that for a moment Carly looked suspicious of his easy capitulation. But then she smiled and said, "Cool. I'll call her tomorrow morning."

As it turned out, Dr. Dalton did have an opening on Thursday afternoon. Sam found himself sitting with his daughter in the same waiting room where he'd first collided with Kate, this time trying to guess what kind of procedure the other patients—predominantly middle-aged women—were going to have done.

When the nurse came out to get Carly, he was disappointed that she wouldn't allow him to accompany his daughter. "No, Dr. Dalton specifically told me she wanted to see Carly alone," the woman said. "She likes to see teenagers by themselves for the initial interview."

He tried to read the waiting room magazines, but he had trouble concentrating. Was Carly right now picking out a pert, turned-up nose that would make her look like some generic, vapid pop star? Would he forever after look at his daughter and instead see a stranger's nose on Carly's face? He wondered—and didn't like the thought at all—if he had capitulated on an important issue partly because he wanted so much to figure out what Kate Dalton was hiding.

About forty-five minutes after she'd left, Carly returned alone to the waiting room. "Aren't we both going to talk to Dr. Dalton now?" he asked her.

Carly shook her head. "No, we covered everything that needed to be covered. Though"—she shot him a sly look—"she did say to tell you hi."

And wasn't that just big of her? He would have preferred a chance to offer his input into his only daughter's major surgery, not to mention an opportunity to ferret out any pertinent information about Josh Edwards's high school activities. But Dr. Kate Dalton couldn't even be bothered to tell him hi in person!

Sam eyed his daughter. "You look happy. How'd it go in there?"

"She is so cool, Dad. I really like her. We tried out a lot of noses on my face. She thinks I'd look best with one of the longer ones—to go with the rest of my facial features."

He managed, with some effort, not to say that she already had a perfectly fine long nose. "So did the two of you pick one out?" he asked as they headed toward the door.

She shook her head. "I haven't decided yet. But you know Dr. Dalton told me that *she* had quite a bit of cosmetic surgery done on her face. She had a nose job—her nose was too long too—and I think she had a chin implant. She used to work part time for a cosmetic surgeon to put herself through medical school. And this doctor gave each person on his staff one free plastic surgery procedure as a Christmas gift. I mean, how cool is that?"

Sam personally thought it sounded revolting. He envisioned a whole office full of cookie-cutter-pretty women with very large breasts. Though from what he recalled of Kate Dalton's trim, compact body, she probably had limited the cosmetic work to her face.

"And she told me that life is so much better after high school, Dad. That people aren't such pack animals anymore. And they're not so mean and intolerant toward anyone who's a little different."

"That's probably true," Sam said, trying not to sound too interested. "Dr. Dalton mention anything else about her own high school experiences?"

Carly cocked her head to one side, thinking about the question. "She said she'd been a real geek—smart and real shy. And some mean kids called her Plain Jane."

"Jane? I thought her name was Kate."

"I said that too. She said Kate is her middle name, and she decided to use that instead of Jane when she went to college." She looked up at her father. "Maybe in a few years I'll decide to go by my middle name. Maybe I'll call myself Elizabeth or Liz."

Sam shrugged and opened the door of the parking garage for her. "I like the name Carly but Elizabeth's not bad." And since he was trying hard to get used to the idea of an entirely new nose on his daughter's face, learning to call her a new name seemed, in comparison, like small potatoes.

An hour later he'd dropped off Carly and returned to his apartment. He found the copy of The Six's high school yearbook that he'd brought home to look at. No Jane Dalton was listed in the index, but finally, after a lot of looking, he found what he wanted.

This Jane was named Murphy. She was a member of the National Honor Society, the orchestra, and the school newspaper: a mousy girl with long straight hair and a long nose who looked like she'd found posing for her yearbook photo acutely embarrassing. Sam probably wouldn't even have recognized her if Carly hadn't given him the heads-up about the different nose and chin. Unlike Kate Dalton, Jane Murphy was a bit plump, wore big glasses, and wore no makeup. The confident woman he knew, a woman no one would call plain, had clearly been a different person at seventeen or eighteen. So was that why she hadn't wanted to talk about her high school life: she didn't want to remember the awkward teenager she'd been?

A lot of people felt that way—couldn't wait to put high school behind them. So what difference did it make that she hadn't wanted to talk about it?

But then, after looking up all the pages listed in the index under the name Jane Murphy, he found what he was searching for. In the front row of the honor society photo stood stoop-shouldered Jane Murphy. And next to her was Josh ("J.R.") Edwards.

Seventeen

Kate's day ended with a tongue lashing by Aaron Glass, who informed her, his voice frigid, that he'd just received a phone call from Lisa Smythe's husband announcing that from now on he'd be taking the family's cosmetic surgery business elsewhere. "And while I understand that you cancelled her surgery because Lisa was still smoking, I do want you to know that Dr. James Goodman, a well-respected, board-certified surgeon, will be doing Lisa's liposuction tomorrow. *He* apparently had no qualms about her smoking."

"*If* she told him," Kate said. "She lied to me, so why not to him too? I only knew because Josh told me she was still smoking a pack a day. She'd assured me on our previous visit that she'd quit."

Aaron nodded. "She also lied to Belinda about her smoking habits. And she's never satisfied with the work she has done. Her expectations are completely unrealistic about how much improvement one can expect from cosmetic surgery."

"She isn't a very reasonable person. Or more accurately, she's a narcissistic and self-absorbed"—Kate started to say "bitch," but stopped herself before she committed professional suicide—"woman who's totally unwilling to follow instructions or accept responsibility for anything that goes wrong. And she thinks that just because she wants to look like a super-model we should be able to make her dreams come true. She seems like the archetype, Aaron, for the type of patient we *should* turn away."

He regarded her through chilly gray eyes. "She also has a husband with a great deal of money that he's willing to spend on making her look younger." Sounding reluctant, he added, "But you do have a point, and Belinda said basically the same thing."

At the beginning of his lecture, Kate had thought that he might be working up to firing her. To her surprise, she, who just a day earlier had thought that she *wanted* to be fired, today found the prospect very upsetting. While admittedly she loathed Lisa, she still believed that refusing to do the woman's liposuction was a medically ethical decision. Now watching Aaron's gaunt, disapproving face, she realized how much she wanted him to value both her professionalism and her medical competence.

He didn't go that far, but he didn't say anything negative like "You don't really seem like a good fit for this practice, Kate." Instead, he said, "I just wanted to touch base with you. Have a good night." He left with a brusque nod.

And good evening to you too, Kate thought. She was so used to being a high achiever—best student, hardest worker, and all-around-boring-good-girl—that the doctor's at-best lukewarm appraisal of her still stung. There wouldn't be any gushing recommendation from Dr. Aaron Glass coming to her next employer.

Kate was in no mood to even consider who or where that next employer would be or what kind of medicine she'd be practicing. She'd always planned on devoting her surgical skills to reconstructive cases rather than cosmetic surgery, and the fact she didn't have the next step planned out, the way she always had before, disturbed her. But, she reminded herself, she had to finish this chapter of her life before she began the next one. After her family obligations here were over, she intended to leave town and her Plain Jane Murphy past forever.

When she got home Betty Sue said her mother had felt so exhausted that she'd already gone to bed. Kate fixed herself a can of soup for dinner and then, feeling unaccountably edgy, went upstairs to her computer to check her e-mail.

She had finally responded to the invitation to her high school reunion, probably prodded by yesterday's confrontation with Lisa Smythe—and the reminder that Lisa would be at the reunion. Last night Kate had e-mailed her regrets to the only name she recognized on the reunion committee, Libby Norman, one of her few high school friends. And for some reason what she'd intended as a brief "sorry I won't be able to attend" turned into a chatty missive, filled with questions about their former high school classmates.

Libby had immediately e-mailed a response:

<Hey, Jane, of course I remember you! How could I forget that brainy, generous kid who let me copy her French homework? Sorry you won't be able to make the reunion, but I do want to point out that even busy doctors often manage to catch one of the dozens of plane flights leaving daily from Chicago to Houston.

<In regards to our classmates, Matt Phillips is an engineer now in Tulsa, married with three children, coming to the reunion with his wife. J.R.—now called "Josh"—and Megan Patterson Edwards are also coming. He's a plastic surgeon and she's a real estate agent with two kids. From the one time I ran into her at a restaurant, I can tell you she is just as much of a mean, arrogant bitch as ever. Lisa Casey Smythe is coming too. She's the too-blonde trophy wife of an old rich guy, though she prefers to think of herself as a "professional volunteer." I wanted to write back that "professionals" usually spend more than four

hours a week on their careers.

<As for the other two of The Six, I don't know if you've heard this already, but Todd Lawson and Allison James were murdered! Todd was killed in his hotel room and Allison was murdered in a church bathroom after Todd's funeral!!! Can you believe that? Hard to take in that anyone in our class would be dead already.

<I too have heard a lot of gossip about The Six and their dirty tricks: you and I were just two of their victims. I think sometimes the price of being bullied isn't always obvious to an outsider. After Megan slipped the Ex-Lax into my Coke at cheerleader tryouts, I just kind of decided to forever boycott all public competitions. Sometimes I think I gave up too easily—I allowed myself to be intimidated by Megan's cruelty.

<And take Stan Perry, our valedictorian, who The Six tried so hard to intimidate. Now he's this incredibly successful New York attorney—as he told everyone repeatedly at our ten-year reunion—but he acts like someone who's always trying to prove that he's the best.

<Then too there are the other victims who everyone lost touch with: that football player whose leg was broken in the car accident that Todd supposedly arranged, and that actress, Maria Somebody or Other, who was harassed by Lisa out of the lead in the school play. Who knows what kind of permanent damage it could have caused that quarterback to know that somebody risked killing him just so one of The Six got to be a starter on a frickin' high school football team? I heard that after Lisa started spreading rumors that Maria got her part in the play because she was sleeping with Miss Harrison, Maria had a nervous breakdown and had to go to a mental hospital for a while. That may just be a rumor, but she DID leave school.

<But enough! I have to finish grading my first period class's personal essays before bedtime. Hope you'll reconsider attend-

ing the reunion. I'd REALLY love to see you. If you come to Houston any time, call me immediately! Libby>

Kate reread the e-mail, trying to dismiss the suspicion that she was opening another door that was better left closed.

Eighteen

She paused outside the door of the outpatient recovery room, feeling unaccountably nervous.

Somehow, she felt more exposed this time, more in danger. Which was ridiculous, really. She'd had just as much chance of being apprehended in the church after Todd Lawson's funeral. More chance, actually, since several people from her high school class had been sitting only a few pews away during the service. Then, as now, she'd been wearing a disguise, but still, you never knew who might recognize you anyway. Both Lisa Smythe and Megan Edwards, for instance, were reported to have a good eye for faces.

Maybe it was the fact that Allison's murder had been so *easy* that was making her feel jumpy, as if her supply of good luck had already run out. Of course it was also possible that she was just being paranoid—expecting people to be out to get her. (Ha! How could she possibly think *that?*)

She took a deep breath, reminding herself that if the room was too crowded with staff or something else didn't look right, she could just walk away and wait for another opportunity. The post-op recovery room was not really an ideal place for a murder. Too many potential witnesses, for one thing. Too much available medical help to save the victim.

But she had to at least scope out the situation. Time was running out and Lisa Smythe had proved a surprisingly elusive target. Once her friend Allison had been murdered, Lisa apparently had freaked. After Allison's funeral, she hardly ventured from her house.

Getting Lisa alone was a definite problem. Drastic measures, she'd decided, were required. Which, unfortunately, meant greater risks.

Another deep breath and she opened the door.

Shit! She'd been hoping against hope that the nurse on duty would be occupied with another patient and she could slip in, quickly deal with Lisa, and get out. But instead there were two nurses sitting there, just shooting the breeze.

You can leave and try again later. Only idiots take needless risks.

But she couldn't leave. Not yet.

She walked briskly inside and headed toward the row of post-op patients. Any minute she expected one of the nurses to snarl at her, "Who are you? What are you doing in here?"

But the women kept talking and ignored the figure in the surgical scrubs who was peering at the half-dozen people sleeping off their anesthesia. Probably the nurses thought she was checking on one of her patients. Or maybe they didn't give a damn what she was doing, as long as she didn't interrupt their discussion of last night's TV shows.

So where the hell *was* Lisa?

Finally, she spotted her. Apparently still asleep, with an IV attached to her arm.

Well, well, well. You have a visitor, Lisa. A specter from your past. Remember me? Here's a hint. Think "high school pranks." Remember me now?

It was a shame that Lisa wasn't awake to witness what was about to happen to her. To feel the terror and realize, with sweaty palms and lurching gut, that she was about to die for her sins.

She paused for a moment at the IV line. Lisa was moaning softly, as if she was starting to wake up.

From the corner of her eye, she checked out the nurses. They still didn't seem to be paying her any attention.

She moved to the head of Lisa's bed. Pulled the scalpel from her pocket.

Suddenly, Lisa's eyes popped open. "Whaat!?" she shouted.

"Sounds like the princess is waking up," a nurse said.

Footsteps were coming in her direction.

For a second she hesitated. Then, turning and nodding at the nurse, she walked quickly away.

As she opened the door, Lisa was still yelling something incoherent and the nurse, in a sickly sweet voice, was saying, "There, there, honey, you need to calm down."

She kept up her busy-professional's walk until she was out of the building. Once she was outside, though, she practically ran to her car.

Tears streamed down her face as she turned on the ignition. She'd failed! The bitch was still alive!

Nineteen

"Someone tried to kill me," a very pale and very agitated Lisa Smythe told Sam. "I'm sure of it."

Propped up by pillows on her sunroom couch, Lisa did indeed look like someone who'd almost died, Sam thought. Without makeup, her face was ashen, her eyes red-tinged. She also appeared to be in pain, though Sam wasn't sure if that was due to the liposuction she'd had four days earlier or to the surgical complications that had sent her briefly into a coma.

He made an effort to keep his voice calm. "What makes you think that?"

Lisa's lower lip jutted out. "I just know it." Her shrill voice rose a few decibels. "Someone hates me and wants me dead. I want you to find him."

Sam reminded himself that the woman had been through a lot. And if the frigid glances he'd seen her geezer husband toss her way when he took Sam to the sunroom were any indication of his attitude toward his young wife, Lisa wasn't raking in a lot of sympathy on the home front either.

"What makes you think someone tried to kill you? Did you see something suspicious?"

He could see her hesitate. "I thought I saw someone in scrubs standing by my IV and then moving toward me, holding something shiny—like a knife. But I didn't really see the face. I was half asleep, but I sensed I was in danger."

Or maybe the fact that your friends were killed with a knife gave you a bad nightmare. And the shiny thing you saw was some medical equipment, like a syringe or a stethoscope.

"Could the person you saw have been your doctor or nurse?"

Lisa shook her head, making her now limp blonde hair spill across her face. She shoved her hair behind her ears and scowled at him. "No, I started shouting and then a nurse came and the person in the scrubs walked away. Right after that I started feeling funny. They told me later that I went into shock."

"Did you tell your doctor about this person you saw?"

She nodded. "I told my doctor and the nurse. They said I probably only imagined it, that sometimes people have strange reactions to anesthesia. The nurse said no one 'inappropriate' came into the recovery room and no one tried to harm me. The doctor seemed to be saying that going into shock was a post-operative complication probably due to lipoing off too much fat—which he implied was *my* fault because I nagged him to take off the maximum amount." She rolled her eyes. "As if *anyone* would say, 'Oh, doctor, take off only a pound or two and let the rest sit there on my hips.' "

She stopped and appeared to check out his reaction to that. Sam maintained his poker face and she returned to her story.

"These medical people apparently think I should feel grateful that I came out of the coma! They don't even grasp that I have grounds for a malpractice suit. 'No harm done' seems to be their attitude. I'm alive and have a smaller butt, so what's there to complain about?"

And I'll bet you're a real favorite of medical people everywhere, Sam thought. "But you don't think that your coma was caused by the doctor taking off too much fat?"

"I know I saw some creep by my IV, and nobody seems to know who this person was and what he or she was doing. And there've been other things too." Lisa glanced toward the doorway, as if to make sure that no one was lurking outside listening. "Right after I got out of the hospital I started getting threatening e-mails," she said, her voice almost a whisper.

Sam pulled out his notebook. "What do these e-mails say?"

Lisa glanced away. "They say 'You're going to pay for what you did to me.' " She turned back to him, glaring. "And before you ask, I don't *know* what I did to him or her. The writer signed his e-mail 'Your Ex–High School Classmate.' When I tried twice to respond, my e-mail was returned because of an address error."

"Do you still have those e-mails? Maybe we could have them traced."

"No, I deleted them. I—I didn't want to be reminded of them or have anybody else read them."

Somebody else like your cold-eyed husband? "How many of these messages did you get?"

"Two. And they both said exactly the same thing—it was payback time."

"So you're thinking that the person at your IV might have been your ex–high school classmate?"

She nodded. "I know it sounds paranoid. When I told my mother about it, she said I was imagining someone was trying to kill me because of Todd's and Allison's murders. Mom thinks the lipo thing was just what the doctor said it was, and the person near my IV was some nurse coming to check on me. She says the e-mail is probably from somebody who I was crappy to in high school—somebody who's just trying to scare me."

"She have any specific candidate in mind?"

Lisa's pale face grew pink. "No, I was kind of mean when I was in high school. It could have been from any one of a lot of people."

"And you didn't recognize anybody from your high school class when you went in for your liposuction?"

Lisa cocked her head to one side, thinking about it. "No,

nobody except Josh Edwards. He was going in to do surgery, but he stopped to tell me good luck."

Dr. Josh Edwards was clearly not happy to see Sam again. The plastic surgeon motioned for him to sit in one of the uncomfortable chrome and leather chairs across from his large, pretentious chrome and glass desk. "I only have ten minutes for you," Edwards said in a voice that clearly indicated his time was worth more than a mere police officer's.

Sam sat. *Okay, fella, I'll cut to the chase.* "Have you or your wife received any threats from a former high school classmate?"

Edwards looked confused. "No. Why are you asking?"

"Others of The Six have." Sam hoped that Lisa Smythe hadn't told her buddies Meg and Josh yet about her e-mail. He wanted very much for Edwards to believe that he'd been in contact with all the remaining members of The Six and had concluded it was only a matter of time before the doctor and his wife would be threatened too.

Sam paused, waited a few beats. "And considering that two of your friends have been murdered, I'm thinking that all verbal or written threats to the rest of you should be checked out."

"What kind of threats?" Edwards asked, sounding a bit less arrogant.

"E-mails suggesting it's payback time for all the dirty tricks you guys played on your high school classmates."

A flush crossed the doctor's angular face. "I don't know what dirty tricks you're talking about."

Right. "Funny, everyone else seems to. From what I've heard, the six of you were notorious bullies who'd do anything to get what you wanted." Edwards blinked rapidly, but said nothing. "None of this would normally interest me," Sam said, "unless, of course, one of your victims decided to press charges. But the fact that your bullying might be connected to two murders makes your adolescent behavior suddenly relevant."

"You think that whoever wrote those e-mails killed Todd and Allison?"

"It's possible," Sam said, maintaining eye contact. "It's certainly enough of a threat that if I were you, I'd want to tell the police every single person who was ever bullied by you and your friends."

He could see the uncertainty in Edwards's eyes change to resolve. "I was never one of the instigators." The surgeon shook his head, anticipating Sam's reaction. "I'm not excusing my behavior. I never tried to stop the others—'The Enforcers,' I called them. Sometimes I even benefited from their stunts. But I never initiated any of the bullying, and I didn't need or ask for their help."

"So who were these enforcers?"

"Mainly Todd, Lisa, and Megan. The other three of us—Allison, Matt, and I—were more the actual achievers of the group, the talented ones. The enforcers kind of made sure we stayed on top."

Sam couldn't decide which group sounded the more disgusting: the thugs who inflicted the damage or the top dogs who looked the other way while they tortured. He didn't even try to hide his disdain when he said, "I'll tell you what I just told Lisa Smythe. You and your wife need to make a list tonight of every single person The Six ever hurt. Because, Dr. Edwards, whoever killed Todd and Allison didn't seem to share your distinction between the enforcers and the achievers."

Twenty

"Dr. Dalton?"

The male voice sounded vaguely familiar. Kate turned to find Officer Sam Wolfe, Carly's father, studying her. "Hello, Mr. Wolfe. What can I do for you?" She wondered what the folded paper in his hand was. It looked very much like the office stationery, a thick, cream-colored linen paper that always struck her as too ostentatiously expensive for a medical practice.

Sam smiled at her, a very nice smile that crinkled the corners of expressive brown eyes that looked like his daughter's. "Is there any chance you could spare a few minutes to talk with me?"

Carly had warned Kate that her father would not like being excluded from the initial rhinoplasty discussion. "I'm sorry, but I have a patient waiting."

Sam nodded. "How about lunch then? I really would like to talk to you."

Kate was about to suggest that they could talk on the phone when she stopped herself. She'd spent way too many lunch hours eating yogurt or a sandwich at her desk while she plowed through a stack of paperwork. She'd promised herself to get out more.

"Okay," she told him. "I should be through by noon."

He looked pleased. "I'll be back for you then."

An hour later, there he was in the waiting room, paging through a magazine. He stood, smiling, when he spotted her.

Several patients and the ever-attentive Mandy noticed too, Kate saw. Why hadn't she thought to tell him they could meet at the corner deli?

"Any place where you particularly want to eat?" he asked as they walked out the door.

She shook her head. "I'm not picky about food, but we're going to have to go someplace fairly close because I need to be back in an hour."

"How would you feel about picking up sandwiches down the street and going to eat in the park?"

"Sounds good to me."

Fifteen minutes later they were sitting across from each other at a picnic table, surrounded by a lot of mothers and toddlers who also were taking advantage of the glorious spring weather.

"I liked your daughter," Kate said as she unwrapped her corned beef sandwich. "She's smart and funny."

"She liked you too. Said *you* didn't treat her like a child. Of course then *I* had to say that if I wasn't responsible for her, I'd treat her like an adult too, and things kind of spiraled down from there."

Kate smiled. "From what I've observed, teenagers often tend to be a lot friendlier toward adults other than their parents. Or at least more polite. That's why I like to see them alone on their first visit with me—to see what they want without any parental intervention."

Sam took a sip of his bottled tea. "I bet they're more receptive to hearing advice from you too. I know Carly seemed to really appreciate what you had to say about your experience in high school."

Kate could feel a sudden tightness in the back of her neck. "High school is a tough time for a lot of people. I think kids who are suffering through it don't know that; they believe they're the only ones who are miserable. They need to hear that life after high school gets better."

Sam nodded. "And I appreciate your telling Carly. When the message came from you, she believed it."

"Only because I'm not her parent."

He leaned across the table to offer her some of his potato chips. "I take it you don't have any kids of your own yet."

The pain in her neck started moving down her spine. "No."

He shrugged. "You still have lots of time. I think we—my ex-wife and I—might have done a lot better if we hadn't had Carly when we were so young. She was twenty-two and I was twenty-three when our daughter was born."

And I had only barely turned eighteen when I gave birth, Kate thought. Would she also have been too young to be the kind of parent she wanted her child to have? She wished to God that she'd had the opportunity to find out.

"I think you and your ex-wife did a better job with Carly than you seem to think. She's a terrific kid."

He smiled. "Thanks. I think she's terrific too—when she's not being a royal pain in the butt."

"That's a teenager's job description."

"Did your parents think you were a pain in the butt when you were in high school?"

She tried to sound nonchalant. "Oh, yeah."

"Funny," he said, sending her a strange look. "I would never have taken you for a hell raiser."

"I wasn't," she said, badly wanting the discussion to end. "In fact, I was shy and studious, the ultimate nerd. I just think all parents have some issues with their teenagers." She hoped she managed to make herself sound so pathetically boring that he wouldn't think of pursuing the topic.

Apparently not. "I've been looking at the Houston West High School yearbooks from fifteen years ago," he said. "And I thought I saw someone who looked like you in the National

Honor Society photo standing right next to Josh Edwards."

She stared at him. "Why—why were you looking at fifteen-year-old yearbooks?" *And how could you recognize me from a fifteen-year-old photo when nobody else can?*

He sent her a level gaze. "I'm looking at them because of the deaths of Allison James and Todd Lawson. They were high school classmates, you know."

"You think their deaths were connected to high school?"

He shrugged. "Maybe. They were in the same school clique. Apparently they, along with Josh Edwards and his wife, were in a group called The Six. You hear of them when you were there?"

What point was there in denying she knew what he was talking about? She nodded. "Everybody knew them. How—how did you know it was me in the yearbook photo?"

The corners of his mouth curved a bit. "If Carly hadn't told me you'd had cosmetic work done I never would have recognized you. There was something about your eyes and the way you turn your head when you smile that reminded me of you. I *did* wonder though why your name was listed as Jane Murphy."

She tried to ignore her suddenly sweaty palms. "Murphy is my maiden name. I decided to keep using Dalton, my married name, even after I got a divorce; it was the name on my medical diploma. And I always hated the name Jane and decided to switch to Kate—my middle name—when I went to college."

He seemed to be buying her explanation. "So you did in fact know Josh Edwards in high school?" he asked.

If he was asking her why she'd lied about it, he was going to have to wait a long time for her answer. "Only casually. We didn't run in the same circles, and he doesn't even know we went to high school together. I—I prefer it that way."

At least he wasn't looking at her as if she was a lunatic. "He won't hear it from me. What I would like to hear is your take on The Six."

Oh, God. How could her shrouded past, the former identity that she'd done so much to obliterate, be so easily uncovered? He'd recognized her when he just happened to glance at an old yearbook!

"They were the golden boys and girls of the high school," she said, not meeting his eyes. "And they seemed to think that they were a separate, superior species from the rest of us."

"From what I've heard, they'd do almost anything to maintain that superiority," Sam said. "Lots of bullying."

She shrugged. "I didn't really have much contact with them. But what does all this have to do with Todd's and Allison's murders? High school, after all, was a very long time ago."

"Maybe nothing. It's just a theory of mine—a way of linking the deaths of two people who didn't seem to have anything else in common."

She ordered herself to detach, to put on her professional demeanor. "It would take a special kind of person to hold a grudge for fifteen years," she said. "Either someone who's psychologically unstable or someone who was very badly damaged by Allison and Todd."

"That's exactly what I was thinking," Sam said.

Kate looked at her watch. "Oh, I'm going to have to be getting back to the office."

"I didn't realize how late it was," Sam said. "I guess I enjoyed talking with you so much I lost track of the time."

Yeah, right. As they collected their trash, Kate realized it was taking every morsel of her self-control not to turn and run as fast as she could from this deceptively soft-spoken man.

Twenty-One

There was still something she wasn't telling him, Sam thought as he drove Kate Dalton back to her office. In fairness, the doctor seemed a reserved and very private woman. Maybe Kate was afraid if she told him why she'd disliked Josh Edwards in high school it might get back to her colleague. Probably whatever she wasn't telling him wouldn't even be pertinent, but in a murder investigation even seemingly innocuous information could sometimes prove helpful.

Still he needed to at least make an attempt at eliciting something more from her. After mentioning his own upcoming twentieth high school reunion—which, he didn't add, he had no intention of attending—he said he'd only kept in touch with a few of his high school buddies. "What about you? You still in contact with your high school friends?"

Her frosty eyes told him she knew exactly what he was trying to do. But she was too polite not to answer. "Not really. This is the first time I've been home for any length of time since college. So basically I lost touch with my old classmates." Her tone said, *And that's the way I want it.*

"So I take it you're not going to your high school reunion?"

"You take it right." She didn't speak again until he pulled up in front of her office building. "Thanks for lunch," she said as she got out of his car.

"Thanks for coming with me." He wanted to tell her he'd like to do it again, but he was afraid she'd laugh in his face. She probably believed the only reason he suggested their meeting was to pump her for more background information for his case—which, granted, was one of his motives, but not the only one.

Sam pulled the paper from his pocket and studied it once more. Josh and Megan Edwards had surprised him. While Lisa Smythe had not yet produced her promised list of high school victims, the Edwardses had overnight provided a detailed listing of the people The Six had wronged in high school, along with a brief description of the dirty trick. Megan Edwards, her husband had explained, was very worried about the e-mailed threats Sam had mentioned. Now that Megan herself felt threatened, she apparently had decided it was in her best interests to cooperate with the police.

So far Sam had managed to locate the first victim on the list, Sean Harris, a one-time high school quarterback who broke a leg his junior year after someone tampered with his car's brakes. According to the Edwards' notes, Harris had been a victim of Todd Lawson, who wanted to make sure that his buddy Matt Phillips had no major competition for the quarterback slot. But by their senior year the recovered Harris was playing well enough to score a college football scholarship.

At first glance, it wouldn't seem that Harris had a lot of reason to be still nursing a grudge against The Six, unless, of course, the broken leg was giving him problems. He now lived in Colorado Springs, was married with two kids, and the owner of a successful ski shop. Sam didn't even see any reason to interview the man, at least not yet.

The next person on the list, Maria Vorgan, was someone Sam hadn't been able to track down with his quick Internet search. Maria had been the promising high school actress who Lisa Smythe harassed in order to get her friend Allison the lead in a school play. After Lisa had spread false rumors that the girl was having a gay affair with the drama teacher, Maria had left the school. Sam intended to find out what had happened to her in the intervening years.

Victim number three was Stan Perry, the class valedictorian, now a successful attorney in a large Wall Street firm. Megan had written that "Stan was quite hostile to us at our ten-year reunion, saying we and our friends made his high school years a living hell." She did not elaborate on what The Six had done to accomplish that.

Perry didn't seem a good fit for the murderer, but the man's open hostility to the Edwardses was intriguing. The fact that Perry was able to verbally confront the pair at the reunion made Sam doubt the lawyer would feel compelled to resort to more violent methods to get his message across, but maybe he just hadn't encountered many articulate murderers lately. The logistics of the crimes—in a Houston hotel and a Dallas church—also seemed extremely difficult for someone living in New York.

And how had the murderer known about the comings and goings of The Six? That was one of the two questions that most perplexed Sam. Aside from Allison James, none of them were exactly national celebrities who might be tracked through the media. Only occasionally did Lisa Smythe and her husband make the Houston society columns, and Todd Lawson hadn't rated newspaper coverage until he died. His funeral arrangements had been in the Dallas newspaper—Sam had checked that—so presumably the killer could have got the time and place from reading the obituary. But the more interesting question still remained: If only one person had murdered both classmates, how had he or she known that Lawson would be in the Houston hotel for the conference?

The second most important question—Why would a person

be so enraged fifteen years after the fact that he'd track down his high school tormentors?—was a matter that Sam intended to purse with the last person on the Edwards' list, Libby Norman.

Ms. Norman was now a high school teacher. The dirty trick that Megan Edwards had played on her—spiking her soft drink with a laxative before a cheerleading tryout—didn't sound, in itself, serious enough to nurse a grievance all these years. But the seriousness of an insult depended a lot on the person hearing it. As Kate Dalton had noted, someone with preexisting psychological problems might be badly damaged by something that wouldn't bother a more resilient person.

The reason Sam wanted to interview Ms. Norman first was her access to The Six. Not only did Libby live in Houston, but she was also one of the organizers of her class's upcoming high school reunion. Even if she had nothing to do with the threats against her classmates, she might prove a good source of gossip.

In person, plump, freckled Libby Norman seemed an unlikely criminal. She'd agreed to meet with Sam at a coffee shop near her school. "After the day I've had, I deserve a latte," she said, settling her large frame on the chair across from him. "You spend much time around teenagers, Officer Wolfe?"

Sam nodded. "I have a sixteen-year-old daughter."

"Then you know what I mean." She sent him a no-nonsense look he remembered from his own student days. "Now why don't you tell me why you really want to talk to me. I've had a very long day."

Sam told her about his investigation into the murders of her classmates and his theory that the killings might be somehow connected to the two victims' high school careers.

"What makes you think that?" she said, looking genuinely astonished.

"I might be wrong," he admitted, "but both victims had their throats slit, which is relatively uncommon. They knew each other, or at least they used to run in the same crowd. And about the only thing the two of them seemed to have in common was high school."

The teacher's eyes narrowed. "Their bullying, you mean. You think someone is paying them back after all these years?"

It's payback time, someone had e-mailed Lisa Smythe.

"Maybe," Sam said. "The question is who would have been so seriously injured by that group that he or she would be enraged enough to kill them fifteen years later?"

Ms. Norman took a long drink while she seemed to consider the question. "You know it's funny that you're asking that. One of my former classmates just e-mailed me about The Six and their meanness. And I was saying that the effects of bullying aren't always obvious. Just because someone isn't bleeding doesn't mean he wasn't hurt. A lot of kids are awfully vulnerable at that age, believe me."

Sam sensed she was about to launch into a lecture about adolescent psyches. "By the way," he interjected before she got started, "what did you and your classmate conclude about The Six's dirty tricks?"

She shrugged. "I guess we decided that they were—and, by all accounts, still are—a bunch of shits. But we, Jane and I, survived their abuse, and probably so did the rest of the kids in our class."

"Jane?" Sam asked.

"Oh, the woman I was e-mailing. Jane Murphy. She's a doctor now in Illinois."

Twenty-Two

It seemed as if she'd been waiting for hours, rather than twenty minutes, in this airless, dimly lit parking garage. She could feel sweat trickling down her sides, under her blouse and too-warm vinyl raincoat.

What if the information she'd gotten was wrong? She'd already had one false start, easing her car door open at the sound of approaching footsteps, then having to duck back when she finally spotted the person's—the wrong person's—face.

Her edginess, of course, was compounded by all the humiliating images that were running through her head of her bungled attack on Lisa Smythe. Just the thought of *that* made her stomach clench. Lisa, the Queen Bitch, had evaded justice and was still free to roam the earth and harm innocents on a whim. And it was all due to *her* failure.

She'd started to think that perhaps her first two attacks, on Todd and Allison, hadn't been the diabolically clever, well-planned maneuvers she'd thought they were, but were instead merely lucky coincidences of time and place. Which *could* mean that her luck had run out. And all the things that went wrong last time—unexpected onlookers showing up, the victim yelling for help—could happen again. Maybe this time the police might even arrive early enough to catch her.

It was even possible that this increasing nervousness was a sign: Time to stop the skulking and slashing and come up with a less-risky plan for retribution. Vengeance, after all, came in many forms. She shouldn't allow herself to get too cocky or too careless, not until she successfully completed her mission.

Then she heard the noise. Rapid footsteps, sounding like a woman in a hurry. She checked her rearview mirror. And this time—finally—she sighted her victim.

So far the two of them were alone in the garage. Carefully she cracked open the car door and slipped out. She wanted to get as close as possible before she was spotted.

Megan Edwards didn't turn around until she was almost next to her.

"You?" Megan said, her eyes narrowed. "What are *you* doing here?" She made it sound as if she was addressing a lazy servant.

"Why waiting for you, of course."

"Me?" Megan's brow wrinkled. But when no further explanation was offered, Megan said, her voice hard, "This is about Josh, isn't it?"

"He is one horny little guy, isn't he? Can't seem to keep it in his pants."

Even in the dim light, she could see the old cheerleader blanch. "You came on to him, didn't you?" Megan said, sounding desperate to believe it.

She laughed. "No, I never came on to him. Is that what he tells you? All those evil, lascivious women are out to seduce your faithful hubby—a long line of sluts trying to tempt St. Josh?"

Megan seemed to be blinking away tears. "He can't help himself," she said in a small voice. "I think he's one of those sex addicts. He needs to get some help, but he refuses. He says the other women mean nothing to him, that his commitment is to me and to our family. And he always—always—comes back to me."

She shook her head. "And that's good enough for you—being the woman he comes back to after screwing dozens of others? I would have thought that you'd have more pride, Megan. I always expected that eventually insecure, not-quite-pretty-enough Megan Patterson would grow up to become something besides J.R.'s girlfriend."

Hands on hips, Megan glared at her. "I'll have you know I'm a lot more than Josh's wife. I'm a businesswoman—a very successful real estate agent—and the mother of two children, for starters."

"But you put up with any abuse, any humiliation, just to keep on being J.R.'s girl. That's pretty pathetic."

Finally what she'd been saying seemed to sink in. She could see the recognition on Megan's pixie face. "How do you know all this about my high school? I just met you recently."

She shook her head, looking rueful. "You don't remember me either. Why, Megan, I *am* hurt."

Megan stared at her, eyes narrowed. "You were in school with me?" Suddenly, her expression changed, her eyes widening. "Why you're that—"

Mid-sentence, Megan stopped. She gasped as she glimpsed her assailant's plastic glove–covered hand. Saw the scalpel. "What—what are you doing?"

But Megan didn't wait for an answer. She turned, trying to run in her successful-realtor stiletto heels.

It required very little effort to tackle her, though once they hit the ground, Megan Patterson Edwards, former cheerleader, put up a good fight.

"What am I doing?" she answered before punching Megan in the face. "Giving you exactly what you deserve."

Megan opened her mouth to scream just as the blade slashed down to silence her.

Twenty-Three

Mandy stopped Kate in the hallway. "You won't believe what's happened."

"What?" Kate said, noticing how pale the young receptionist's face was.

"Dr. Edwards called this morning to ask me to cancel his patients for today. When I asked if he was sick, he didn't answer for a long time and then it sounded like he was crying. His wife was murdered last night! Somebody killed her in the parking garage outside her office. Isn't that terrible?"

Kate stared at her. "Megan is dead?"

The woman nodded. "Dr. Edwards said someone stabbed her."

First Todd in the hotel room, then Allison in the church bathroom, and now Megan in her office parking garage. Could there be any doubt now that someone was targeting The Six? There were only three of them left: Josh Edwards, Lisa Smythe, and Matt Phillips, the quiet jock who Kate had once tutored.

"Dr. Dalton? Are you okay?"

The receptionist's high-pitched voice finally penetrated the kaleidoscope of her thoughts. "I—I'm just startled, that's all. What a terrible tragedy."

"I know. Thinking of those two little kids without their mother—it just makes me want to cry."

Kate took a deep breath. She couldn't think about those children right now. "Is there anything we can do for Josh?"

"Oh, yeah, Dr. Glass said you all might have to see Dr. Edwards's patients if he decides to take some time off."

Another funeral and another casket filled with a member of her high school class, Kate thought as she said the expected words about being happy to see any of Josh's patients if required.

Fortunately, her day was so busy that she didn't have a lot of time to think about either Megan or Josh Edwards. She'd been with a patient when Sam Wolfe first phoned, leaving a message for her to please call him at her earliest convenience. It wasn't going to be convenient for a long time, Kate decided, at least not until she figured out what this charmingly manipulative police detective wanted from her.

The last time she'd seen him, during that awkward picnic in the park, she felt as if Sam wanted to interrogate her but had to settle for taking her to lunch instead because he didn't have cause for official questioning. His explanation—that he only wanted her take on her high school classmates—just didn't make sense. And his story about paging through her high school yearbook and just *happening* to spot her in the National Honor Society photo—amazingly, with a different name and a significantly less attractive face—was pretty pathetic. Why was he so interested in her past?

Now that another of The Six had been murdered, Sam should be able to convince his superiors that his oddball homicide theory—a revenge killer getting rid of former high school bullies—might well be on target. Which meant that her old classmates would be put under even more scrutiny, their adolescent injuries and grievances unearthed, the cruel social roles—jocks, popular kids, nerds, losers—revisited. The past Kate had worked so hard to obscure and the persona she'd tried to obliterate would be dredged up, discussed, perhaps even snickered at. She didn't know if she could stand that.

Kate glanced again at the yellow phone message from Sam.

What information did he think she was keeping from him? Scowling, she wadded the paper into a ball and tossed it into her wastebasket.

At least, Kate thought as she left the office, she'd managed to avoid Sam Wolfe's three phone calls. Eventually, of course, she'd have to talk to him, but not today.

Before she went home she needed to stop at the grocery store. Her mother wasn't eating much these days, but they were running out of the few foods—tomato soup, ginger ale, vanilla ice cream, strawberry popsicles—that she seemed to like. Maybe Kate would pick up a roast chicken and potato salad from the deli too. Eating sandwiches or take-out food every night was getting old, but it seemed too much effort to cook a real meal just for herself.

She pulled into a space at the farthest end of the parking lot, telling herself that walking briskly back and forth to the store would count for at least a few minutes of aerobic exercise.

She wouldn't have paid attention to the black sports car parked a few spaces away if it hadn't had the vanity license plates: JRE MD. Josh Edwards was grocery shopping today?

Well, people still had to eat, particularly if that person was now the sole parent of two small children.

She'd only moved a few more steps when she spotted them. In the row behind the black sports car, seated in an old-model station wagon, was Josh Edwards himself. Kate couldn't see the woman's face, but she'd bet a year's salary that the dark-haired female he was kissing was not a grief counselor.

Twenty-Four

"And *I'm* probably the killer's next victim," Lisa Smythe was yelling. "What are you planning to *do* about that?"

Sam moved the phone further from his ear. Lisa was bordering on hysteria. At the beginning of the conversation, a good five minutes ago, he'd started out sympathetic to her fears for her safety, but now, after her insinuation that Megan Edwards would be alive today if Sam had been a more competent investigator, all he wanted to do was hang up. Or, better yet, tell her what he was really thinking: *Maybe you should have thought of this when you were bullying all of your classmates. Not much fun being a victim, is it?*

"And did you manage to learn anything about those threatening e-mails I was getting?" Lisa asked.

"We found out they came from a dummy account we couldn't track." Which meant that the sender was clever and computer savvy.

"So you can't determine who's harassing me. Why doesn't *that* surprise me?"

It took quite a lot to make Sam angry, but Ms. Entitlement here had managed to push him over the edge. "Perhaps, if you'd given me the list I asked for of kids you'd bullied—doing *your* part in this investigation—we might have made more progress."

When she answered, her voice was a tad less shrill. "I knew Megan and Josh gave you their list. Megan read it to me. I thought that was enough."

"You didn't have any other names to add?"

"I—I didn't want to think about it."

"Well maybe it's time you did." *And while you're at it, start placing the blame where it belongs.*

Sam had seen a lot of grieving family members in his job, so the fact that Josh Edwards looked more angry than sad didn't really surprise him.

Edwards led him into the tasteful, antique-filled living room Sam had first seen when he'd talked to Megan Edwards. It was messier today, with a plastic dump truck and some blocks on the floor and the front section of a newspaper lying on the couch.

The doctor sank into an upholstered chair. Sitting opposite him on the couch, Sam noted the dark circles under the man's eyes and his unshaven face. "I wanted to learn more about Mrs. Edwards's normal routine. Did she normally leave work so late?"

Edwards shook his head. "Usually she left earlier, but that day she had an afternoon closing and then had to come back to the office to finish some paperwork. She called to say she'd be late so that I'd get home by six when our nanny left."

Sam made a mental note to get the nanny's name. "Any ideas how the killer could have known that Mrs. Edwards would be working late that night?"

The hostility that Sam had sensed when Edwards opened the door flared back to life. "Of course this is only an educated guess, detective," he said, enunciating each word, "but maybe the killer just staked out her car and waited until she came out."

"That might be quite a wait in a fairly busy garage, at least during rush hour. The other real estate agent I talked to, who'd been working late that night too, said Mrs. Edwards didn't leave the office until almost eight."

"Maybe we're talking about a highly motivated killer,"

Edwards said, looking as if he'd like to take a swing at Sam. "Or who knows, maybe the killer called Megan's office and found out she was still there."

"Or maybe the killer was someone she knew," Sam said.

To his surprise, Edwards took the bait. "Just what exactly are you inferring?"

Sam had expected him to be more of a shrewd chess-player type. But then the doctor-as-god syndrome sometimes cancelled out innate intelligence. "I'm not inferring anything. In a homicide investigation we just have to explore all possibilities."

"Maybe if you'd explored all the possibilities on the list I gave you, there wouldn't *be* any homicide investigation now."

Or once you gave me a list of people who might want to murder Megan, you felt confident in getting rid of your shrewish wife, knowing the police would suspect a serial killer. "The question that really puzzled me is how the killer—or killers—seemed to know all of the victims' schedules: where your wife parked her car and how late she was working. For that matter, how did the murderer know Todd Lawson would be in town for a sales conference?"

Sam couldn't be absolutely sure, but there seemed to be something about the questions that upset the surgeon. His body stiffened and he blinked rapidly before quickly recovering his righteous indignation.

"I guess it's *your* job to find that out," Edwards said, rising from his chair. "I want to hear the results of the forensic evidence as soon as you get them. And now if we're through here, I have an appointment."

It was almost five by the time Sam got around to phoning Matt Phillips in Oklahoma. Phillips was the only living member of The Six he hadn't talked to yet. From what the others said, the Tulsa engineer hadn't had much to do with his old high school friends since they'd graduated, but maybe his take on their past history might offer a badly needed new perspective.

"Phillips," a deep-voiced man answered his work phone.

"Mr. Phillips, this is Officer Sam Wolfe." He told the man why he was calling.

"Megan's dead?" Phillips was either a good actor or he was genuinely shocked. "My God."

Sam waited.

"I—I knew that Todd and Allison had died. That was in the last update about our high school reunion. But now another one . . ."

"Another of The Six," Sam said.

"The Six," Phillips said bitterly. "I'd pretty much forgotten that nickname. It—it was a long time ago."

"Someone seems not to have forgotten."

"What do you mean?"

"It's just a theory. I think that someone might be murdering members of your high school clique."

The man was silent for so long that Sam began to wonder if he was still there. "I guess that doesn't really surprise me," he finally said.

Twenty-Five

"Won't you please try to eat just a bit of this soup, Mom?" Kate said.

Her mother attempted a smile. "That's what I used to say to you when you were a little girl."

"So you know then how important it is to me to see you eat something. And as I recall, I was a very cooperative child."

"Yes, you were." Obediently her mother opened her mouth and allowed her daughter to spoon-feed her a few mouthfuls of tomato soup.

"Now that's better," Kate said after she'd finished. Trying to sound pleased and optimistic rather than what she really felt: helpless, depressed, terrified that at any minute this skeleton who only faintly resembled her mother was going to close her paper-thin eyelids and never open them again.

She was almost relieved when the doorbell rang. "I wonder who that could be," her mother said.

Kate went to find out. Opening the door, she stared. "Officer Wolfe?"

"You weren't returning my phone calls, so I decided we needed to talk in person."

"It—it's not the best time," she said, though it was fairly obvious this wasn't a social call. "My mother is very ill."

"Jane, who is it?" her mom called from inside, probably not even realizing that she'd used the old name.

Sam met Kate's eyes. "I'm sorry, but I have to insist we talk now." He didn't look sorry. He looked cool, professional, beyond sympathy—a different man from Carly's wry, self-deprecating father.

Shivering, Kate stepped aside to let him in.

Her mother, dressed in her pink quilted robe and slippers, shuffled to the door. "Kate, who's there?"

"Mom, this is Sam Wolfe. Sam, my mother Ellen Murphy."

Sam, to his credit, managed to look friendly and unthreatening as he greeted her mother. "I'm sorry to interrupt your dinner, Mrs. Murphy, but I just wasn't able to catch Kate at the office, and I needed to get some information from her."

The pre-cancer Ellen Murphy would have asked some follow-up questions: "Oh, do you two work together? No? So how *do* you know her?" But today she just nodded. "Nice to meet you, Sam," she said before retreating to her bedroom.

Reluctantly Kate led the detective to her mother's plant-filled living room and sat across from him on one of the overstuffed chintz chairs.

"I just talked to one of your old high school classmates. He said you used to tutor him. Matt Phillips—remember him?"

The best Kate could do was nod. She took a deep breath, fighting a wave of nausea.

Sam's gaze was cold, unflinching, a predator surveying his prey. When Kate didn't respond, he said, "Matt told me that you'd been a victim of The Six. One of their more vicious tricks: Todd Lawson asking you out on a date, getting you drunk, and then telling everyone that he'd had sex with you."

"I believe 'Plain Jane Gets Laid' was the catchphrase."

He winced. A good-cop ploy? "So it was true?" he asked.

"Oh yeah. It was fast, groping, awkward, painful sex—but yes."

For a moment Sam Wolfe's brown eyes registered the empathy she remembered from their previous conversations.

"That's date rape, you know."

Kate tried to blink away the tears welling in her eyes. "Back then it wasn't called that. And even if I'd been aware that rape wasn't only a total stranger holding a knife to your throat and forcing you to have sex, I probably wouldn't have pressed charges. I wanted to forget it happened." *Which became impossible once I learned I was pregnant.*

"That must have been hard when Lisa and Todd were spreading those rumors around school."

He couldn't have learned about the baby, could he? No, of course not, not if his information was coming from Matt Phillips, she decided. And if she kept her wits about her, the detective would never know.

"It *was* hard. But I got tougher," she said in her calm doctor's voice. Oh, wouldn't Officer Wolfe like to know about all the lessons she'd learned during that terrible senior year in high school: how to pretend the pain didn't matter, how to never again let others know what she was really feeling, and—the biggie—how to turn herself into a strong, invulnerable, totally different person.

"Eventually, the whole thing died down. I wasn't that interesting, and the school moved on to new gossip." And she'd made very sure her classmates missed out on the biggest scandal of all: Plain Jane's pregnancy. By the time she graduated she'd made herself so invisible that no one even suspected her recent weight gain might have come from something other than a few too many doughnuts.

Sam looked as if he wasn't buying it. Tough, she thought. Let him prove otherwise.

He studied her silently for a minute, then said quietly, "It sounds pretty painful to me. In fact, as a father of a teenage girl, it sounds excruciating."

She glared at him, happy to segue into anger at him for this cheap shot—using his daughter to trap her.

She decided to call his bluff. "I didn't kill Todd Lawson, detective. And I didn't kill Allison or Megan, or anyone else, for that matter. I certainly didn't feel sorry when I heard someone murdered Todd—the world is probably a better place without an amoral sadist like him in it—but I didn't have anything to do with his death."

For a moment, she wanted—desperately wanted—for him to understand. "Don't you see? I kept myself sane by getting as far away as possible from my high school and everyone in it. I forced myself to leave all that behind—to start in a new place and become the kind of person I wanted to be. I had no contact with anyone from my high school years, and that was the way I wanted it."

He nodded. "Can you verify where you were on Saturday, March second, the day Todd Lawson died?"

So much for understanding. "Yes," she said coldly. "I was in the process of moving out of my apartment in Chicago. The next day, I flew to Houston so I could take care of my mother. My plane arrived at one-fifteen, as I recall. That night Mom and I heard on the TV news that Todd had been killed." She paused. "Would you like me to go get her so she can back up my story?"

Sam glanced away. "That's not necessary right now."

But it might be necessary in the future? She wanted to scream at him to get out of her house. How dare he violate her privacy for this obscene fishing expedition, callously probing into the dark corners of her psyche on the off chance he might glean a few tidbits for his investigation! An investigation that seemed every bit as disorganized, inept, and ineffective as Sam Wolfe himself.

"For what it's worth," he said quietly, "Matt Phillips feels terrible about what happened to you. He said he didn't have anything to do with The Six after that. He broke up with his girlfriend Lisa when he figured out she launched that attack on you because she got jealous when she saw you and Matt talking in the hall. He said he tried to find you to say how sorry he was and to tell you he had nothing to do with what happened, but you always ran away from him."

"He wanted to tell me he was *sorry?*" She shook her head, trying to clear away the many hurtful images she'd worked so hard to pack away and never take out again. Trying to sound calm. "I never thought Matt had anything to do with siccing Todd on me. But you know what? He didn't stop Lisa or Todd or all the sniggering afterward. So while he may have felt *sorry,* I always thought of Matt as being like those thirty-eight people who watched that woman in New York being stabbed. They might have felt guilty later, but at the time they didn't do anything because they were too scared to get involved."

Sam was still studying her, looking as if he wanted to say something.

Whatever it was, she didn't want to hear it. "So if that's all your questions about my painful adolescence, detective, I suggest you leave." She stood up, dismissing him.

Twenty-Six

The worst thing about Megan Edwards's funeral, Kate thought, was having to watch the Edwards children sit through it. The older child, a boy of around six or seven who looked like Josh, sat ramrod straight next to his father, staring ahead. But the boy's younger sister, a tiny blonde of about three or four, made no effort to rein in her grief. She sat, thumb firmly in her mouth, sobbing quietly as a gray-haired woman Kate assumed was her grandmother attempted to comfort her.

Five rows behind them, Kate was fighting the headache from hell. She surveyed the mourners around her, some of them at least pretending to listen to the elderly minister's lengthy sermon about life after death. Kate, glancing in the direction of the grim-faced new widower, wondered if Josh believed in that.

The people sitting in her row were mainly from the medical practice. Dr. Aaron Glass, in a navy pin-striped suit, appeared appropriate and solemn. Dr. Emily Stone, sitting next to Kate, looked as if she was thinking about something else. On the other side of her, soft-hearted Mandy, in the black skirt and gray sweater she often wore to work, swiped at the tears streaming down her freckled face.

From the corner of Kate's eye, she saw a woman slip into the end of their pew. It was Annette, office manager and Josh's lunch friend. Kate glanced her way just as the woman turned to pick up a hymnal. She'd had a haircut since Kate had last seen her. Annette's once-long dark hair was now cut short, showcasing the back of her long, slender neck. My God, why hadn't Kate realized it before? Annette was the brunette she'd seen only a few days ago, locked in a passionate embrace with Josh Edwards in a car in the supermarket parking lot. Kate had been so intent on hurrying into the store before Josh spotted her that she'd only had a quick glimpse of the back of the woman's head.

Annette seemed to sense Kate's scrutiny because she turned suddenly and met her gaze. Abruptly Kate turned away and pretended to listen to the sermon.

Two rows ahead of her she saw Lisa Smythe seated next to her elderly husband. They seemed to be sitting as far away from each other as possible without moving to a separate row, the old coot with his arms folded across his chest, Lisa's body posture so rigid she might have been playing a game of statues.

Kate wondered what was going on. One would think that even a marginally sensitive husband would be sympathetic to Lisa today. Not only had another of her friends just been murdered, but at this point it was starting to look like someone was systematically killing off members of Lisa's snotty high school clique. Half of them were already gone, and Lisa was one of the only three remaining.

So shouldn't Mr. Smythe at least feel a bit concerned about the welfare of his young wife? He didn't look it; he appeared annoyed. Maybe that was the thing about trophy wives: in exchange for all that money and social status, they were supposed to be decorative and take good care of their geezer spouses. Having a wife who might predecease you was apparently not part of the bargain.

The minister at last had stopped talking, and a soloist, a soprano, stood up to sing "Amazing Grace."

Kate wondered if Megan Edwards had particularly liked that song. She could hear crying throughout the church now. Music could do that to you, touch the raw emotions that mere words would bypass. Even Josh's broad shoulders seemed to be shaking as he draped an arm around his small son.

Lisa seemed to be crying too. Kate did an unofficial head count. In her row, Aaron was blinking rapidly, Mandy was swabbing her cheeks with a crumpled tissue, and Emily, Kate, and Annette were dry-eyed.

At the end of the row across from her Sam Wolfe nodded at her. When had he come in? Could he possibly be expecting another murder in a church bathroom? Or did he think Megan's killer would identify him- or herself at the funeral by some bizarrely inappropriate behavior peculiar to serial killers? And if that was the case—Sam scoping out Megan's killer—why was he looking so intently at *her?*

Abruptly Kate jerked her head toward the pulpit. She needed to get out of here fast, she thought, as the service drew to a close. She had no intention of dealing with Sam Wolfe and his suspicious eyes today.

As soon as Josh, his children, and Megan's parents filed down the aisle, Kate stood up and moved to the side aisle.

Unfortunately, Lisa Smythe and her husband seemed to have the same idea. Lisa, barreling forward on four-inch stilettos, stopped in front of Kate, glaring. "This," she told her husband, "is Dr. Dalton, the one who refused to do my lipo."

Her husband barely glanced in Kate's direction. "Let's get out of here," he muttered.

But Lisa was not about to be sidetracked. "Do you realize," she said loudly, "that I almost *died* because you refused to operate on me, and I had to go to some hack surgeon to get the procedure done?"

Kate grew aware that mourners were turning to stare at them—most noticeably, her colleagues from the practice, the people she least wanted to witness the scene. She was surprised to realize she didn't care.

"Don't blame me for your decision," she said, staring into Lisa's cold blue eyes. "You were the one who refused to follow medical instructions and quit smoking. Your behavior endangered your health. It's time you started taking some responsibility for your own actions."

Lisa turned to her husband. "Are you going to let her get away with talking to me like that?"

The look he sent his wife could have formed ice crystals in hot chocolate. "I didn't hear her say anything that wasn't true."

Scowling, Lisa opened her mouth to respond, but before she got the words out, her husband grabbed her elbow and propelled them down the aisle.

"You refused to operate on her?" a familiar voice from behind Kate asked.

For the briefest moment she wondered if she could pretend not to have heard, instead just turn on her heel and flee from the church. Probably not a good idea. Knowing Sam Wolfe, the dogged detective would run right after her. She swiveled around to face him.

"I refused to do a liposuction procedure when she lied to me that she'd stopped smoking. I explained to her when she first consulted me that smoking could compromise the results of her surgery and she assured me she'd quit." Kate briefly considered whether she was violating patient–doctor confidentiality, but decided that technically Lisa wasn't her patient anymore.

"And then she found another physician who didn't have your scruples?" Sam asked.

Now *that* was a question she was smart enough not to touch.

Sam tilted his head slightly, studying her. "The much more interesting question is why would she want to be asleep on an operating table, at the mercy of a classmate she victimized in high school? Mrs. Smythe doesn't strike me as that trusting of a woman."

Kate met his gaze. "She never made the connection. I told you, for her and for everyone else, Jane Murphy and Kate Dalton are two separate people. And that's the way I want it."

Or did she? The detective, she was irritated to see, didn't look as if he believed her either.

Twenty-Seven

God, Sam wanted to believe Kate Dalton's version of events. Dr. Dalton, after all, had had a golden opportunity to kill Lisa Smythe, and she'd refused to grab it. She could have performed the liposuction on Lisa, and when some surgical complications occurred, Kate could have tried—unsuccessfully—to save her. Hundreds of people each year died during routine liposuction procedures, and no one would have called Dr. Kate Dalton a cold-blooded murderer.

Instead, she had refused to operate on her old classmate. If Kate didn't want to exact revenge on Lisa, the member of The Six who'd instigated the attack on her, Sam couldn't see her going after Allison or Megan, who, as far as he could tell, were only peripherally involved in the Plain Jane Gets Laid incident.

Todd Lawson, of course, was another matter. Sam had no problem imagining Kate wanting to punish the guy who'd asked her out, got her drunk, and slept with her, then gleefully spread the story around school. But if Kate had been Todd's killer, wouldn't she have then gone after the other classmates directly involved in her attack? The next logical targets would be Lisa, who'd sent Todd on his mission, and maybe Matt Phillips, if Kate blamed him for not trying hard enough to stop Lisa's abuse. But Matt hadn't mentioned any problems, and the only documented attacks against Lisa had been written ones. Sam was still inclined to believe that the threatening person with a scalpel that Lisa had reported—and no one else in the recovery room had seen—was probably an anesthesia-fueled hallucination.

In any case, he was moving Kate to the bottom of his suspect list. He guessed it was possible she might have sent Lisa those anonymous e-mails. But if that was the only retaliation Kate ever took against her, Lisa was damn lucky.

Walking to the back of the church, Sam studied the group of well-wishers clustered around Josh Edwards and his in-laws. Josh's small daughter clung to her grandmother like she was grasping for the last lifeboat. The Edwards son, older and more reserved, stood, white-faced and silent, next to his father, who was fielding the condolences with determined politeness. The older couple who stood next to Josh—Megan Edwards's parents, Sam assumed—looked as if they were summoning every ounce of energy to remain upright and respond to the line of condolence-givers.

Lisa Smythe and her husband were talking to Josh now, Lisa leaning down to pat the little boy's head, then standing to enclose Josh in a tight hug.

Sam glanced back into the sanctuary. Kate was no longer there. Probably she'd slipped out the side door. When he'd talked to her, she'd seemed eager to cut short their conversation.

Sam couldn't blame her. His questions about her past—the painful high school years she seemed so determined to put behind her—had clearly upset Kate. The fact that he'd only been doing his job when he dredged up her pain today didn't seem like a good excuse. Maybe it was just wishful thinking, but he'd had the sense that before he started grilling her, something—the first whiff of romantic interest, perhaps, or maybe just the cautious tentacles of friendship—was starting to develop between him and the pretty doctor. But whatever the budding relationship was, it sure as hell was squelched the night he showed up at her mother's house to play bad cop.

Sam took a last look at Lisa Smythe fawning over the new widower. It crossed his mind that in the course of her day Kate Dalton had to put up with a lot of assholes: arrogant, womanizing Josh Edwards, who one day might suddenly recognize Plain Jane from their honor society meetings; Lisa Smythe, teenage sadist turned into rich-bitch Patient from Hell; and, since he was wallowing in it today, Sam Wolfe, nice-guy-turned-police-bully.

How, he wondered, did Kate cope with the people from her past who she encountered so often? Did she have to work to hide her personal history from Josh, invent another place where she'd grown up and gone to school in case the topic came up at an office party? Wasn't she afraid that she'd let some detail slip, that someone from her high school class might put together the pieces and say, "Isn't Kate Dalton living in the same house where that nerdy Jane Murphy used to live?" Or "Isn't that Dr. Dalton in the car with Mrs. Murphy? What are they doing together?"

And how did Kate feel about her former classmates not recognizing her? Relieved, certainly. But Sam wouldn't be surprised if there was also an undercurrent of anger that old Plain Jane Murphy was just too insignificant for anyone to remember very clearly.

Though from the furious expression he'd seen on Lisa Smythe's face when she and Kate spoke in the church, the former Jane Murphy had grown a lot more assertive in the years since high school. She wasn't going to be pushed around by a bully any longer. And the bully didn't like it one bit.

As if she could read his mind, Lisa moved from the Edwards' family group, said something to her impatient-looking husband, and marched over to Sam. "I need to talk to you." Predictably she made it sound like an order issued from the top. "But let's do it outside. I only have a few minutes."

He nodded, following her to a quiet courtyard on the side of the church. "What's on your mind, Mrs. Smythe?"

"I didn't realize that you knew Dr. Dalton. I saw the two of you talking a few minutes ago."

What was *this* about? Sam wondered. Was it possible Lisa had realized that Kate was Jane Murphy?

But no, there was something in those malicious blue eyes that told him she was only scavenging for gossip. He considered how much he wanted to tell her and settled for half the truth. "My daughter consulted Dr. Dalton about corrective surgery." Corrective only in the sense that Carly didn't like the look of her nose, but the curious Mrs. Smythe didn't need to know that.

Lisa raised her perfectly plucked eyebrows, clearly surprised. "I should warn you, as a plastic surgeon, Dr. Dalton is a bad-tempered tyrant. Sometimes these brand-new doctors are a little too full of themselves."

Sam almost laughed in her face. "That wasn't Carly's experience with her. But I'm sure this isn't what you wanted to talk to me about, Mrs. Smythe."

"You're right." Lisa glanced around, as if making sure no one was within earshot. "I decided those e-mails I've been getting aren't just a pissed-off classmate trying to scare me. Now I think it's more serious than that."

"What made you change your mind?"

Lisa turned around, looking nervously to a doorway where Mr. Smythe stood glowering at them. "My husband got those e-mails too. At his work. From the same person."

An expression Sam couldn't quite identify crossed Lisa's face. Was it guilt? Embarrassment? Neither were emotions he'd witnessed in her before. "What did your husband's e-mails say?"

Apparently the thought of their content set Lisa back on more familiar emotional territory. Her eyes narrowed with rage.

"They said I was a monster who'd taken immense pleasure in torturing innocent classmates in high school. They asked if my husband wanted to subject his own innocent adolescent daughters—innocent, my ass!—to my evil scheming."

She looked, Sam thought, as if she were about to explode on the spot. "You've seen these e-mails? You're sure it's the same person who wrote you?"

Lisa nodded. "Same style, same signature. Except this time it was signed Your Wife's Ex–High School Classmate. And it was dated yesterday."

She glared at him. "So obviously I was wrong about those messages being no threat to me. They *are* personal. Someone went to a lot of effort to learn my husband's e-mail address and the names of his daughters. Now I realize I *am* in danger."

"Did the writer make a specific threat against you or your husband?" The e-mailer still didn't sound to him like the knife-wielding killer of Todd, Allison, and Megan. None of the three victims, as far as he knew, had received any threatening e-mail. Lisa's poison-pen correspondent undoubtedly wanted to frighten and embarrass her, but that was a far cry from murder.

Lisa glanced back at her scowling husband, who, Sam saw, was motioning to her that he wanted to leave. "And I also got another e-mail last night. The writer said the same thing as before: I'd get what was coming to me. But this time they added a P.S."

Sam raised his eyebrows in interest.

Lisa shuddered. "It said, 'I'll see you tomorrow at Megan's funeral.' "

Twenty-Eight

Her mother had started calling her Jane all the time now. Kate knew she wasn't even aware she was doing it. Ellen Murphy was visibly weakening, sleeping more, talking less, and the few words she managed usually conveyed barebones information: "Could you get me more water, Jane?"

Kate did what she could, which wasn't much besides sit with her or coax her mother to eat a little. How could she feel so devastated, so pole-axed when she'd known for months that this moment was coming? The fury she'd felt toward her mother only a few weeks ago seemed to have disappeared as her mom's health deteriorated. The woman who'd once lied to her daughter about her critically ill baby was not the gaunt, vacant-eyed parent Kate now shared a house with. The main thing she felt was helplessness: She was a physician, damn it; she wanted to cure her mother. But she couldn't.

Today she had taken time off to accompany her mother to her appointment with her oncologist. Both of them liked Dr. Bly, an empathetic, prematurely white-haired woman who managed to gently tell them the harsh truth.

"I think you might start to think about moving to a hospice," Dr. Bly told Ellen Murphy after her examination. "They'll be able to make you more comfortable. It's a very fine facility with extremely caring staff."

Kate closed her eyes, wondering if her mother was hearing what the doctor was really saying: There was no hope of cure at this point, little chance of remission. All they could do was offer palliative care to make her feel as good as possible.

"I don't want to go there," her mother said, a spark of defiance in her tired eyes. "I want to die at home. In my own bed."

Kate took a deep breath. Of course her mother knew. How could she not?

"How do you feel about that, Dr. Dalton?" She looked up to see Dr. Bly studying her.

How *did* she feel? Now that was a subject Kate really didn't want to contemplate. But she could answer Dr. Bly's question. "If that's what Mom wants, we'll manage it."

"You still have the private duty nurse at your home during the day?" the oncologist asked.

Kate nodded. "But I'm planning on cutting back on my work hours, going in part time for a while." Although she hadn't yet informed her boss of that decision.

"I think that might be a wise idea," the oncologist said.

In other words, it won't be long now, Kate thought as she tucked the new prescription into her purse and then followed her mother out through the clinic waiting room.

She'd only walked a few steps when a woman's voice said, "Jane? Jane Murphy?"

For the briefest of moments, Kate considered the wisdom of not stopping. *Don't look back. Just keep moving.*

But her mother was already looking questioningly toward a row of seats behind them.

Feeling as if she were facing a firing squad, Kate swallowed and turned too. She gasped. It was Libby Norman, looking like an older, plumper version of the gregarious girl who'd sat behind her in three years of French class. Mademoiselle Murphy sitting in front of Mademoiselle Norman. How had Libby recognized her?

They stared at each other for what seemed like hours, Libby

giving her face such intense scrutiny it seemed as if she intended to catalogue every feature.

"I wasn't sure it was you," Libby finally said. "Your face is different, but you still walk the same way, and I thought I recognized your mother. You got a nose job, right? And your chin is shorter, and of course your hair looks a lot better too." She grinned at Kate. "God, you look great!"

Kate could feel sweat trickling down the back of her neck. "So do you."

"Yeah, right. I still haven't lost the baby fat, and my baby is almost seven."

"No, I mean it," Kate said, studying her old friend's face. Once a bit gawky, Libby had become a handsome woman.

She turned to her mother. "Mom, do you remember Libby Norman from high school?"

Libby smiled at her. "I certainly remember your oatmeal cookies, Mrs. Murphy. They sustained Jane and me through several joint French projects, as I recall."

"Nice to see you again," her mother said.

Kate could see Libby trying to hide her shock at Mrs. Murphy's appearance. "I'm here with my dad." Libby nodded at a white-haired man napping in his chair.

"Well, I guess I need to get Mom home," Kate said, taking her mother's arm. "Great seeing you, Libby."

"Wait!" Libby touched her shoulder. "We need to get together while you're home. How long are—" She glanced at Mrs. Murphy and apparently decided the question was too tactless. "Well, call me," she said instead. "I'm in the phone book. We're the Norman-Stevens, Libby and Paul."

"I'll do that," Kate said, knowing she never would and wondering why she didn't feel more relieved to have gotten away so quickly.

★ ★ ★ ★ ★

The next day Kate made arrangements to cut her work schedule. She could tell Aaron wasn't happy about her decision, but realizing that the alternative was her quitting altogether, he consented. "We always strive to be as accommodating as possible in helping our staff cope with family emergencies."

"And I appreciate that," Kate said. As she walked down the hallway to her office, she fought to squelch the tears that always seemed to be welling in the corners of her eyes these days. At least, she reminded herself, she was honoring her mother's wishes to die in her own home. At least there was that.

She was surprised to hear voices behind the closed door of Josh Edwards's office. She'd thought everybody had gone home, and she hadn't even known Josh had come in today. He'd been taking a lot of time off, to be with his kids, he said.

The raised voice was Josh's. "I'm only saying that maybe we need to take a break for a while."

"You are such a hypocrite," a woman's voice replied. "Why don't you say what you really mean for once—that you want to dump me?"

Kate had just reached her own office at the end of the hall when Josh's door banged open. She turned in time to see Annette, who only a few days ago had been kissing Josh in a grocery store parking lot, stalk out of his office.

Twenty-Nine

Lisa Smythe's voice, high and shrill at the best of times, today sounded as if it might shatter glass, Sam thought as he pulled the phone away from his ear.

He swallowed two more aspirin for his increasingly intense headache. "Uh-huh," he said into the receiver. "And you're sure this e-mail is from the same person?"

"*Of course* I'm sure. It's the same style of writing, the same accusations, and—here's a great clue—the same signature: Your Ex–High School Classmate."

God, she was a bitch. "But you say it's from a different e-mail account than the others?"

"Yes, that's what I've been telling you." She was practically shouting now, enunciating the words slowly and carefully, as if he were mentally challenged or hard of hearing. "This message comes from Studmuffin@hotmail.com."

"Studmuffin?" Sam tried to imagine the kind of guy who'd use that as his screen name. A college kid in a fraternity? A wannabe Don Juan? Or somebody who wanted Lisa Smythe to assume she was receiving hate mail from a swaggering ladies' man?

"I know, interesting choice of name. Makes me wonder if it's from one of the losers in high school who couldn't buy himself a date to the prom."

"You have any particular loser in mind? Say one who felt especially mistreated by you?"

Lisa sighed. She clearly didn't enjoy thinking about the dozens of people she'd hurt, who had good reason to hate her, but that was just too damn bad. "I *was* quite nasty to Stan Perry when he asked me to the homecoming dance senior year. I'd just broken up with my boyfriend, so he knew I wasn't going to be going to the dance. But I told him I'd rather spend the night alone in my bedroom than show up in public with him."

Nice. And the woman wondered why her old classmates sent her hate mail? "Isn't he the guy who was your class valedictorian?"

"That's right. And he showed up at our ten-year reunion with a flashy girlfriend, bragging about what a hotshot Manhattan lawyer he is. Stan probably thinks of himself as being a studmuffin, though let me say *that* is a major piece of self-delusion."

He jotted down Perry's name. He had intended to check out the guy when he appeared on the Edwards' list of people The Six had bullied. But the facts that Perry lived in New York and seemed to have done well for himself didn't make him sound like a likely killer of three classmates in Texas. He didn't seem like an anonymous poison-pen e-mailer either. Stan Perry had obviously relished rubbing his classmates' noses in his success. What was the point in writing another message?

"Can you think of any other guy who might have it in for you?" Sam asked.

"Not off the top of my head. But I think you're missing the point. This is an account that might actually be traced. I think whoever is sending this stuff finally made a big mistake."

Sam hadn't missed that, but he was finding it hard to believe that a correspondent who'd previously been so cyber-savvy that none of their experts could trace the e-mails would suddenly send a message from an individual account.

"We'll look into it," Sam said. But he wasn't as optimistic as she about finding her cyber-stalker.

Four days later he was stunned to read the report on that e-mail. Could finding the poison-pen writer really be this easy? Still even clever criminals sometimes got sloppy or complacent.

Before he entered the office building, he stopped to read the paper one more time. He needed to reassure himself that their very competent investigator had determined that Studmuffin was the screen name of one Joshua R. Edwards.

The same friendly receptionist was on the phone when he walked into the plastic surgeons' offices. Sam waited as she explained to someone that Dr. Dalton was only seeing patients in the afternoons now.

When she hung up she smiled at Sam. "May I help you?"

"I'm Officer Sam Wolfe, here to see Dr. Edwards. He's expecting me." Expecting him only after some arm-twisting on Sam's part, along with a reminder that this was not a social visit.

The receptionist cocked her head to one side. "Oh, I remember you now. You're the guy who took Dr. Dalton to lunch, aren't you?"

Sam nodded, amused by her nosiness. "How *is* Kate these days?" he asked. "I heard you just say she's only working in the afternoons."

She leaned toward him and whispered, "It's her mother. She's very sick, and Dr. Dalton wants to spend as much time as possible with her."

"I'm sorry to hear that."

Another person walked up to the desk. "I'll tell Dr. Edwards you're here," the receptionist said.

Josh Edwards was wearing his poker face when Sam entered his chrome-and-glass office. "Have you found out who murdered my wife, detective?" he asked as Sam seated himself in an uncomfortable chrome-and-leather chair.

"Still working on that. I'm here on another matter. Do you have an e-mail account with the screen name Studmuffin?"

Sam could see two red splotches spread across the doctor's face. "What—what does that have to do with anything?"

"You admit that's your screen name?"

Edwards's eyes narrowed. "What is this about? It's just a private account. I'm not doing anything illegal."

"Actually that's open to interpretation. A judge might be inclined to see your messages as less innocuous, particularly with the pattern of repeated threats."

This time the plastic surgeon's entire face grew red. "What the hell are you talking about? Admittedly, some of the language might have been raunchy, but these are consenting women I was writing to—adult women I knew personally who sent me back equally, uh, explicit replies."

So apparently Dr. Studmuffin kept up an active correspondence. Sam took the copy of Lisa Smythe's latest e-mail out of his jacket and handed it to Edwards. "This is the particular e-mail I'm interested in."

The doctor's eyes widened as he read it. He glanced up, shook his head, and then scanned the message again. Either he was a gifted actor or Josh Edwards was genuinely shocked, Sam thought. Though maybe what had shocked him was that he'd been found out.

"You can't possibly believe that I sent this to Lisa?" He pointed to the paper on his desk as if it were radioactive.

"It's from your account. Who else would have sent it?"

Edwards's eyes frantically scanned the room, as if trying to discover a hiding e-mailer. "Why, anyone who had access to my computer." He pointed to a laptop at the corner of his glass-topped desk. "It could be anyone who came into my office when I wasn't here."

"You usually leave your office when your personal e-mail is still on the screen?"

"Of course not."

Sam studied him. "So who knows your password?"

"Right offhand I can't think of anybody. But I'm telling you I *didn't* write that message."

"And yet it came from your computer."

"Maybe another person uses the same screen name."

"No, we already checked on that." Sam raised an eyebrow. "So we've established that the e-mail is from your account, to a woman you've known for years, and it discusses your high school clique's bullying."

Edwards had the look of a man who suddenly realizes he'd better start thinking fast. "But it doesn't make sense. *Why* would I send something like that to Lisa? She never did anything to me, and I'm not exactly in any position to be judgmental about those high school pranks."

Sam had already considered that question, and the answers he'd come up with weren't entirely satisfactory. "Maybe you blame Lisa for instigating a lot of those dirty tricks. You might figure your wife and friends could still be alive today if it weren't for Lisa's sadism."

He stared into the doctor's angry eyes. "Or maybe you just wanted to scare Mrs. Smythe for some reason." *Perhaps because you know that Lisa Smythe suspects you killed your wife and you want to warn her to keep her mouth shut.*

"Those are nice little theories, Officer Wolfe. But there is one very large hole in them. If I wanted to threaten Lisa—which, for the record, I do not—I wouldn't be stupid enough to send the e-mail from my own computer."

And that was exactly the problem Sam had with the Edwards-as-poison-pen-e-mailer theory.

"Which means, detective, that someone is setting me up."

THIRTY

The expression on Kate Dalton's face as she glanced at the pizza box he'd brought to her house was not encouraging. Either she was worried about food poisoning or she was transferring all her Sam-based hostility onto the pizza he was carrying. Sam himself was betting on the second interpretation.

"I hope you're hungry," he said. "I didn't know what you like so I got one that was half vegetarian and half supreme—a little of everything."

"I've already eaten dinner," Kate said.

The woman hates your guts, Wolfe. And coming here expecting a nice friendly visit was a major piece of self-delusion.

"But I might be able to eat one piece," Kate said.

"Great." Sam followed her to a round oak table in the cheerful, old-fashioned kitchen with white painted cabinet doors that had bright yellow handles. He watched as she set yellow plates on the table.

"What would you like to drink? I have iced tea, diet soda, water, or a fairly decent bottle of Chablis."

"I'm off duty, so I guess I'll go for the wine."

She raised an eyebrow: At the unsubtle off-duty comment? At her suspicion of his incipient alcoholism? But she retrieved two wine glasses from the cabinet and filled them both without comment.

She waited to speak until they were seated across from each other and he'd taken his first bite of pizza. "So why did you really come here tonight, Officer Wolfe?"

He swallowed. "You think you could call me Sam?"

"Why did you come here tonight, Sam?"

He could tell from those flinty eyes that there wasn't a chance in hell that she'd buy his explanation, but he had to try anyway. "I feel as if I've treated you badly, even though I didn't intend to. That my probing into your"—he searched for a tactful word—"past caused you pain. And I'm sorry about that."

Her face was impassive, giving nothing away. "You were doing your job, investigating your case. I never thought you were being gratuitously mean."

And yet he felt as if he'd been slicing into her old wounds without benefit of anesthesia. He nodded. "I have to follow all leads, even if they come to nothing."

Something seemed to soften in her eyes. "Are you telling me I'm no longer a suspect in my classmates' murders?"

"You're not a suspect." Which, Sam rationalized, was roughly a ninety-seven percent truthful statement. He never entirely crossed anyone off his mental suspect list until the killer was behind bars.

"And this pizza is your idea of an apology?"

He shrugged. "More or less."

"Okay." She picked up her piece—the supreme, though he would have guessed she'd opt for the vegetarian—and took a big bite. It wasn't exactly an acceptance of his apology, but at least she wasn't throwing him out.

"How's Carly doing?" she asked.

"Carly's good. She started taking fencing lessons and, amazingly, she loves them. Said fencing makes her feel as if she should be in a Zorro movie."

Kate smiled. "Fencing does sound like fun, at least once you get good enough at it to fight."

He shook his head. "Probably it's the cop in me, but it just seems too much like playing with weapons. I'm glad, though, that she's found something she likes to do. I keep reading that participating in sports raises girls' self-esteem."

"I read that too, about organized sports preparing girls for the work world by teaching about winning, losing, and being a team player."

"Did you play sports as a kid?" he asked.

Her body visibly stiffened. "No."

Did she think he was trying to trick her into talking about high school again? Or maybe she just didn't want to talk to him about anything personal because she didn't trust him.

He tried another tack. "How's your mother doing?"

"Not very well. But today was one of her better days. She got all excited about looking over old family photos."

"My mom loves to do that too—pull out the old albums and tell us all the stories from when a picture was taken."

Kate nodded. "Mom was just talking about a trip to Yellowstone National Park we took when I was seven. I hadn't thought about it for years, but it all came back: me getting carsick, the sulfur smell of the park, my parents trying to convince me how great Old Faithful was. The high point of the trip for me was eating a hot fudge sundae."

Sam grinned. "Oh yeah, those good old family vacations. My little sister got carsick too. My brother and I used to call her Pukey-Lukey."

"Such empathetic children."

"It's hard to be empathetic when someone throws up in your lap."

Kate laughed. "I see your point." She seemed to hesitate for a moment as she looked questioningly at him. Then, apparently reaching a conclusion, she said, "Josh Edwards was going around interrogating people in our practice today, trying to discover who snuck into his office and sent an e-mail when he wasn't there."

"And did he come up with any likely candidates?"

"Not that I know of. Mandy, our receptionist, was very upset that he accused her. She said Josh even suspected the janitorial staff because they had keys to his office."

"Did he accuse you?" The minute he said it, Sam wished he could take the words back. He could see her eyes change, that look of distrust returning.

"No. Why would he?"

He considered a few innocuous answers: "I thought you said he was asking everyone in your office." But he opted for the truth. "Because the e-mail sent from his office was to Lisa Smythe, someone you know."

Her face was blank, unreadable, when she asked, "And what exactly did this message say?"

"Basically that she was going to pay for all the terrible things she did in high school. And it was signed Your Ex–High School Classmate."

She glared at him. "And you think that *I* sent it to Lisa, using Josh's computer? I can see now why you came over here tonight with your let's-be-friends bullshit. That's really despicable."

He started to answer, to assure her he'd had no such thought. But was he kidding himself? Just because he didn't want Kate Dalton to be guilty didn't mean she wasn't. "I didn't—"

She cut him off. "Take your damn pizza and get out."

He stood, feeling like a bastard. "I really came over just to see you."

"Yeah, right." She handed him the pizza box.

"Keep it," he said.

She shook her head. "I'm not hungry anymore."

As he headed toward his car Sam heard the deadbolt lock behind him.

★ ★ ★ ★ ★

His pager was buzzing when he walked into his apartment. He glanced at it and groaned: Lisa Smythe. Maybe God was punishing him for being a cold-hearted workaholic who got everything right except his personal life.

He phoned her, trying to keep the annoyance out of his voice. If he wasn't such an obsessive–compulsive, he would have waited until tomorrow to return her call. But there was a possibility—a slim possibility—that she had something more urgent to tell him than her need for another progress report.

"Josh Edwards just left my house," she said as soon as he identified himself. "He was really angry. I've never seen him like this."

Sam set down the bottle of beer he'd just opened. "Did he threaten you?"

"Not exactly. He yelled a lot about not being the person who sent me that e-mail. Said since he'd been one of our crowd, it wouldn't even make sense for him to blame me for stuff we all did. He thinks someone is setting him up, trying to make him look guilty."

Which was basically what Edwards had also told Sam. "So did he convince you?" While he had grown to dislike this woman intensely, he'd also come to appreciate that she was a lot brighter than he'd originally believed.

"I'm not sure. He could be trying to intimidate me because he knows I think he might have killed Megan. He's also so damn cocky that he figures no one would ever suspect brilliant Josh Edwards of doing something so idiotic as sending a threatening e-mail that could be traced to his office computer."

Sam guessed it was possible. If Edwards felt desperate enough, who knew what convoluted stunt he might pull?

At the other end of the line Lisa gasped. "Oh, my God."

He stiffened. "What's wrong?"

"I—I just got another e-mail. This one says 'Your time is up. I didn't get you in the recovery room, but next time I won't be so careless.' "

Thirty-One

Josh Edwards hurried toward her. "Kate, do you have a minute?"

"Sure," she said, not seeing any way to avoid talking to him.

He followed her into her office and sat down. "Someone got into my office and used my computer."

"Really? Do you know who?"

He narrowed his eyes. "No, but I thought you might have some ideas."

"Me?" It came out a squeak, at least to her own ears.

Josh nodded. "I noticed you're often here late, after everybody else has gone home."

So he must have seen her in the hall the night he and his girlfriend were having their big argument. "Not that often," she said, sounding defensive. Was he trying to accuse her of sending that e-mail from his computer? "Since I've only been coming in the afternoons, sometimes I have to stay to get caught up on my work."

"I just thought you might have seen something unusual, like somebody who shouldn't be there coming out of my office."

You mean like your mistress, the office manager, who was shrieking like a banshee when you decided to dump her? Kate wondered if she should suggest that Annette might have hijacked his computer. The only problem was that it didn't sound at all like a spurned-lover's revenge tactic. Why send a fake e-mail when you could slash the guy's tires or accuse him of work-related sexual harassment?

Kate shook her head. "I haven't seen anybody go in or out of your office when you weren't there." She focused on a spot just over his shoulder as she asked, "What did this person do to your computer?" It seemed like the question she would have asked if she didn't already know the answer.

"Sent a threatening e-mail that was supposed to have come from me." An unamused smile crossed his face. "Sent it, in fact, to your favorite patient, Lisa Smythe."

"Lisa?" She hoped she looked surprised. "Why would you be threatening her?"

"I wouldn't." He scowled. "Coming from me, the message doesn't even make sense. Lisa never did anything to me in high school. I can't believe she even *thought* I'd sent it. The bitch even reported it to the police."

"Must have said something that scared her."

"Not really. It's just that it was sent to a paranoid nutcase with too much time on her hands. And Lisa always loved meddling with other people, making them squirm. She probably called the police just to get some attention."

His malicious smile returned. "She's getting a little long in the tooth for a trophy wife; that's why she's so desperate to maintain her looks. Not that Lisa was ever that great-looking to start with, especially in comparison to the other girls in our group."

Kate could feel herself stiffen. "Oh, what group is that?" Had Officer Wolfe told Josh that she was the nerdy girl standing right next to him in the National Honor Society photo in their yearbook? He didn't act as if he knew he was speaking to Plain Jane Murphy.

Josh waved his hand dismissively. "Just a high school clique Megan and I were in. Allison James, the actress, was in it too. Lisa was definitely the dog of the girls."

Kate wondered who was more disgusting: Josh or Lisa. "Well,

got to get going. Sorry I couldn't be of more help."

She thought he was looking at her strangely, but maybe she was just imagining it.

Her mother was already asleep by the time Kate got home. It hadn't been one of Ellen's better days, Betty Sue said as she left. Increasingly her mother was spending the major part of each day sleeping.

The house seemed much too silent. Kate made herself a sandwich, ate a few bites, went upstairs to check on her mother, and then returned, restless and with no appetite, to the empty kitchen.

She needed a distraction. There were too many things she didn't want to think about right now: her mother's health, Officer Wolfe's callous manipulation and his obvious suspicion that she'd had something to do with the attacks on her former classmates.

She was even starting to have problems differentiating between Jane Murphy and Kate Dalton, probably because the roles seemed to be blurring now that her mother had started calling her Jane and Sam Wolfe had discovered her dual identities. Over and over she had to remind herself that things would be better once she got back to her old, work-centered life. When she was no longer living in her childhood home, surrounded by memories she only wanted to forget, Plain Jane Murphy would be a footnote from her past. In another city she'd be Kate Dalton again. All the time. Only Kate.

She decided to phone Libby Norman. Betty Sue had left a message that Libby had called this afternoon. It seemed only polite to return her old friend's phone call, even though at their last meeting she'd had no intention of even trying to maintain the relationship. Now, she wasn't so sure . . .

"Hi, it's Jane," she said when Libby answered. "Am I catching you at a bad time?"

Libby chuckled. "No, you're giving me a perfect excuse to let my husband finish preparing dinner." Speaking to someone else, she said, "Just keep stirring that, honey, until it gets thicker."

Kate felt a stab of envy. "Maybe I should call back later." What was coming over her? It never used to bother her to be alone.

"No, I have fifteen minutes before dinner. How's your mother doing?"

"Not very well. But, thank God, she's not in pain, just incredibly tired. How's your dad?"

"Relieved that he's finished his last round of chemo." Libby apparently turned to talk to one of her children. "Mommy's on the phone now. Sorry," she told Kate. "So what else is up with you?"

Kate who, before she'd dialed, had invented several evasive replies to just such a question, astonished herself by saying, "I just heard that someone is sending threatening e-mails to Lisa Smythe—she was Lisa Casey to us—saying she'll pay for what she did in high school."

Libby squealed. "Really? How did you find that out?"

"I talked to the detective who's investigating Todd's, Allison's, and Megan's murders. I think he talked to you too."

"Oh, yeah, Officer Wolfe. Nice guy. Were they able to trace the e-mails?"

Kate scowled. *He's not as nice as you think.* "I don't believe so," she said, remembering just in time that she'd have to explain how she'd encountered Josh Edwards if she said anything about the message sent from his computer. As far as Libby knew, she was Dr. Jane Murphy who still lived and worked in Illinois. Libby certainly wouldn't know Kate was now working with Josh. "Officer Wolfe asked me who I thought might have sent them. I told him I had no idea. Apparently they all were signed Your Ex–High School Classmate."

"There are probably a dozen people who hated her guts enough to send that e-mail. Hell, I may have even helped them do it."

"What do you mean?"

"My committee decided to list contact information for everyone who said they're coming to the reunion. So anyone who RSVPed got a list of our classmates' phone numbers and e-mail addresses. If I remember right, Lisa only wanted her e-mail information printed. She was probably afraid that one of her former victims would start making crank calls to her in the middle of the night."

"So how many people would have received that list?"

"So far about one hundred twenty people have said they're coming." Libby paused. "I wonder which one of them was still pissed off enough at Lisa to send those e-mails."

Thirty-Two

"I hope you remember that I saw Josh at the hospital the day I had my lipo," Lisa told Sam during the latest in their series of interminable one-sided phone conversations. "He told me he was going into surgery, but he could have returned later when I was in the recovery room. Nobody would have questioned a doctor coming in to check on me."

She and Sam had gone over this before, but Lisa's latest e-mail seemed to have compelled her to rehash her every memory of the recovery room. "But you said before that you didn't recognize the person who approached you," he said.

"I didn't see his—or her—face. I think he was wearing a surgical mask. All I really remember was someone standing by my IV and then walking toward me holding something sharp. I was drifting in and out of sleep, and it didn't occur to me until later that that person might have been trying to harm me."

Or maybe the person in the white coat was only doing his or her job, Sam thought. "Was there ever any evidence that something toxic was put in your IV?"

"No, but that doesn't mean anything," Lisa said, sounding defensive. "Dr. Goodman and his associates have a vested interest, after all, in *not* uncovering any medical malfeasance. They want everyone to believe it was just a normal surgical complication, which they handled and now want to forget about. They even had the nerve to imply that the whole thing was my fault for continuing to smoke and insisting they remove the maximum amount of fat."

Sam had been inclined to agree with the doctor's conclusions. The fact that Lisa admitted she'd been half-asleep when she spotted her potential assassin and no one else in the recovery room had seen anyone suspicious near her bed seemed to point to an anesthesia-produced hallucination.

But now someone else was saying that Lisa's surgical complications had not been accidental—someone, in fact, who claimed to have attempted to murder her. Even if it wasn't true and the e-mailer was merely trying to scare her, how many of Lisa's former classmates would have even known that she'd had liposuction and briefly lapsed into a coma? Lisa didn't seem like the kind of woman who'd casually spread the news that she planned to have her extra fat removed.

The only explanations Sam could think of were that either the e-mailer was somebody very close to Lisa or someone who actually had been there during her medical procedure. Someone who perhaps *had* tried to kill her.

"What about the people in the operating room?" Sam asked. "Maybe the attempt on your life was during the surgery, not after. Do you remember who was there?"

"Dr. Goodman, an anesthesiologist, and a nurse. I don't know their names. But I don't remember anyone looking familiar, as if I knew them from high school. And the two doctors are considerably older than I am."

"What about the nurse?"

"She looked as if she was in her mid-twenties, too young to be in high school with me. Anyway, wouldn't it have been awfully hard to try to kill me with two other people watching?"

Sam was less sure of that, especially since no one seemed clear about why Lisa had lapsed into a coma.

"I'm assuming that you'll be interviewing everyone who was in the operating and recovery rooms the day of my procedure,"

Lisa said in her issuing-orders-to-the-servants voice.

Sam mentally counted to ten, reminding himself that she might actually be in danger. "How many people other than medical staff knew that you were having liposuction on that day?"

He could hear her intake of breath. "Why, no one. It wasn't something I was likely to announce to the world."

"You didn't tell your family or your close friends?"

"Well, my husband knew and our maid. She took me to the surgery and picked me up."

Sam wondered if she treated the maid with the contempt she showed almost everyone else and if the maid were computer literate. But the maid as the poison-pen writer seemed like a long shot. Lisa's husband, on the other hand, might be a better bet. He was probably comfortable with computers and, from the times Sam had seen him with Lisa, was not all that happy with his young wife. But the man had seemed too domineering, too much of an in-your-face, swaggering Texas oil man to bother with anonymous e-mails. He would consider that a tactic for sissies.

"What about your stepdaughters? Did they know?"

He heard her gasp. "I—no, I didn't tell them. I'm sure I didn't."

"Do you see a lot of the girls?"

"Not a lot. Usually they meet their father for lunch. On Wednesdays when I have my Pilates class."

He could tell from her tone that it was a touchy topic. "Are the girls close to their father?"

"Very," she snapped.

So during their weekly lunch Daddy could have told his daughters that Lisa was going in for another round of fat-sucking. "What's their relationship with you like?"

"When we see each other, we're very civil."

He knew she was lying. "Think one of the girls could have sent you the e-mails?"

It took her a long time to answer. "Of course not. How could they get into Josh Edwards's computer?"

"Maybe I should talk to the two of them," Sam said.

"They—they're out of town right now," Lisa said. "And I need to go." Then she hung up on him.

Sam shook his head. He'd need to talk to the stepdaughters.

Right from the start, he'd thought Lisa's e-mails were sent by a woman—probably a woman who had nothing to do with the murders.

Sighing, he ran a hand through thick hair that was badly in need of a haircut. None of this, though, was getting him one iota closer to finding the killer—or killers—of Todd Lawson, Allison James, and Megan Edwards. He was even starting to doubt his high school revenge theory.

Why would a killer wait fifteen years to get back at high school bullies? It would make more sense to seek justice years ago when the memory of those old injuries should be more vivid, more painful. Was there some reason the murderer hadn't been able to strike earlier: out of the country perhaps, or serving a prison sentence? Sam hadn't spotted any convicted felons in the list he'd received of The Six's victims, but maybe some other commitment had kept the killer away from old classmates.

Or maybe the killer had a more current grudge. The only reason Sam had linked the crimes to the victims' high school activities was that seemed to be the only thing connecting Todd and Allison and Megan. From what Sam could tell, The Six had had very little to do with each other in recent years.

He could imagine a number of more current reasons for wanting to get rid of those three. Todd, the debt-ridden womanizer on the brink of being fired; Allison James, a has-been actress desperate to wring a hefty divorce settlement from her ruthless producer husband; and Megan Edwards, the pathologically jealous wife of a pathologically cheating husband—all of them could have provoked someone close to them into murder.

A homicidal spouse could easily have known about their husband's or wife's high school life—and figured out how to use it to his or her advantage. If, for instance, Todd's death had been a random homicide—a drug deal gone wrong, a hooker who'd tried to rob him—Allison's or Megan's husband could have seen a way to get rid of an annoying wife while pointing the blame toward a throat-slashing serial killer with a grudge from high school. Both Josh Edwards and Ethan Fox seemed ruthless enough to not mind killing a few extra people to get what they wanted.

The problem, of course, was finding some hard evidence. But even clever killers, he reminded himself, slipped up eventually.

Sam walked into the real estate office where Megan Edwards had worked.

The office manager bristled when she saw him. She apparently wanted everyone to forget that one of their colleagues had had her throat slashed in the garage next door—probably didn't want to distract anyone from nailing the next big commission. "Officer Wolfe," she said, "I'm surprised to see you again so soon."

He sent her a brooking-no-nonsense look. "I want to talk to Ms. Sheffield. She was on vacation the last time I was here."

She nodded to a very young woman at the receptionist desk who was sporting what used to be called a buzz cut. "Victoria, will you come over here for a minute?"

Victoria came, looking curious. "Officer Wolfe wants to ask you a few questions about Megan," the older woman told her, putting the emphasis on "a few."

They moved to the small office where Sam had last time

questioned the others.

"I'm really sorry, but the only thing I remember about that day is that I was going to Acapulco the next morning," the receptionist said. "I left work early to get packed."

Mentally Sam groaned. "Did Ms. Edwards seem especially upset that day? Can you recall anything unusual about her?"

The young woman tilted her head to one side, thinking. "Megan *was* pissed off. I remember that. Someone phoned to make an appointment to see this really expensive mini-mansion in River Oaks. Megan was going to show it to her at four, but then at three-thirty the woman called to say she couldn't make it then, she wanted to come at six-thirty instead. Megan had to call her husband to make sure he'd get home early to relieve the nanny, and I gather he wasn't pleased. I heard her say something like, 'As much as you'd like to think otherwise, I'm not the children's only parent.' The two of them were always fighting about him not doing his share."

"But then someone cancelled an evening appointment with Megan that night," Sam said.

Victoria shook her head. "So that woman must have bailed out of the second appointment. I bet Megan was furious. She said the woman sounded like one of those self-centered socialite types."

"She mention the woman's name?" Sam asked.

Victoria narrowed her eyes. "The only thing I heard Megan call her was Juliet-the-Rich-Bitch."

Thirty-Three

Again Kate had stayed later than she'd intended at work. It was harder than she thought to fit a full-time job into part-time hours, especially if you were a conscientious physician. The unfortunate result was that she was always feeling guilty about *something:* neglecting her mother to finish her work or neglecting her patients because she was home with her mother.

As she hurried down the hallway, she thought that her ex-husband, who'd once accused her of being "the worst workaholic I've ever known, and that's saying a lot when we're talking about surgeons," would be amused to learn that her boss had just informed her she needed to put in more hours at the office.

Kate almost didn't see the woman backing out of Josh Edwards's office, a woman who was obviously paying more attention to Josh than to the hallway traffic. "See you tonight, lover," she said with a flirtatious smile as she closed Josh's door. And stepped directly into Kate's path.

It was their office manager Annette, Josh's on-again-off-again girlfriend. Apparently today the two of them were on. Kate skidded to a halt to avoid slamming into her.

"God, I'm sorry," she told Kate. "I wasn't looking where I was going."

Kate took a deep breath. "It's okay. I wasn't paying much attention either."

"You're Dr. Dalton, right?" the woman said, sounding almost shy. "I think we met at the office party, but we didn't really get to talk. I'm Annette Williams, by the way." She offered Kate her hand.

Kate shook it, smiling. "I remember you from the party. You said you'd come from Boston."

The woman nodded. "I've been in Houston about a year now. I came last January, just in time to avoid the endless Massachusetts winter. I sure didn't miss that."

"Of course the trade-off is Houston's endless summer." Kate glanced at her watch. "But I need to get moving. Enjoyed talking to you."

Annette nodded. "I—I heard about your mother," she said, tentatively patting Kate's arm. "I think it's great that you're cutting back your work to spend more time with her. It's important to cherish the people you love while you can."

"Thanks." Kate was touched by her words. Heading down the hall, she thought how this young woman seemed so sweet and vulnerable, the polar opposite of aggressive, sharp-tongued Megan Edwards. But maybe that was what Josh found appealing about Annette. She just hoped Annette knew what she was getting into with Josh.

Kate was reaching for the door to the waiting room when it opened. She found herself face to face with Sam Wolfe. What was he doing here? Had he come for another session of official interrogation masked as a social encounter?

She narrowed her eyes. "Officer Wolfe, what a surprise."

He nodded. "Dr. Dalton, nice to see you again." His eyes darted past her down the hall.

He must be here to see Josh, she decided. Did he have some new information about Megan's killer? Or maybe he suspected Josh. A disproportionate number of homicides, after all, seemed to occur at the hands of the victim's spouse.

"Goodnight." She started to walk by him.

"Do you have a minute for a quick question?"

Afraid not, she wanted to tell him. "I can only give you a minute. I need to get home."

"Can you remember anyone in your high school class named Juliet?" he asked. "Maybe someone who'd been bullied."

Kate shook her head. "I remember a Julia, but no Juliet. But you might have better luck asking Libby Norman. She knew a lot more people than I did."

Sam nodded. "Good idea. I'll call her."

"Libby told me, incidentally, that everyone who registered for our reunion received phone numbers and e-mail addresses of the others who are coming. Libby said that's probably how someone learned where to e-mail Lisa."

"Interesting theory," Sam said.

And of course, Kate thought, feeling irritated, he wasn't going to volunteer any information to *her.* Hers was not to wonder why, only to answer.

He looked amused at what she assumed was her peevish expression. "I'd tell you if I could," he said.

Sure you would. Kate saw Annette in the hallway, watching the two of them, obviously curious. Probably she'd report everything she heard to Josh. "I've got to go."

"Give your mother my regards. How's she doing, by the way?"

She turned back to answer. "About the same."

His brown eyes studied her face with an expression she couldn't identify. "I hope I'll see you again soon."

This time she kept moving. *Not if I can help it.*

Her mother was asleep by the time Kate got home—a pattern that was becoming increasingly familiar. At least she was usually awake in the mornings when Kate was there. They'd gotten into the habit of talking at breakfast. Some days they just discussed what they'd read in the newspaper, but on others, like today, her mother told Kate stories about her life. Today she was describing how she met her husband-to-be in their college Spanish class. "He kept looking at me and smiling, too tongue-tied to talk," her mother had said, and Kate, who'd never remembered her father at a loss for words, chuckled.

Kate scrambled some eggs and settled down for a solitary supper. She was washing the few dishes when the phone rang.

"Hi, Jane, it's Libby. Just called to see how you and your mom are doing."

"I'm okay. Mom is the same, sleeping a lot." She knew that Libby expected her to say more, but talking about her mother's obviously deteriorating condition made Kate feel even more depressed. "By the way, I saw Sam Wolfe today and told him to call you. He asked if I knew anyone in our class named Juliet. I didn't, but I told him you might."

"Let me think. There was a Juliette who was a foreign exchange student from France. Remember her?"

"Nope. I told him you knew more people than I did. Was she bullied by The Six?"

"I don't think so. She was a year ahead of us and she was only at the school for a year. Why? What does this Juliet have to do with The Six?"

"Don't know. Officer Wolfe is not good at sharing."

Libby laughed. "No, he's not, is he? He phoned me a few days ago to ask about the reunion. But I got the idea that that wasn't what he really wanted to talk about. He spent most of the conversation asking me questions about you."

"Me?" Putting away the dishes, Kate noticed suddenly that her hand was shaking. "What—what kind of questions?"

"Kind of general stuff: What were you like in high school? Had I seen much of you lately? Did I know if you were dating anyone?"

Libby paused. "He's divorced, you know, has a teenage daughter." She giggled, sounding very much the way she had in high school. "I think he likes you, Jane."

Kate doubted that very much. "Well, I'm not all that fond of him." *And stop telling him things about me! Especially not about high school.* But there was no way she could say that to Libby—that Sam was gathering information, not planning a date.

"Oh, my mother's calling for me, Libby. Got to go."

As she hung up the phone, Kate noticed her hands were still shaking.

Thirty-Four

Josh Edwards was doing a poor job of hiding his hostility, Sam thought as he sat in the uncomfortable chrome-and-leather-chair in Edwards's sleek office.

"I don't understand why you think *I* would know who Megan was going to meet that evening," Edwards said, sounding like a whiny teenager.

Maybe because I assumed—apparently erroneously—that you might want to help find her killer, Sam was tempted to say. Instead, he said, "I was under the impression that the two of you spoke on the phone that afternoon."

The doctor nodded. "She said she had a late appointment to show a house in River Oaks and that I'd have to get home to take care of the kids. Our nanny leaves at six."

"Did she say anything at all about the person she was going to show the house to?"

"Some woman from out of town whose husband was being transferred to Houston in a month. I didn't get any more details."

"I just learned that this client's name was Juliet. That name sound familiar? Maybe someone in your high school class?"

Josh stared at him. "Did Megan tell someone at her office that she knew this woman?"

"No, she didn't say much of anything about her except that she sounded like a rich bitch."

"I don't remember any Juliet from our class, though I seem

to remember one from the year ahead of us."

"Was that Juliet someone your little group bullied?"

Edwards's normally pale face turned crimson. "Not that I know of," he said coldly. "As I mentioned before, *I* was not personally involved in any of those incidents."

Sam could have argued that point: There were many ways to be personally involved in crimes without inflicting the actual violence. He studied the furious, red-faced doctor. Could he have arranged his wife's murder? Hiring someone else to do the job would ensure that Josh had an alibi at the time of Megan's death. Perhaps too he was queasy about slashing the throat of the mother of his children. This "Juliet" might even be his paid assassin.

"Are you saying you think this woman had something to do with Megan's death?" Edwards asked.

"She was one of the last people to talk to your wife. I'm just checking out all the angles." He wasn't going to tell the man that Juliet's phone call canceling her second appointment with Megan had originated from a pay phone across the street from the parking garage where his wife died—ten minutes later.

As Sam stood up to leave, the doctor said, "By the way, I don't appreciate you interrogating our nanny. She told me she was upset by your questions."

"She didn't appear upset to me," Sam said.

"She seemed to think you were accusing her of lying about the time I got home."

Sam studied him, wondering if any of that anger had to do with the nanny's emotional well-being. Not much, he'd guess. But if Edwards had really arrived home at a few minutes before six, the time the girl repeatedly insisted he had, why did he seem so suddenly anxious? Megan Edwards had not even left her office until almost six-thirty.

Sam kept his voice purposely bland. "As I said, I'm just

checking out all the angles."

He waited for Edwards to reply. The man looked as if there were a lot of things he'd like to say, but he was too smart to say them. Instead, he pointedly glanced away as Sam nodded and headed out the door.

Sam could understand now why Lisa Smythe was not fond of her two stepdaughters. The young women, who'd agreed to meet him at a coffee shop on Westheimer, were blonde, trim, and trendy in molded-to-their-bodies designer jeans and those skimpy, midriff-baring sweaters that made Sam go ballistic whenever his daughter chose to wear one. The sisters—Ashley and Meredith—had that supremely confident, snotty air of popular college sorority girls. They were a good ten to fifteen years younger than their stepmother. Lisa must have hated that Ashley and Meredith—at this point in their lives, at least—didn't need plastic surgery to look good.

Her stepdaughters also were clearly not fond of Lisa. "I printed all the e-mails I got about her," said Ashley, the older, less blonde, and more bossy sister, a law student. She pushed two pages across the table to Sam. "Meredith and I got the same e-mails, three of them."

Sam scanned the papers while the young women sipped their lattes. The first message informed the girls that their stepmother was a sadistic bully who'd preyed on weaker students in high school, spreading vicious lies about them while she secretly lusted after her best friend Allison. The second message detailed Lisa's later years: her failed modeling career; her unrequited love for Allison, who no longer returned her phone calls; and Lisa's subsequent marriage to their father. "At least he offers me financial security," Lisa reportedly told an unnamed friend. "And while he's not the sharpest tack in the box, I do look very good when I'm standing next to him." Both e-mails were signed

"Your Stepmother's Former Classmate."

Sam glanced up at the girls. "They're quite malicious, aren't they?"

Ashley, apparently the official spokeswoman, nodded. "Which doesn't mean they're not true. Lisa is still a witch."

"Bullying sounds like something Lisa would do," said Meredith, the younger, blonder sister. "She tries to come across as this loving wife and our understanding big sister, but anyone can see that she's a gold-digger who hates our guts—almost as much as we hate hers."

Ashley shot her sister an annoyed look and took back the conversational reins. "Though to be fair, the first e-mails didn't give any conclusive evidence that Lisa is a sadistic, bullying lesbian who sneers at our father behind his back."

Sam bit his lip to keep from laughing. Fortunately, Ashley didn't seem to expect any response.

"We wanted to give Lisa the benefit of the doubt," Ashley said.

I'll bet, Sam thought, noticing that Meredith looked as doubtful of that statement as he. But he managed to nod.

"Then we got this last message." Ashley handed him another paper.

"After this one," Meredith added, "we decided we had to show them to Daddy."

This e-mail came with photos attached. The first was from Lisa's high school yearbook: Lisa, according to the caption, helping her "good friend Allison James learn her lines" for a school play. The camera had caught Allison emoting and Lisa gazing at her with undisguised adoration.

The next photo was more recent. It showed Lisa, dressed in a black suit with tears streaming down her face, speaking at a podium to a church audience.

Sam stiffened. He knew where this picture came from. He'd

been there, in the church, watching Lisa give the eulogy at Allison James's funeral. Who, sitting with him in the church that day, had taken this photo?

The last picture had been taken in another church. Another funeral that Sam had attended: this one, Megan Edwards's. The camera had caught Lisa waiting in a line of mourners to talk to Josh. She was glancing back at her scowling husband, a look of undisguised loathing on her face.

The message accompanying the pictures was simple: "I figured you'd want proof."

Thirty-Five

The nurse ushered Kate's next patient into her office.

"Carly," Kate said, trying to hide her surprise, "it's nice to see you again. What can I do for you?"

Sam Wolfe's teenage daughter blushed. "You said I should let you know if I had any more questions about my nose—uh, rhinoplasty. And I do, kind of."

Kate smiled encouragingly. The girl really did remind her of herself at that age—so shy and self-conscious that you just wanted to pat her on the shoulder. "I'll try my best to answer them. What do you want to know?"

"How long after the surgery will it be before I look as if I haven't been in a car accident?"

"You'll be in a cast for around twelve days. Healing takes awhile, but you'll probably look okay after a few weeks," Kate said. She would have sworn that information was included in the booklets she'd given Carly to read.

"I was thinking I'd like to do the surgery soon so you can be the one to do it. I have a week off at spring break. You *will* be here next month, won't you?"

Kate nodded. Probably—if Aaron didn't fire her or she didn't quit. "But don't base this decision on my schedule. There are a lot of doctors here who do excellent work."

"No, I want you to do it, and I've almost convinced my parents. I know I need to bring in a parent for the pre-surgery consultation. My mom has a hard time getting away from her job during the day so my dad will probably be the one to come."

"Fine, though I'm here late some days so you and your mother could schedule an appointment for after she gets off work." *I'll happily stay here an extra hour to avoid having to deal again with your father.*

"Oh, Mom trusts my dad to handle things. She always says what a responsible, caring man he is. Charming too."

Kate raised her eyebrows. "Funny that she divorced such a paragon."

"She isn't in love with him anymore, but she still likes him. And he *is* a very nice man. You think my dad is nice too, don't you?"

No, actually I don't, Kate thought. But it didn't seem professional to mention it. "I'm more interested in answering your medical questions now, Carly."

The girl smiled. "Oh, you've already covered those. But I wanted to tell you my dad really likes you, and he seemed upset that he made you mad when he came to your house. He said he acted like a cop; he does that to me sometimes too, kind of interrogates me. Or else he thinks I'm a little kid out in the big bad world of criminals."

So maybe the kid wasn't so shy after all. "Does your father know you're here?"

Carly shook her head. Her eyes widened. "You're not going to tell him that I told you he likes you, are you?"

In the best of all possible worlds I won't ever have to talk to your father again. "No, I won't tell him," Kate said. "I think *both of us* should let him manage his own social life."

"Oh, he needs help with that. Big time. I mean he's working these incredible hours, and then he tries to spend time with me—he's a very conscientious father. He used to date this assistant D.A., but they broke up last year, and he hasn't gone out with anybody else since then."

Kate reminded herself that the girl meant well. "Carly, as much as you want to offer your matchmaking assistance, I am *not* the person to match with your dad. The two of us just aren't right for each other." She stood up. "And I have another patient now."

Carly stood up too. "Okay. I'll be back with a parent for the pre-surgery thing."

"Good." Kate had a feeling Carly might decide to bring her mother after all. She opened the door. "Bye."

Carly took a step, then turned back. "It's the cop thing you don't like, isn't it? That's what Dad thinks."

The cop thing? She glared at the girl. "I suppose I'm *not* especially fond of the way your father tries to pump me for information while pretending to be making a social visit. And yes, I find it quite off-putting when he keeps acting as if I'm a crime suspect. So if that's the cop thing, you're correct; I'm not crazy about it."

Carly seemed unfazed by her anger. "But you're not, are you? Involved in a crime, I mean."

"No, I am not."

"That's what I thought." Carly shot her a grin as she finally walked out the door.

Kate closed the door firmly and returned to her desk. She took a deep cleansing breath, then slowly exhaled. Was it possible that Sam Wolfe actually did like her? He must have told his daughter something positive about her, and it sounded as if he was embarrassed by his botched pizza-bearing visit.

But even if Sam was attracted to her, that didn't mean he didn't also suspect her of committing a crime. Kate opened her eyes, sighed, and got up to meet her next patient.

Talk about making a bad day worse, Kate thought as she walked into the examination room. Lisa Smythe perched on the table, looking pleased.

"Mrs. Smythe, this is a surprise." *Not a good one.*

"Not half as surprised as you're going to be." Lisa paused, waiting for Kate to reply. When she didn't, Lisa smiled. "I know who you are, Jane."

Kate could feel her stomach lurch.

"I thought you looked familiar the first time I saw you, but then Megan told me you were from Illinois and were only here because of your sick mother, and I figured I was mistaken. But yesterday I talked to your good friend Libby Norman, and she let it slip that you were back in town caring for your mom and—guess what?—Jane Murphy is a plastic surgeon in Illinois now. She didn't seem to realize you're using an assumed name, but she did mention how good you looked; she almost didn't recognize you, she said."

Kate shrugged, trying to look indifferent. "It's not an assumed name. I'm Jane Katherine Murphy Dalton. In college I started going by Kate, my middle name, and my married name is Dalton. Katherine Dalton is what's on my medical diploma, and after my divorce, I just decided to keep calling myself that."

Lisa, she was happy to see, looked somewhat less smug. "It was funny that you didn't mention to anyone—Josh, Megan, or me, for instance—that you'd gone to high school with us."

Kate sneered. "Why would I do that? We weren't friends. And it was years ago. For *some* of us, high school was not the high point of our lives. In fact, for me it wasn't even a very significant part."

It was a direct hit. Her old classmate flushed angrily. So the bully didn't much like being bullied.

"Oh, I'll bet it was more significant than you're letting on," Lisa said. "Who could forget 'Plain Jane Gets Laid'? I started thinking that a brainy girl like you is undoubtedly very skilled with computers. And you probably even have a key to Josh

Edwards's office. So you could use his computer when you didn't feel like going to another public library to send me those anonymous e-mails."

"I've never sent you any e-mails," Kate said. "Anonymous or otherwise. Frankly, I prefer to avoid contact with you."

"Is that why you cancelled my surgery?"

"No, you cancelled your surgery when you refused to quit smoking." Kate wondered what Lisa would say if she revealed the rest of the answer: *And I was damned relieved that I didn't have to fight the temptation to injure you on the operating table.*

Lisa had the look of a cat cornering a mouse. "Then I thought, Could my old classmate Jane have snuck into the recovery room after another doctor did the surgery, trying to finish me off? Whoever I saw skulking around my bed with some sharp instrument was wearing scrubs."

Kate stared at her. "That's ridiculous! I didn't even know you were having the liposuction. I'm amazed that you found another surgeon willing to take the risk—unless, of course, you lied to him about your smoking."

Lisa opened her mouth to respond, but Kate turned her back on her and stalked to the door. "Get out of my office. I have nothing more to say to you."

Slowly Lisa stood up. "Do not think that I'm through with you, Plain Jane Murphy," she said before she marched out.

Thirty-Six

"I want you to arrest her," Lisa Smythe told Sam, her arms folded across her chest.

Something was clearly very wrong. She'd shown up, unannounced, at the station—something she'd never done before. Today the Queen of Good Grooming looked like hell. Her eyes were red-rimmed and devoid of makeup, and the blouse and slacks she had on were wrinkled enough for her to have slept in. She was also so nervous she was practically twitching. Sam found it hard to believe that learning Dr. Kate Dalton was one of her former high school victims was enough to provoke this kind of reaction.

"I can't do that," he said. "The law requires me to have a good reason for arresting someone, not just a vague suspicion that she might have committed a crime."

"It's not a 'vague suspicion.' " Lisa looked as if she'd like to rake her blood-red fingernails across his face. "The woman has a motive, she's been hiding her identity, and she probably had access to Josh Edwards's computer. It sure makes a lot more sense that Jane would have sent those e-mails rather than Josh. Like Josh said, I didn't do anything bad to him in high school, so why would he e-mail me saying I'd pay for what I did?"

Her pale eyes, Sam noticed, looked rabbity without mascara. "What did Dr. Dalton say when you accused her of sending you the e-mails?"

"She denied it, of course. She also said she wasn't anywhere near the hospital the day I had my lipo, that Kate Dalton is her real married name, and high school was an insignificant part of her life that she barely remembers."

Maybe that was what Kate wanted to believe about her high school years, but Sam didn't buy that they'd been insignificant. He'd seen the wounded look in her eyes when she mentioned the Plain Jane Gets Laid incident.

The memory of Lisa's casual cruelty to a shy girl she barely knew made his voice come out harsher than he'd intended. "So you have no proof that Kate Dalton has done anything to you, aside from not mentioning that she was in your high school class?"

Lisa's eyes narrowed. "I wonder if you're a bit too attached to Dr. Dalton to see this situation objectively, Officer Wolfe. I remember your little tête-à-tête at Megan's funeral."

Sam made an effort to keep his face expressionless. "No competent police officer I know of would arrest Dr. Dalton on what you've told me." Which was true. He was grateful, however, that Lisa wasn't aware of his daughter's single-minded campaign to spark a romance between Kate and him.

"Don't think, detective, that I don't realize what you think of me: a self-absorbed, shallow socialite who's making a big deal out of a few nasty e-mails. I suspect you also think I'm a mean bitch getting exactly what she deserves. But, unfortunately, you don't really have the luxury of being that judgmental, do you? You don't get to protect only the people you approve of."

Sam nodded. It was a valid point—and also a surprisingly spot-on assessment of his feelings about her.

The glare she was shooting his way was enough to cause frostbite. "And those little messages did more than simply embarrass me. I just learned that my ex–high school classmate sent my husband and two stepdaughters several e-mails I didn't get. They were vicious lies, claiming I'm a lesbian who was in love with Allison and I only married my husband for his money. It also said I'd been overheard calling John an old coot and laughed about how good I looked standing next to him—which is totally untrue!"

For a moment Lisa looked suspiciously close to tears. She took several deep breaths before speaking again. "And I *never* had a sexual relationship with Allison—we were just close friends. But when I told John that, he didn't believe me. He seemed to think that since I admitted I'd done the cruel high school tricks the e-mailer accused me of, then the rest of her claims must be true too."

Sam couldn't believe that this was the first time Lisa's husband might have wondered if she'd married him for his money. The one time he'd seen Mr. and Mrs. Smythe together, it hadn't looked like a love match.

Lisa apparently sensed what he was thinking. "Hard as it is to believe, I married John because I loved him. I felt protected by him, taken care of. But when I said that to him, he laughed. Then he told me he was filing for divorce. So the way I see it, Jane or whichever of my classmates sent those e-mails did a hell of a lot of damage. She ruined my life."

"I'm sorry about your husband," Sam said. He wondered what part Smythe's daughters had played in his decision to divorce Lisa. Whoever had sent the girls those e-mails must have had a fairly good idea of the sisters' antipathy toward their stepmother.

Would Kate Dalton have known about the Smythe family dynamics? From what he'd heard, the two women had only met a few times in Kate's office. The e-mailer, though, seemed very well acquainted with Lisa. Either the writer was someone personally close to Lisa or someone so consumed with hatred of her that he—or she—had spent a lot of time spying on her. Maybe Sam was kidding himself, but he didn't think that Kate

Dalton fit either profile.

"I want you to find out who's doing this to me," Lisa said. "You're right that I don't have proof that it's Dr. Jane-Kate. But think of this: whoever sent those e-mails intended to spread malicious rumors that would humiliate me—exactly what I did to Jane fifteen years ago. I'm sure she'd see this as fitting revenge."

"But Dr. Dalton wasn't the only person you spread rumors about. As I recall, there were quite a number of others."

Lisa's thin lips pressed together. "True, but, as far as I know, I haven't laid eyes on any of those others in years. This former classmate seems to have a lot of inside information about me. Jane could have learned some of this stuff from Josh; he's a big gossip. It's also possible that Jane didn't start out seeking revenge, but then I walked into her office and all those bad memories suddenly came back."

Sam stared at her. Her scenario sounded almost plausible. It would explain so much: why someone had waited fifteen years to take Lisa to task for her adolescent cruelty, why Lisa had been the only one of her group to receive the accusing e-mails. Perhaps something in Kate—a tightly wound, self-disciplined woman who'd consciously distanced herself from her past—had snapped when she saw her old nemesis. Maybe the pain that had been locked away in some remote corner of her psyche had returned with such overwhelming force that even the doctor's vaunted self-control couldn't contain it.

"I hadn't thought of this before," Lisa said, "but maybe Jane killed Todd too. He was the one who got her drunk and seduced her, you know."

On your orders, Sam thought. "I believe it's called date rape these days."

Lisa apparently didn't hear—or chose to ignore—the accusation in his voice. Her own voice was tense with excitement.

"She's a surgeon, after all. I bet she wouldn't have any problem slashing someone's throat."

And the thin-bladed murder weapon could very well have been a scalpel. Sam took a deep breath. "What about Allison James and Megan Edwards? Did they do anything to her?"

Lisa shook her head. "They might have passed along the rumors, but they weren't really involved." She had the grace to look embarrassed. "It was a terrible thing for me to do to her. I realize that now."

Sam wasn't sure he believed her, though undoubtedly, she was sorry that the fallout from her high school pranks had ended up hurting her.

"Although I think Todd was already dead the first time I saw Dr. Dalton." Lisa sounded as if she was talking to herself as much as to him. "Which I guess would shoot down my theory that the shock of seeing me unleashed all these repressed violent impulses. Of course maybe she really moved back to Houston just so she could murder Todd—and the others." Her face turned pale as she realized what she was saying. "Maybe Jane intends to kill me too, but she wanted me to suffer first."

"More likely," Sam said, "the person who's sending you the e-mails is not the one who killed your friends."

He could see on her face how much she wanted to believe that her ex–high school classmate was happy to break up Lisa's marriage, but didn't intend to slit her throat.

Sam hoped his own thoughts weren't as transparent to her. Because while his gut told him that Kate Dalton was not a killer, he had no problem believing she might be Lisa's anonymous e-mailer.

When Lisa finally left, Sam made the phone call he'd been about to make when she walked in. He just hoped that Megan Edwards's colleague was still in her office.

She was. "Ms. Johnson, this is Officer Wolfe again. I have a quick question. Do you recall the kind of shoes you were wearing when you found Megan Edwards's body?"

"Black leather pumps," the woman said.

"Can you tell me what size shoes you wear?"

"Eight-and-a-half wide. I've got big feet. And now are you going to tell me, officer, why you want to know this?"

Sam guessed he owed her that much. "Our forensic experts have been working on a bloody footprint found in the garage that night. I wanted to make sure it wasn't yours."

"So what size shoe print was it?"

"I'm afraid that's classified information at this point. All I can tell you is it's not yours." He paused. "Have you remembered seeing anyone at all in the garage that night?"

"No. Remember, I left the office half an hour after Megan did. Then when I saw her lying in a pool of blood, I was so shocked that anybody could have walked right past me and I wouldn't have noticed."

Sam thanked her for her help and hung up. He stared at the forensic report in front of him. The bloody footprint found near Megan's body was from a rubber-soled shoe, probably a sneaker. Whoever was wearing it had a small, very narrow foot, probably a woman's size six narrow.

It was looking more and more likely that Megan's killer was a woman. Or a man with tiny feet. Sam just wished he knew what size shoes Juliet, Megan's no-show client, wore.

Thirty-Seven

Josh Edwards leaned against the door of Kate's office. Grinning, he shook his head. "I can't believe I didn't figure out you were Jane Murphy from high school."

From behind her desk, Kate stared at him. "Didn't take Lisa long to get the word out, did it?"

He chuckled. "Sure didn't. But you'll be happy to know that I told her you didn't have a key to my office or the password to my computer."

She closed her eyes. How had it all come to this? Josh, she could tell, expected her to feel grateful to him. But there was a flirtatious undercurrent, an unspoken threat, to his words that she didn't appreciate one bit.

He was openly studying her face. "I can see you had rhinoplasty. And I'd guess a chin implant?" When she nodded, he added, "After Lisa told me who you were, I looked up your photo in our yearbook. With the cosmetic work on your face, the different hairstyle, and your losing weight—what? twenty, twenty-five pounds?—you look like a different person."

Which had been her intent, Kate thought. But she didn't want to start that discussion with him. Instead, she tried to keep the conversation professional. "I worked for a plastic surgeon throughout college. He gave everyone who worked in his office one cosmetic procedure of our choice as a Christmas gift. I chose to have my nose done, and he suggested he do the chin implant at the same time."

"A very generous man." Josh's tone and raised eyebrows gave the words an ugly innuendo.

Kate glared at him. "He was a very kind man—went on missionary work each year to South America to fix kids' cleft palates. Working with him was what made me want to do reconstructive work."

Josh was still inspecting her. "He also was a very good surgeon. Your face looks great."

In contrast to the way I used to look? Kate was tempted to ask. "He was an excellent surgeon," she said. "He died last year."

Josh moved closer, making Kate edgy. There was something predatory about the man. She tried hard not to react when he perched on the edge of her desk.

"So why didn't you mention our shared past before?" he asked. "Why did you lie about going to school in Illinois?"

"I *did* go to school in Illinois—college and medical school. As for why I didn't discuss high school with you, I guess it seemed like a very long time ago." *And it wasn't any of your damn business.*

"And maybe you'd just as soon forget high school?"

Kate tried to smile, wondering if it looked more like a grimace. "Wouldn't we all?"

To her surprise, Josh laughed. "Isn't *that* the truth? I can never understand why everyone gets so hyped up about these high school reunions. I figure if you haven't laid eyes on your classmates in fifteen years, maybe those are relationships that don't need to be revisited. Adolescence, after all, isn't the finest moment for most of us."

This time Kate's smile was genuine. "I couldn't agree more." She was just surprised that someone whose high school life seemed right out of the pages of a teen magazine felt the same way.

He leaned toward her. "I remember you from National Honor Society meetings. I always thought you had a great sense of humor."

Oh, spare me. You didn't know I was alive.

"I might have looked like one of the most popular kids in school, Kate, but I felt lonely, like a nerdy outsider."

She made a valiant effort not to roll her eyes. "I talked to Annette the other night. She seems like a very nice woman."

He leaned back, looking almost pained. "Yes, she is, but we're just friends."

I'll bet that's not what Annette thinks. Or what you say when you're alone with her. "Oh, I had the impression the two of you were more than that." *For instance, when I saw you and Annette playing kissy-face in the grocery store parking lot the day after your wife died.*

"I'm not sure what Annette told you, but from my standpoint, our relationship isn't serious." He hesitated. "I have no intention of ever getting married again."

"Not a big fan of marriage?" she asked, knowing she would be better advised to just drop the subject.

He shook his head. "Once was enough. What Megan and I had together was great at first, but we got married too young. I'm not going to be trapped again. I have my kids to raise and I'll have girlfriends, but not another wife."

He was looking at her as if he was about to offer her one of the girlfriend slots. Kate stood up quickly. "Well, I'm glad you stopped by, Josh."

He stayed seated. "I want you to know that I don't even like Lisa."

That makes two of us. But why was he telling her this? It was possible Josh was only angling for sex or was simply curious, out for gossip about Plain Jane Murphy. Or maybe she was just suspicious of anyone who'd been part of The Six.

When she didn't respond, he said, "I was never part of that stunt that Lisa and Todd pulled on you. I didn't even know about it until after the fact."

When everybody in school knew Plain Jane Got Laid. She nodded, unwilling to discuss the incident, only indicating that she'd heard him.

He didn't seem to require any more encouragement to continue. "Lisa and Todd were the sadistic ones in our group, always ready to turn on other kids to make sure they—we—got what we wanted. Maybe it was because they were so unexceptional in every other way. Think about it: Allison was a gifted actress, Matt an amazing football player, Megan was head cheerleader, and I was an excellent student. But Todd and Lisa weren't especially good at anything. Todd became president of our class because of his attachment to us, and Lisa's only real claim to fame was her meanness. She was the enforcer, willing to do anything to help The Six keep our power."

Kate's jaw clenched. "And yet none of the rest of you did anything to stop Lisa and Todd, did you? You all benefited from their brutality—The Six eliminating all your competition for those lead spots on the football team, cheerleading squad, and class plays. But you could tell yourself that you weren't involved in any of that behind-the-scenes nastiness."

"I didn't need their help to do well," Josh said.

But you didn't turn it down either. Maybe Josh hadn't done anything directly to her in the way Todd and Lisa had, but he'd sat back and let it happen. Now years after the fact, he might be feeling embarrassed, but all those months when Kate was so mortified she had to force herself to even enter her high school, the only thing Josh Edwards had been feeling was indifference. His sympathy was fifteen years too late.

"I can understand now why you dislike Lisa so much," Josh said.

Kate's eyes narrowed. "I had the impression that everyone here disliked Lisa. Weren't you the one who said she was the patient from hell, that no one wanted to work on her because she was never satisfied with the results?"

Josh nodded. "Lisa *is* impossible to work with. But your dislike always seemed more intense than that—more personal." When she didn't respond, he added, "I can understand too why you might want to get even with her."

Was he really trying to manipulate her into admitting that she'd sent Lisa those anonymous e-mails? Is that what had prompted this sudden visit?

Kate stalked to the door and pulled it open. "Actually, Josh, you don't understand me at all."

Kate stared at the phone she'd just hung up. Was her encounter with Josh that morning making her suspicious of everyone? Or was the conversation she'd just had with Sam Wolfe as bizarre as she thought?

Ostensibly Sam had phoned to ask if she had any printed information about the rhinoplasty his daughter was lobbying for.

Kate had replied—with eminent common sense—that she'd already given Carly all the pamphlets; maybe he could read those. Except Sam, his voice suddenly strained, had said he'd like to get his own copies. Would it be okay if he came now to get them?

No, it was *not* okay. Whatever game Sam Wolfe was playing, Kate didn't intend to play along. She took the booklets to the reception desk and told Mandy that if Officer Wolfe requested to see her, the receptionist should say she was unavailable.

Twenty minutes later Mandy phoned to say Sam had come and gone. "He really wanted to see you, but I told him you were with a patient."

"Thanks, Mandy. I appreciate it."

"I got the idea he really likes you. He was asking me a lot of questions about you."

"What kind of questions?"

"How late you usually work, what your schedule is like, do you ever go home in your scrubs. He's a very chatty guy. He even told me how much he liked my shoes and said he remembered your feet were small like mine. But I said, no, your feet were much narrower."

Now she knew that Sam Wolfe was either crazy or after something. "He's gone now? I need to leave, but I don't want to get in some long-winded conversation with the man."

Mandy giggled. "He *is* a big talker. But don't worry, he left over ten minutes ago."

Kate waited another five minutes before going to her car. She walked quickly through the garage, keeping her eyes straight ahead.

She hoped Sam Wolfe didn't realize that she'd seen him sitting in his car near the parking garage elevator.

Thirty-Eight

Libby Norman reminded Sam of his favorite high school teacher, a wry, book-loving woman who had insisted he go to college. It made no difference, Mrs. Hess said, that no one else in his family had ever set foot on a college campus or that he'd probably end up being a cop just like his dad; he still owed it to himself to get an education. And, to her delight, Sam had, even trudging through a year of law school before deciding he'd rather be a detective.

Sitting behind a desk in her closet-sized office, Libby was interrogating him with the sardonic relentlessness that Mrs. Hess would have brought to the task. "Why don't you just tell me what this is really about, Officer Wolfe?" she said, sending him a don't-even-try-to-bullshit-me teacher look.

Sam reminded himself that he was the one supposedly in charge here. He glanced once more at Libby's feet, reassured that his original impression had been correct: her shoes were huge, probably a size nine or ten wide. She clearly was not the person who killed Megan Edwards.

So why not level with her? He met the teacher's gray eyes. "There's some new evidence that makes me think the killer we're looking for is one of the girls victimized by The Six."

Libby stared at him. "What new evidence?"

"A woman's bloody shoe print was found near Megan Edwards's body."

"But what connects that print to someone from my high

school class?"

"It's just a theory on a possible link between the three murder victims." When she raised her eyebrows inquiringly, he explained. "Once it was established that Megan Edwards's killer was a woman, I got to thinking about the other victims. Allison Lawson was killed in a ladies' restroom. That's certainly no proof that her murderer was a woman, but I think that a smart male killer would figure that following Allison into a women's restroom was awfully risky. As for Todd Lawson, there was no evidence of forced entry or sign of a struggle in his hotel room. He apparently invited his murderer in and wasn't expecting the attack."

"Maybe he let a man—someone he knew—inside."

"He was found in bed, naked. The autopsy said he died in the bed after he ingested a lot of sleeping pills, which is probably why he didn't try to fight off the killer."

Libby shrugged. "Still could be a man, couldn't it? Maybe he was gay or bisexual."

"I looked into that possibility. If Todd was homosexual, it was a well-kept secret. He had quite a reputation as a womanizer. And several people mentioned he was trying to pick up women at the hotel bar that night."

The teacher shook her head. "That doesn't surprise me at all. Even in high school, he was a sexual predator." Her eyes widened. "But you're saying maybe one of the teenage girls he preyed upon decided to get even?"

"That's my guess."

"And you came here today to ask me which girl in my class would be that vengeful?"

Sam nodded. "I know I asked you before about who'd been bullied, but I thought that now we're focused on female victims, you might remember something else."

Libby's eyes fixated on the table as she considered his question. "I already told you that Megan put laxatives in my drink at cheerleader tryouts and Jane Murphy was bullied by Lisa and Todd."

"Plain Jane Gets Laid," Sam said. "I remember."

"Then there was that actress, Maria Somebody—I don't remember her last name. She was going to get the lead in our school play until Lisa spread it around school that Maria was having a lesbian tryst with our drama coach. Maria was so mortified she dropped out of school and Allison got the part. And I told you about that other girl, Meredith, who transferred to another high school after Megan started harassing her for flirting with Josh."

"Meredith Lewis," Sam said. "She lives in Boston, a married social worker with three kids." Sam hadn't been able to locate the actress, Maria Vorgan, though her old high school drama teacher had told him Maria had written that she'd gotten some off-Broadway parts and was thinking of moving to LA to break into film.

Neither Meredith nor Maria sounded like the kind of person who stalked and murdered people who'd hurt them fifteen years earlier. Both of these women seemed to have moved on with their post–high school lives.

Libby leaned forward. "There *is* someone else who I'd forgotten about: Tanya Greene. I just talked to her; she called about our reunion. She's just gotten divorced—I heard about *that* at length—and moved to her parents' house with her kids. She reminded me that she'd dated Todd Lawson during our sophomore year. When she broke up with him, Todd apparently spread it around school that he'd been the one who ended it because she was such a slut."

Libby rolled her eyes. "As if anyone who knew Todd would believe he'd break up with a girl because of *that.* But the really interesting thing is how Tanya responded. She confronted him in front of a group of guys and punched him. Gave him a black eye. And with all those witnesses, Todd couldn't very well punch her back."

She chuckled and Sam couldn't help grinning. He wondered if he would have found the story so amusing if he hadn't had a daughter in high school.

"I thought your classmates were too afraid of The Six to retaliate," he said.

"They usually were. But the group's bullying was later, during our junior and senior years. This was only Todd. I think he got meaner after that. Tanya humiliated him, and he wanted to make sure it never happened again."

"So the whole clique didn't pick on Tanya?"

Libby shook her head. "Tanya started dating a guy in the class ahead of us—the man she just divorced—and they hung out with the older kids. That's why I didn't think of her when you asked about people in our class who'd been bullied. But she certainly is still hostile toward Todd. She told me that whoever killed him did the world a favor."

Sam raised his eyebrows. "She say anything to make you think she has a grudge against the rest of the group?"

"Not really. If she were going to kill anyone, I'd think it would be her ex-husband. She told me she broke his nose when she found out he'd been cheating on her."

Tanya sounded like a long shot as their killer, but Sam said he'd look into it. Whoever had murdered the three was undoubtedly mentally unstable, and maybe this woman was paranoid enough to blame her marital problems on her high school experiences.

"Do you remember what Tanya looked like?" he asked.

Libby appeared puzzled. "I only talked to her on the phone. She used to be very tall with short curly red hair, kind of big-boned and athletic-looking."

"Big feet?"

Her eyes narrowed. "Oh, I get it. You want to know if her shoe matched the bloody footprint. Actually Tanya was one of the few girls in gym class who had bigger feet than me."

Sam pulled out a tape recorder from his pocket and set it on her desk. "I have something I'd like you to hear."

Libby nodded and listened intently as an animated female voice said, "Megan, hi, this is Juliet Montague. My husband and I are going to be moving to Houston in two months, and I'm in town looking for a home, probably in River Oaks or Memorial. You were recommended as a fabulous realtor who's very knowledgeable about the high-end housing market. Unfortunately, I don't have a lot of time. I'm flying back to St. Louis tomorrow afternoon. My cell phone isn't working so I'll call you back in an hour."

"Do you recognize that voice?" Sam asked.

"I don't think so. You were asking me if I remembered someone in our class named Juliet. Is this the same person?"

"Yes."

"This woman could have been in my high school class, but I don't think she was someone I knew well. I'm sorry."

Sam tried to hide his disappointment. Megan Edwards, after all, had spoken to the woman several times and she apparently hadn't recognized the voice. Or if she had, she hadn't mentioned it to her husband or coworkers.

The odd thing was that Sam could have sworn he'd heard that breathy, alto voice before. But, for the life of him, he couldn't remember where or when he'd heard it.

Thirty-Nine

"Any more questions?" Kate glanced from Sam to his daughter, the two Wolfes sitting next to each other in her office.

"I'm a little worried about the pain," the girl admitted. "I've never had surgery before. Is it going to be excruciating?"

Kate smiled at her. "You won't feel anything at all during the surgery; the anesthesia will take care of that. But afterward, when you wake up, it will be uncomfortable. Not excruciating, though; we'll give you medication for the pain."

"What am I going to look like a few days after the operation?"

"Your face will be swollen, and you'll have bruises around your eyes. I'll pack the inside of your nose with gauze to stop the bleeding, and that packing stays in for several days. There will be a cast on your nose for around twelve days. That's to protect it during the early healing and to keep the bones of the nose together."

Sam looked as if he was trying not to wince. "How long before she's completely healed?"

Kate glanced at him. Why was the man continually looking at her feet?

She swiveled back to the daughter as she answered the father's question. "You'll look much better—presentable—a few weeks after the surgery. But the swelling won't disappear entirely until another six to twelve months."

Carly moaned. "That's a long time. And going to school with

a cast on my face—I mean, talk about broadcasting that I've had a nose job."

Kate nodded sympathetically. "It really might be a better idea for you to postpone the surgery until the summer. That way by the time you go back to school the cast, the bruising, and most of the swelling will be gone. You'll feel a lot less conspicuous."

She could see the indecision in the teenager's eyes. "I would sort of like to wait. But I want you to do the surgery, and you won't be here next summer. Or will you?"

Two sets of brown eyes studied Kate. But there was something about the elder Wolfe's curiosity, the way he was watching her, that was making her acutely uncomfortable.

"I'm not sure yet where I'll be. It's possible I'll still be here." To Kate's astonishment, Aaron Glass had suggested yesterday that she take a permanent position with their group; Kate told him she needed to think about it. "And if I'm not, I promise to help you find an excellent cosmetic surgeon before I leave."

Carly looked uncertain. "So you might be here in the summer?"

"Yes, and if I am, I'll be happy to do your rhinoplasty."

"So if you're going to be here for a while you'll be able to go to your high school reunion," Sam said.

And where had *that* non sequitur come from? "Actually, I'm quite sure that no matter where I'm living, I won't be attending my reunion." She glared at him. "And why are you constantly staring at my feet?"

"I was wondering what size shoes you wore."

"What size *shoes?* Why do you want to know that?"

"Tell me your shoe size first."

Kate didn't answer, wishing she could throw him out of her office.

"Oh, come on," Carly said, glancing at Kate's feet. "They look like a size five, triple A."

"Double A," Kate said. "Five, double A."

"Thank you," Sam said, though Kate was not sure which one of them he was thanking.

"So now tell her, Dad, why you want to know her shoe size."

He sent his daughter an irritated look. "A woman's bloody footprint was found in the parking garage where Megan Edwards was murdered," he told Kate.

She could feel her fists clench at her side. "And you thought it was *my* footprint?" Sam opened his mouth, but she wouldn't let him interrupt her. "You ask the receptionist what my shoe size is, you sit in our parking garage spying on me because you think *I* killed Megan Edwards?"

"I know now that you didn't kill her," Sam said in what he probably assumed was a soothing voice.

"Only because I apparently have the wrong-sized feet!"

"They are the wrong size," Sam said. "Too small."

"This is how you conduct a murder investigation—check on shoe sizes?" Kate asked. "It sounds like the search for who fit into Cinderella's glass slipper."

"It's only *one* thing I'm checking on. It's a piece of new evidence."

Carly leaned toward her father and whispered, loud enough for Kate to hear. "Tell her about the other new evidence. Maybe she can help you figure out who the real killer is."

Was Carly part of this duplicitous scheme to pry information out of her? Kate stood. "You can let me know later when you want to have the rhinoplasty." *Now, both of you, leave my office.*

Neither of the Wolfes seemed to take the hint. "Tell her," Carly told her father.

He shrugged and turned to Kate. "The other new evidence was a phone message Megan Edwards received from a woman who might be her killer. She said she was from out of town and wanted to set up an appointment that day for Megan to show her homes. She said her name was Juliet Montague."

Kate stared at him. "Juliet Montague?"

He nodded. "Do you know her?"

"No, it's just that Juliet Montague would be the married name of Juliet in *Romeo and Juliet.* Remember? Juliet Capulet secretly marries Romeo Montague. It's very strange to hear of a real person with that name. The last time I heard anyone mention the Montagues and the Capulets was in our high school play."

She could see the excitement on Sam's face as he leaned toward her. "Do you remember who was in your high school production?"

Kate thought about it. "A guy named Jonathan Trilby was Romeo. Allison James was Juliet."

"Allison was Juliet? Was this the play where Lisa Smythe spread rumors about another student who was up for the same part?"

"That's right," Kate said. "There was a new girl in school, Maria somebody, who was a wonderful actress, and she, not Allison, was originally cast as Juliet. But after it started going around the school that Maria was gay and had only gotten the part because she was sleeping with the drama teacher, Maria quit and Allison took over the part."

"*That* really sucks," Carly said.

Her father ignored her. "Did you know that girl, Maria Vorgan?" he asked Kate.

"No, I never met her. I didn't get involved in the play until later; I was on the stage crew. I heard from some kids who saw the tryouts, though, that she was an incredible actress—unlike Allison who was pathetic in the role. It was pretty obvious that Allison had invented the rumors about Maria and the drama teacher because she was jealous that Maria beat her for the role."

Sam studied her. "Do you think most students thought the rumors were lies?"

"Well nobody really knew Maria. She'd just transferred to the school and, from what I heard, she was kind of standoffish or shy." Kate hesitated. "But it didn't make much difference whether or not kids thought the rumors were true. This was more about teenagers' malicious glee in watching someone else be humiliated.

"After all," she said, hearing the bitter edge to her voice, "people knew me and they knew Todd, and they still laughed at me for being stupid enough to believe that Mr. Popular actually wanted to go out with me—for any reason other than a dare. No one seemed especially concerned that he'd tricked me, gotten me drunk and had sex with me—basically he date-raped me. I thought at the time, how can these people be so cruel? I'd never done anything to them. And what I finally decided was their reaction really had more to do with relief that it hadn't happened to them. If jeering at the designated scapegoat was the price they had to pay for not being picked on, then, by God, they'd jeer."

"But unlike Maria, you stayed in school and took the abuse," Sam said softly.

"I wish Maria had stayed and gone ahead with the play. I would love to have seen a real actress in the part. And it would have been great if for once The Six's intimidation didn't work." She stared at him. "But what does all this have to do with Megan's murder?"

"I'm not sure yet, but I intend to find out."

FORTY

Lisa Smythe was obviously surprised to hear from Sam. "Why, Officer Wolfe, do you actually have something to report to me?"

Sam glanced around the hotel where Lisa had moved after her husband kicked her out of the mini-mansion. "There's some new evidence that I wanted to discuss with you," he said coolly. "I'm in the lobby right now. Do you want to come here or should I come to your room?"

There was a pause. "Give me five minutes and then come up to my suite."

"Fine."

When she opened the door six minutes later, Sam walked into an opulent suite with floor-to-ceiling windows offering an impressive view of downtown Houston's skyscrapers. Had Lisa picked the most expensive place she could find because the geezer was footing the bill? Or maybe she'd chosen a hotel rather than an apartment because she was hoping that she and Smythe would reconcile.

She motioned for Sam to sit in one of two matching mauve upholstered chairs while she sat across from him on the mauve and turquoise sofa. "What did you want to tell me so early in the morning?"

Ten-fifteen was early in the morning? Sam wondered if she'd been asleep when he called. Her face seemed devoid of much of its usual makeup. Without it, the dark circles under her eyes looked like bruises against the pallor of her skin. Even her clothes—black slacks and a gray sweater—looked wrinkled, as if she'd worn them before.

"I wanted to ask you if the name Juliet Montague means anything to you," Sam said.

"It sounds like *Romeo and Juliet.* If you're asking if I know a real person by that name, I don't. What does this have to do with anything?"

"That's the name a woman who may have killed Megan Edwards was using."

Lisa's eyes widened. "How do you know that?"

"She left a message on Ms. Edwards's answering machine arranging a meeting." Before she could ask more questions, Sam added, "Can you think of anyone from your high school class who might choose to call herself that?"

"I guess it could have been someone who was in our school's production of the play." She swallowed. "My friend Allison played Juliet."

"Do you think Megan Edwards also would have associated that name with Allison or the school play?"

Lisa shook her head. "I doubt it. Megan was never into drama. She went to all the athletic stuff, but I don't think she ever attended a school play." She paused. "Did this Juliet woman mention anything that would connect her to our high school? You know it *is* possible that there is a real woman named Juliet Montague. Maybe her parents had a strange sense of humor."

"No, she didn't mention your high school." He expected her to continue her questions, but instead she was silent, looking like a woman fighting a wave of nausea.

Finally, she took a deep breath and said, "There was a girl who tried out for the part of Juliet in the school play. Maria seemed as if she actually was Juliet, very young and passionate—and poetic. She didn't sound awkward or stagy saying all those Shakespeare lines."

"Sounds perfect for the role."

Lisa looked away, her face flushed. "Allison wanted the part too; she said she needed to show that her acting had more depth. She kept thinking that some director might come to our play and discover her."

Sam met her eyes. "And your job was to get Allison whatever she wanted? What was it that Allison's sister called you—The Enforcer?"

Lisa's face, pink before, darkened to crimson. "Allison was just as involved in this as I was. It was her idea to say Maria got the part because she was sleeping with the drama teacher. It really bugged her that Miss Harrison was spending so much time with Maria. I think she figured that this was a way to get even with both of them."

"So she was hoping Maria would drop out of school?"

"All she wanted was her to quit the play." She glanced up at Sam. "But the whole thing kind of backfired on her."

"In what way? Maria quit and Allison got the part."

"Yeah, but Miss Harrison refused to cast Allison in any other play after that. She blamed Allison for Maria's breakdown. Maria came to the first performance of the play, then went home and slashed her wrists. Her mother found her in the bathtub and called an ambulance. From what I heard, Maria ended up in a mental hospital."

Lisa actually looked guilty. It was about time, Sam thought. "Do you know what happened to Maria after she got out of the mental hospital?"

She shook her head.

Sam stood. "Thanks for the information."

"No, wait! You can't go yet!" Lisa said, looking alarmed. "It sounds like Maria is the person who e-mailed me and my husband. Think about it: I spread false rumors about her having an affair with a woman and she did the same thing to me—

saying Allison and I were lovers. My lies got her to drop out of the play, and hers—hers cost me my marriage." She scowled. "My husband didn't care if I'd been mean in high school, but the minute he heard I might be gay—which is totally untrue—he wanted me out of his life."

It sounded to Sam like eminent justice. And Maria Vorgan made more sense as a poison-pen writer than Kate Dalton. "We're trying to locate her."

"You don't know where she is?"

"Not yet."

The woman leapt off the couch and grabbed his arm. "Don't you see? Maria's had her fun with me, showed me what it feels like to have people you trust believe lies about you. But now she's going to carry out her threats: she's going to murder me!"

Forty-One

"Hold on a minute, Kate!"

Oh, lovely. In the hallway outside her office, Kate wished she could pretend she hadn't heard him. But knowing Josh Edwards, he'd probably just come running after her. She turned to face him.

He was with Annette, his arm draped around her shoulders, as the two of them moved toward her. Apparently they were now more than just friends. "Did you know someone in high school named Maria Vorgan?" Josh asked.

"Nope. Never met her." Then, not wanting to admit that she knew why he was asking, Kate added, "Why? Did you know her?"

Josh shook his head. "Never heard of her. Officer Wolfe was asking me about her. Thought you might know something."

He didn't say why Wolfe was interested, Kate noticed, and she didn't intend to ask. She was keeping contact with Josh to a minimum, being polite but slightly distant whenever they were forced to talk. She wanted to make clear to him that they'd never be anything more than colleagues.

Apparently Josh was fine with that, cordial but slightly distant to her too.

"This Officer Wolfe, did he show you the woman's picture?" Annette asked him. "Maybe Kate would recognize her if she saw the photo."

"He doesn't have a photo. This girl was only in our class for a couple months before she dropped out of school. Apparently the only person who even remembers laying eyes on her is Lisa Smythe." He turned to Kate, his smile malicious. "Your old buddy."

So maybe he wasn't as friendly as Kate wanted to believe. "I was just on my way out," she told both of them. "Good night."

Annette, at least, smiled back. "Good night, Kate. Nice seeing you."

An unfamiliar car was parked in front of the house when Kate pulled into the driveway. Who did her mother know who drove a Mercedes convertible?

As she unlocked the kitchen door, she heard the female voices in the living room. *Oh, no, it couldn't be . . .*

She hurried to the front of the house. Unfortunately, it could. Lisa Smythe sat on a corner of the couch chatting with her mother and Betty Sue.

Three sets of eyes turned her way when Kate walked in, all of them showing varying degrees of relief.

"Look who's here, dear," her mother said with forced gaiety. "Lisa says the two of you were in high school together."

"We were," Kate said. *And she made my senior year a living hell.* She turned to her old nemesis. "What brings you here?"

"I needed to talk to you," Lisa said, "and I thought it might be easier here than at your office."

Kate frowned. "There's always the phone."

"Jane—uh, Kate!" her mother said. "There's no need to be rude."

Oh, but there was. Turning her back slightly so her mom wouldn't see her expression, Kate sent her former classmate a frigid look. "What did you want to tell me?" *What compelled you to come, uninvited, to my home and disturb my critically ill mother?*

Lisa stood. "Perhaps we could talk somewhere else so we

don't bother your mom."

She sounded, Kate realized, quite unlike the shrill, arrogant woman who'd confronted her in her office. Lisa seemed more tentative today, almost vulnerable. Devoid of makeup and with dark circles under her eyes, she looked less like a pampered trophy wife than a depressed middle-aged woman.

"We can go into the kitchen," Kate said. *Where I'll give you five minutes to tell me what you want before I kick you out the door.* "Will you be okay, Mom?"

"I'll be just fine," her mother said with a be-nice look.

In the kitchen, the two of them sat at the butcher-block table. "So what prompted this visit?" Kate asked.

Lisa swallowed. "I finally realized how much . . . harm I've done to other people. I wanted to apologize to you."

"Why?"

Lisa looked confused. "Why am I apologizing?" When Kate nodded, she said, "Because it seemed the right thing to do and because, I guess, I've been pretty miserable myself lately since my husband and I separated. It made me realize how it feels to be attacked for no reason and to have people you trusted believe malicious lies about you."

Why couldn't Kate believe that? After all, suffering sometimes transformed self-involved, mean-spirited people into more caring, empathetic ones. Perhaps she was allowing her personal dislike for this woman to color her judgment, but she didn't think so. Her instinct told her that Lisa was an unrepentant bitch who wanted something from her.

"Okay," Kate said coolly. "I appreciate your apology, even though it's fifteen years late. Thanks for stopping by." She stood.

"Uh, there were a few other things I wanted to discuss too," Lisa said quickly.

Kate remained standing. "What things?"

"I want to find out what you know about Maria Vorgan from

high school."

It was the second time in the last hour that she'd been asked that question. She gave Lisa the same answer she'd given Josh. "I never met her."

"I'm convinced she was the one who sent me and my husband those horrible e-mails from Your Ex–High School Classmate."

"A couple weeks ago you were sure *I* was the one sending them to you."

Lisa's pale skin displayed sudden red blotches. "Well, I was wrong. I admit it."

"Maybe you're wrong about her too. Perhaps Maria isn't involved with any of this."

Lisa shook her head. "No, it has to be Maria. It makes perfect sense. She's doing to me exactly what I did to her: discrediting me with untrue lesbian rumors."

When Kate didn't respond, Lisa said, "But I keep asking myself, Why wait fifteen years to do this? Why now? And the only answer I could come up with is it has to be connected somehow to our high school reunion. Maybe Maria read about us in that 'What Your Old Classmates Are Doing' piece the reunion committee sent out, and that triggered something. Maybe it infuriated her that Allison, Todd, Josh, Megan, Matt, and I were more successful than she was, and she didn't think we deserved to be happy. Or maybe she blames us for whatever went wrong in her own life."

"That's a lot of maybes."

Lisa scowled. "I realize that. The other thing I've been wondering is how could Maria have so much personal information about us? How could she possibly know where Megan worked or the hotel where Todd was staying? I had Libby Norman check the mailing list for our reunion and Maria isn't on it. So how did she learn so much?"

Kate shrugged. "Good question."

"And the only explanations I came up with are either she's on the mailing list under another name, she's getting information from someone who is on the reunion list, or she's friends with somebody who knows the six of us quite well." At the end of her little speech, Lisa narrowed her eyes, as if she were monitoring Kate's reaction.

So that was it! "And you decided *I* might be the person who's feeding Maria this information?" Kate gave a bitter laugh. "You think there's a support group we both belong to for Former Victims of The Six? Or maybe you thought the two of us met at a meeting of Outcasts Anonymous?"

"Very funny." Lisa glared, suddenly looking like her old self. She pushed up from the table. "I should have expected this. You don't want to help me, do you? I came over here to apologize and to ask for your help, but you just don't care what happens to me."

Kate considered the matter. "No, I really don't."

The lethal glare Lisa shot at her as she pushed back her chair made Kate wonder how she'd ever imagined that this woman was vulnerable. Lisa was about as defenseless as a feral cat.

Fortunately, her mother was no longer in the living room when Lisa stalked to the front door. Kate's hand was trembling as she bolted the deadbolt—one more thing she was glad her mother hadn't seen.

Forty-Two

It seemed as if Maria Vorgan, one-time high school actress and possible murderer, had fallen off the face of the earth. Sam massaged the bridge of his nose as he talked on the phone to Maria's father.

Ted Vorgan didn't have a clue where his daughter was. He hadn't, he said, seen Maria for at least ten years.

"So when was the last time you spoke to her?" Sam asked. He tried to imagine what it would be like to not see Carly for that long and couldn't conceive of it.

"She called to tell me her mother had died. That was last year, around Christmas. I think she was in New York then, but I could be wrong. We didn't talk much. My ex-wife died of cirrhosis of the liver, and Maria seemed to blame me for that—as if my leaving the woman turned her into a crazy lush. I told her I'd divorced her mother because she was a boozer and a nutcase and I couldn't take it anymore, and Maria hung up on me. So much for a little compassion for her old man."

Unlike all the compassion her old man had shown for his teenage daughter when he'd left her in the custody of a "crazy lush."

Her father had no idea what might have motivated Maria to return to Houston. Didn't seem to care a lot either, Sam thought. Hearing Vorgan's slightly slurred words, he suspected that Maria's father might also have some substance abuse problems. Could the daughter have inherited her parents' addictions? Was her murder spree fueled by drugs or alcohol as well as rage?

His head ached as he hung up the phone, thinking of all the vital questions he had no answer to: Where was Maria Vorgan at this moment? How had she learned all the logistical information about her victims? And who did she plan to kill next? Because all his instincts told him she planned to murder another classmate. And soon.

His phone rang. "Wolfe," he answered, still scanning his list of questions.

"Officer Wolfe," an unfamiliar female voice said, "this is Daphne Harrison. I've been out of town for the last month. I understand you've been trying to reach me."

It took him a moment to place the name; she was the former high school drama teacher of both Allison James and Maria Vorgan. Trying to tamp down his growing excitement, Sam said, "I was calling to ask about a former student, Maria Vorgan—do you remember her?"

"Of course. But why do you want to know about her?"

"I'm trying to locate her, but nobody, including her father, seems to know where she is. He apparently hasn't laid eyes on her in the last ten years."

There was silence on the line. Was she too going to tell him that she'd lost touch with Maria, that she couldn't be expected to remember a student who she'd taught over fifteen years ago? Sam didn't realize he'd been holding his breath until the teacher spoke again.

"I'm not sure where Maria is living now, but I occasionally get an e-mail or phone call from her. She tried acting in New York for a while. Got some parts in a few off-Broadway plays and commercials, but finally gave up. She phoned me and we talked about it. She's very talented, but it's a hard life, full of constant rejection, and emotionally she wasn't equipped for that." She laughed, a humorless bark. "Not that many people are."

"Do you know what she did after she gave up acting?"

"Went back to finish college. Said this time she was going to prepare herself for a practical career, maybe something with computers. I e-mailed her a few months ago, but my message was returned. She changed e-mail accounts a lot. I always had to wait until she decided to contact me."

"You don't happen to remember what her last e-mail address was, do you?"

The teacher laughed, this time sounding genuinely amused. "She kept changing screen names. Last time she was Chameleon and before that Drama Queen—both of which she was, by the way."

"A drama queen?" Sam's associations with the term were not positive, but maybe a drama teacher felt differently. "Was she very emotional?"

"Oh, yes. Maria felt everything very strongly, which was one of the reasons she was such a good actress."

"I know about Maria's high school suicide attempt," he said. "Did you get the idea she was more emotionally stable when she got older?"

"Stable?" The woman snorted. "That is *not* a word I'd use to describe Maria. She was diagnosed with paranoid schizophrenia when she was hospitalized. I think she was fairly stable when she stayed on her medications. And to most people, she probably wouldn't seem disturbed. Maria is very bright and articulate. Plus, as I mentioned, she's an excellent actress."

"Did you notice this paranoia when she was in high school?"

"When Maria was in high school, someone, in fact, *was* plotting against her. Two mean-spirited girls who were envious of her talent spread rumors that Maria had only gotten the part in a school play because she was sleeping with me—and no, I am *not* gay and neither is Maria. But she was new to the school, already under a lot of pressure trying to take care of her needy, alcoholic mother; she just couldn't handle the harassment."

Sam closed his eyes. Now was not the time to feel sorry for Maria Vorgan, he reminded himself.

"Did you know that schizophrenia usually doesn't show up until a person is in their late teens or early twenties?" the teacher said. "Often, until the mental illness suddenly shows up, the kid seems okay, maybe high-strung or odd, but not crazy. I always thought that if Maria's life at that point hadn't been so stressful—if her parents hadn't divorced, her mother hadn't been so dependent, and she hadn't moved here and been picked on for no reason at all—maybe she would never have become schizophrenic. Perhaps mental illness doesn't work that way, but Maria had too much thrown at her all at once."

"It certainly sounds that way," he said.

Ms. Harrison sighed. "Just tell me this, detective. Is this attempt to find Maria at all connected to the death of Allison James?"

Sam took a deep breath. "It is. But why would you think that?"

"The last times I talked to her, maybe a year ago, Maria phoned me in the middle of the night. She was obviously off her meds, and she was just raging—this stream-of-conscious ranting I'd never heard from her before. She claimed her time here in high school was what pushed her over the edge, started her life on a downward cycle. Said it was like she'd been clinging to the edge of a cliff, barely holding on, when someone came along and stomped on her hand."

"Did she say who she thought did the stomping?"

"Oh, yes. I thought it was only Allison and Lisa who'd started the rumors about her, but Maria seemed to think that more of that clique was involved. The Six Sadists, she called them. The Junior Marquis de Sade Society."

Forty-Three

Kate heard the arguing the minute she opened her office door. Josh, obviously—his deep voice was distinctive and, when irritated, quite loud—and what sounded like Annette. The woman's voice was softer, but she too was clearly annoyed.

Which was pretty much par for this couple's course. Annette had apparently decided she and Josh were ready to take their previously quiet affair public—a decision Josh didn't seem too happy about. Had Annette convinced herself that Josh would marry her? Because Kate tended to believe what Josh had told her: from now on, he intended to have lots of girlfriends but no more wives. And if their recent arguments were any indication, it didn't look like Annette would even be one of those girlfriends.

Kate was tempted to stay holed up in her office until the two of them finished their battle or moved it to another location. But she didn't have the luxury to wait around for them; she had to get home to her mother.

Taking a deep breath, she hurried down the hall, trying to act as if she hadn't heard Annette just shout, "I know why you don't want to take me to your precious reunion. You're ashamed of me!"

Josh replied, "I don't want to go at all, Annette—with or without you. Apparently it hadn't occurred to you that my wife's murder might make me feel disinclined to socialize."

The door to his office was open, Annette leaning against the doorframe, Josh standing next to his desk. Annette, her face red with fury, glanced at Kate, then turned back to Josh. "That *isn't* the way you felt before."

Josh's face contorted in disgust. "It's the way I feel now."

Kate kept walking. As—at last!—she opened the door leading to the waiting room, she heard Annette ask, "Has anyone mentioned lately what a pathetic excuse for a man you are?"

Fortunately, Kate did not hear the answer.

Mandy looked up from the reception desk. "Are those two going at it again?" She rolled her eyes. "I think he fights as much with her as he did with his wife—which is saying *a lot.* My sister worked here a few years back and boy, would she tell the stories about Josh and Megan going at it whenever Megan decided to visit him at work."

Luckily, Kate hadn't had to be around Megan and Josh much. But she remembered vividly a coworker warning her to steer clear of Josh's pathologically jealous wife. "Did Megan use to stop by a lot? I don't think I ever saw her here."

"No, thank God. Josh apparently told her she couldn't drop in like that. He was too busy seeing patients."

And Megan accepted that? "I thought someone told me that Megan was always checking up on Josh, that she'd even gotten a woman fired for flirting with him."

Mandy snorted. "Can you imagine! Ruining another woman's career because her husband has a wandering eye. And I bet no one even reprimanded Dr. Josh for *his* flirting."

Kate sighed. "I bet you're right." In fact, she doubted if Golden Boy Josh had ever experienced many negative repercussions for any of his bad behavior.

Mandy stood up. "I'm just leaving. I'll walk out with you."

As they headed out the door, the gatherer-of-office-information asked her, "How's your mother doing?"

"About the same. She's weak and tired, but she's hanging in there."

The receptionist nodded. "And how are things going with you and your police detective?"

Kate glared at her. "He's not *my* police detective. And things between us are not going at all."

"Okay, there's no reason to get testy."

Easy for you to say. "So how's *your* love life?" Kate inquired. "You ask a lot of questions, Mandy, but you're not very forthcoming about giving out personal information yourself."

"That's because nobody is interested," Mandy said, looking unperturbed.

"I am."

The receptionist, to Kate's surprise, blushed. "Not much to tell, really. I broke up with my boyfriend six months ago. He said I wasn't fun anymore; I was spending too much time studying."

"What are you studying?"

"I'm taking a physiology class at night so I can apply to nursing school." She glanced at Kate, looking suddenly shy. "Eventually I'd like to be a surgical nurse."

"That's great. I didn't realize . . ." But she should have shown enough interest to learn that Mandy, a woman she talked to several times a day, wanted to go to nursing school. "How do you like the class?"

"Kind of dull, actually. I was hoping we'd be doing a lot more dissecting."

They entered the parking garage. "My car's parked on the next floor," the receptionist said. "See you tomorrow."

Without a backward glance, she hurried to the stairwell, barely giving Kate time to call after her, " 'Night, Mandy."

Kate phoned home from the car. "Anything you want me to pick up, Mom?" *Something that might tempt you to eat?*

"No, thanks, dear." Her mother sounded more energetic than

she usually did at this time of day. "Officer Wolfe has brought me some tortilla soup. Wasn't that nice?"

Oh, yeah, he's a regular Good Samaritan. "Is Officer Wolfe at the house right now?"

"Yes." Her mother, at least, sounded happy about it.

Damn. Kate briefly considered spending the next hour window shopping. Let Wolfe cool his manipulative heels waiting for her. If he was still there when she finally got home, she could say, "Oh, but I thought you'd come over to visit with my mother. Did I misunderstand?"

Except she couldn't do it. Her mother and Betty Sue, who wouldn't leave until Kate arrived, were counting on her. So she'd have to face Officer Wolfe, whether she wanted to or not.

The soup was simmering in a big pot on the stove when Kate walked in the back door. Apparently the detective had brought enough to feed them for a week.

"Oh, good, you're here." Her mother smiled at Kate from her usual seat on the living room couch. "Now we can eat. I was just telling Sam how much I love tortilla soup."

Sam, is it now? It irritated her that her mother seemed so pleased with his gesture. *Just don't ask what he wants in return, Mom.* Whatever it was—more information about Kate's former classmates? a confession to the murders? a date?—Kate was sure she didn't want to give it to him.

Her mother insisted that Betty Sue and the detective join them for dinner. Kate was gratified to see her mother eat a bit more than usual. She seemed quite animated, asking Wolfe questions about his daughter and her newfound love of fencing. Betty Sue whispered to Kate that today had been one of her mother's good days, "and she sure perked up when that detective called."

As soon as they'd finished eating, though, her mother said she was going to her bedroom to rest and Betty Sue went home.

Kate was alone with Sam.

He sent her an amused glance. "You didn't look very happy to see me, Dr. Dalton. You had a *what-does-he-want-NOW?* expression on your face."

"I *was* wondering that."

"I brought the soup over because I like your mother, and she'd mentioned it was her favorite. But I also came to ask you something."

And why doesn't that surprise me?

The detective seemed oblivious to her silent hostility. "The woman I told you about, Maria Vorgan, is possibly our murderer. The problem is finding her. She's obviously both intelligent and wily. From everything I've learned about her, she's probably using another name, established an entirely new identity."

"Why do you think that she's reinvented herself?"

"Because after her mother died, when Maria was nineteen, all records of her seemed to stop: no more college transcripts, no more tax returns, nothing. Her drama teacher, Ms. Harrison, said Maria told her that she'd graduated from college and had been in some off-Broadway plays, but we can't find any proof of that. It's as if Maria Vorgan ceased to exist."

Kate arched one eyebrow. "And you're thinking because I changed my name, I'd have some special insight into her?"

He shook his head. "I want you to help me catch her."

She stared at him. "How?"

"I think she's planning to kill again, maybe finish off the remaining members of the high school clique: Lisa Smythe, Josh Edwards, and Matt Phillips. Keep in mind that Maria is a gifted actress—and also, unfortunately, mentally ill. I keep thinking how theatrical it would be to kill her old enemies in front of an audience of classmates at your high school reunion."

Theatrical? She guessed that was one way of putting it. But

why was he telling her this? What did he want?

Sam leaned toward her. "I intend to be at the reunion, Kate. I'd like to be there as your date."

Forty-Four

"But I'm not going to the reunion," Kate said.

No surprise there, Sam thought. He needed to somehow convince her to change her mind. "Don't you think it's time to stop hiding from your past?"

"Hiding? I'm not hiding. I'm moving on with my life."

"By letting your classmates think you're still living in Illinois? By not telling them that you've changed your name from Jane Murphy to Kate Dalton?"

She glared at him. "You make it sound as if I'm using an alias. I told you my married name is Dalton and my middle name is Katherine—it's not a pseudonym I invented."

Did she really believe that? Or was she just trying to get him to back off? Because it was one thing to forge your own life and quite another to pretend your past never existed.

When he raised his eyebrows, she added, "Look, I don't want to see my old classmates. I don't want to hear what they've been doing since graduation, chuckle over stories from the good old days. Because those days were a nightmare for me—and I'm grateful that I've awakened from it."

"You don't want to show everyone how successful and attractive you are now?"

She sent him a contemptuous look. "Why? So I can win the achievement competition? Libby told me how at our ten-year reunion our valedictorian—another classic, lonely brainiac—made a point of rubbing our classmates' noses in his success.

He made sure everyone knew he was a partner in a big Manhattan law firm and had a blonde and beautiful girlfriend. He wanted them to envy him."

"And did they?"

"Apparently a lot did, according to Libby. Of course she thought his bragging was kind of pathetic, but then she wasn't the type of person he was trying to impress. He was going for revenge on all the kids who'd called him The Nerd and didn't invite him to their parties."

"I take it you don't think you'd find it satisfying to see your classmates green with envy?"

"It would be much more satisfying not to see my classmates at all. The only one I wanted to see, Libby, I've seen already."

Sam wondered if she was also thinking about the former classmates she'd rather not have seen—Lisa and Josh. She probably hadn't found those encounters particularly satisfying, though she'd apparently managed to stand up for herself. A less self-critical person might have given herself credit for now being able to hold her own with people who'd intimidated her in high school, but Kate hadn't seemed to take much pleasure from the experience.

So how could he convince her to face an even bigger group of those classmates? "If you really want to move on with your life, as you say," he said, "you'll go to the reunion and show everyone who you've become. Not to impress them, but to connect who you were as a teenager to who you are now, to integrate Jane and Dr. Kate."

Her eyes flashed. "You've missed your calling, detective. You should have become a psychotherapist."

He smiled. "And right now you're thinking I'm only using this psychological bullshit to manipulate you into accompanying me to my stakeout."

She widened her eyes, mocking him. "And you're intuitive too!"

Okay, so she didn't believe him. Never mind that he was telling her what anyone with a modicum of insight could see: Smart, driven, secretive Dr. Kate Dalton needed to come to grips with her painful past. And if at the same time she also assisted him with a criminal investigation, well, so much the better.

"If you won't go for your own benefit," he said, "then go for other people's: help us save some lives by capturing this killer."

She stared at him. "What makes you think that I'd be any help? I wouldn't recognize this woman if she walked right up to me. I told you she wasn't someone I knew."

"No one else knows for sure what she looks like either. The description I've got is very vague: medium height, slender, brownish curly hair. That could describe dozens of women at the reunion."

"If you don't know who you're looking for, why don't you just tell Lisa, Josh, and Matt not to come to an event where someone might try to kill them? That they'll be a lot safer by just staying home."

"If Josh, Lisa, and Matt are her targets, she'll just go after them somewhere else," he said. "Think of where she cornered her victims before: a hotel room, a church bathroom, a parking garage. At least at the reunion, they'll have some police protection."

"I still don't see what I can do."

"You can provide another pair of eyes and ears. No one will be suspicious of what you're doing there. And being your date will provide me with an excuse for attending."

She still did not look convinced. He added, "Who knows? Maybe other people in your class might be at risk too. At one time Maria was diagnosed as a paranoid schizophrenic, which could mean she isn't necessarily rational about deciding who's persecuting her. She apparently blamed all six of the clique for what happened to her, but, from what I could tell, only Lisa and Allison were involved in it."

Kate narrowed her eyes. "It isn't as simple as that. Maybe Lisa and Allison were the ones who instigated the false rumors about Maria, but I can see why she also blamed the rest of the group. It's like what happened to me. Some people might say that only Lisa and Todd were responsible: Lisa devised the trick and enlisted Todd to carry it out. But does that mean that the other four were innocent? I don't think so. They didn't stop Lisa and Todd from telling everyone, Hey, guess what, Plain Jane finally got laid. In fact they probably helped to spread the news."

"By those standards, anyone who laughed at you would be guilty."

"No, I'm saying anyone who could have stopped Lisa and Todd but didn't was complicit in the bullying. The other four were the only ones who Lisa and Todd might have listened to. From what I've heard, none of them ever tried to stop the others' malicious pranks. Maybe they were too afraid the rest of the group would turn on them or they wouldn't be popular anymore."

Sam nodded. "Maybe that's why Maria holds all of them culpable. Though she seemed especially angry with Lisa. She's the only one of the group who was threatened beforehand, the only one whose family was contacted."

Kate smiled grimly. "Spreading rumors was Lisa's specialty. I guess Maria wanted Lisa to taste some of her own medicine: You spread lies saying I'm gay and I'll do the same to you. A fitting revenge, I'd say. It's unfortunate that she couldn't stop with just sending the e-mails."

"Profilers often say that once a serial killer murders the first victim, it becomes increasingly difficult to stop killing."

Kate stared at him. Finally, she said, "Okay, I'll go with you to the damned reunion."

He smiled. "And I accept your gracious invitation."

Forty-Five

The minute she saw the cutesy name badges—high school graduation photos pasted above names—Kate knew that coming here was a big mistake. What an idiot she'd been, letting Sam talk her into assisting him with his undercover investigation. He'd probably be *more* conspicuous just because he was with her—the number one oddity of the reunion.

Almost every person she encountered stared at her—first her face, then her graduation photo and name, then back to her face. "All the girls' last names change," one guy she didn't remember said. "But you're the first one who's changed both her names."

Kate gave her standard answer: Kate was her middle name, Dalton her married name. The man still looked puzzled.

"Are you *sure* you're Jane Murphy?" the man's already-drunk companion asked her. "Because Jane was in my chemistry class and she was a dog. You don't look anything like her."

This guy Kate *did* remember. "Well, at least *I* changed for the better," she said and walked away.

She spotted Sam talking to Josh and Annette, who must have just arrived. Kate hurried to join them. At least they wouldn't tell her how different she looked.

Josh was putting on his name badge and scowling. "So Wolfe made you come tonight too?" he said to Kate.

"Yeah, I had to twist both of your arms to get you to the party," Sam said before she could answer.

"Well, *I'm* happy to be here," Annette announced.

"Nice somebody is," Josh muttered. He peered at Kate's name badge photo. "At least you can say you've improved with age. All I can claim is losing a lot of hair in the last fifteen years."

Kate glanced at his graduation photo. Fifteen years ago he had had a lot more hair. "But you didn't have that wonderful aura of sophistication you have now," she said with a grin.

Josh rolled his eyes. He turned to Sam. "What does this Maria woman who we're watching for look like?"

"Unfortunately, we don't have any photos. All we know is that she's about five-five or five-six, Caucasian, fairly slender, light brown hair. I also gather that she's somewhat of a chameleon who can change her appearance and demeanor easily."

"Well, that sure narrows it down," Josh said sarcastically. "I guess I should walk the other way every time a five-foot-six white female comes toward me tonight."

Annette smiled. "Sounds good to me."

Josh ignored her. "So what's the game plan?" he asked Sam. "Considering that no one knows who we're looking for, I think I'd be better advised to turn around and go home."

Sam's mouth thinned into a taut line.

He wants to tell Josh to stop whining and think of someone besides himself, Kate thought. *Probably he wants to say the same thing to me.* She straightened her shoulders. "So what do you want us to do?" she asked Sam. "Besides circulate and be on the lookout for anything unusual."

"If you notice anything suspicious or if even your conversation with someone just feels wrong, walk away. Phone me on your cell or come get one of us." He nodded toward two plainclothes officers now standing near the sign-in table. "And for God's sake, don't wander down any deserted hallways or go out for a private talk with a classmate. Stay with the crowd."

Josh looked as if he was about to protest, but Annette patted his arm. "Come on, Joshie, let's go mingle. You can tell everyone what a big-shot surgeon you are."

Josh frowned. Then, looking martyred, he followed her into the crowd congregating around the sign-in table.

Kate turned to Sam. "Okay, I guess it's time that I mingle too." It came out sounding more fearful—less stoically resolved—than she'd intended.

"Wait," he said as she turned to leave. "I'm coming with you. I'm your date, remember? You have to introduce me to your classmates."

Kate hated to admit it, but she felt a little less miserable when Sam took her arm.

"Kate!" somebody called. She turned. "Mandy? What are you—I mean I didn't expect to see you here."

The receptionist grinned. "I'm here with my sister, who was in your class." She glanced over her shoulder, obviously gauging if the red-haired woman behind her could overhear, then whispered, "Meredith is going through a bad divorce and she wanted me to come with her for moral support."

"That's nice of you," Kate said. It was bad enough having to come to your own reunion, much less somebody else's.

Mandy smiled as her sister joined them. "Meredith, this is Dr. Kate Dalton, who I told you about, and Detective Sam Wolfe. Kate and Sam, my sister Meredith Vidal."

Meredith looked like a much-older version of her sister, with dark circles under her eyes and no trace of Mandy's effervescence. "I'm sure you don't remember, but I was in your French class senior year," she told Kate. "You and Libby sat in the front and I was in the back. I was Meredith Green then."

"Oh, of course." Kate vaguely remembered a tall, red-haired girl at the back of the room.

Meredith's eyes narrowed. "It must have been very strange finding yourself working in the same office as J.R. Edwards."

You don't know the half of it, honey. Kate sent the woman a cool smile. "I guess it is a little strange to see people you knew as teenagers, all of us pretending to be grownups now." *How's that for politely evading a question?*

Meredith did not appear inclined to drop the subject. "J.R. doesn't seem to have improved with age, does he?"

Kate shrugged.

"Though you have, Dr. Dalton," she added, growing more animated. "I really admire that. I remember how awful things were for you our senior year, how depressed you looked and how you blimped up after the Todd Lawson thing. But you turned it around. Not like J.R., Megan, and Lisa, who basically stayed the same disgusting, entitled brats. They grew old but never grew up. You know what I mean?"

Kate nodded, hoping she didn't look as mortified as she felt. Was Sam wondering right now why she'd "blimped up" after her "date" with Todd? They'd better find this killer damn soon because Kate was absolutely convinced she was not going to make it to the end of this reunion.

Mandy looked embarrassed. "Isn't that your friend Helen?" she asked her sister.

Meredith turned. "No, but that's J.R. Edwards over there with that blonde woman. Let's go say hi, Mandy. And look, isn't that Lisa Smythe who just came in with that young hunk? I thought you told me that she was married to some old geezer."

Yes, go, Kate thought. Please.

"And I see someone who wants to talk to you, Kate," Sam said. "Nice meeting you, Meredith."

Kate glanced at her watch as she followed him toward a cluster of people in the corner. Only half an hour at the reunion and she'd already been called a (former) dog, an imposter, and been reminded how depressed and fat she'd been after Todd raped her. *How much better could the evening get? And here was her least-favorite patient, Lisa Smythe, probably eagerly waiting to pile on some additional abuse.*

"Who's the guy with Lisa?" she asked Sam.

"Her paid bodyguard. She said she didn't feel safe with only our police protection, so she hired someone to only look out for her. Though unlike you and Josh, she didn't have to be persuaded to come to the reunion."

Of course not. How could Lisa miss this event when she'd gone to so much trouble to impress her classmates with the reduced size of her butt? Kate studied Lisa in her tight black dress. Yes, Lisa's backside was definitely smaller, her body trim, her face unwrinkled. And yet, despite skillful makeup and the Botox injections, Lisa's face looked hard and sleep-deprived. Kate scolded herself for her decidedly petty and mean-spirited surge of satisfaction. But she couldn't help thinking that Lisa's face accurately reflected who she was: a bitter, self-absorbed, and perpetually dissatisfied woman.

Sam stopped next to a tall man who still had the body of an athlete. The man glanced at Sam, then at Kate's name badge. "Just the woman I wanted to see," he said with a grin. "Though I don't think I would have recognized you without your name tag."

Now this was one old classmate she'd recognize anywhere.

"Kate, you remember Matt Phillips, don't you?" Sam said.

"Of course." She offered him her hand, smiled politely, feeling as if she were watching herself perform in a play.

Matt seemed to sense her coolness. He turned to a trim woman with short auburn hair, a mass of freckles, and no visible makeup. "This is my wife, Lauren. Lauren, Dr. Kate Dalton."

Lauren offered Kate the guileless smile of a nursery school

teacher. "I am so pleased to meet you, Dr. Dalton. Matt can't seem to stop talking about you."

Really? Kate would have liked to pursue that topic, but decided against it. "Nice to meet you too, Lauren, and please call me Kate. Do you two live around here?"

Lauren's hazel eyes twinkled. "And here I thought you'd say, 'What exactly could that butthead have to say about me? He hasn't laid eyes on me in fifteen years—thank goodness.' "

Kate laughed. This woman, with her no-nonsense haircut, sensible cotton sundress, and her lack of social airs, was the antithesis of Lisa Smythe, Matt's high school girlfriend. She reminded Kate of a friendly puppy who hadn't yet been taught not to jump on the guests.

Matt shook his head. "We're working on her shyness," he told Kate. "Trying to coax her out of her shell."

Kate looked at Lauren. "Okay, so tell me, what *does* the butthead have to say about me?"

Matt's wife turned to him. "Can you manage this? Or do you want me to tell her?"

"I think I can handle it." Matt looked at Kate, his expression solemn. "Our oldest child, Julie, started middle school this year. And it's been hell for her. She's a sweet kid, smart, kind of a tomboy. She's never mean to anyone."

"But she's young for her age," his wife added. "Not ready to be a teenager yet. And because of that the other girls pick on her. At least once a week she comes home from school crying."

"I'm sorry," Kate said.

Matt nodded. "What I'm trying to say is seeing this happen to my kid made me realize how terrible you must have felt." He scanned the room as if searching for words. "Sure, I always knew what Todd and Lisa did to you was terrible, but I didn't know anything about their stunt until it was over, and I told myself it was too late for me to do anything—so I didn't. I figured it was like a football injury—it hurts, you recover and go on. But now, seeing my own kid being picked on, I just wanted you to know that I'm really, really sorry."

Kate smiled at him, this time a true smile. "Thank you," she said. "I accept your apology."

A look of relief crossed Matt's face. His wife, her eyes wet, patted his arm.

From somewhere behind her, Kate heard Josh say, "Isn't that the drama teacher, Miss Harrison? Wasn't that her name?"

She turned to see who Josh was talking about, but stopped instead at the expressions on Mandy and Annette's faces. They were staring in shock at a regal, white-haired woman in a flowing violet pants suit.

Forty-Six

She could see the instant when Josh figured it out: saw the moment of recognition, the emotions—disbelief, revulsion, anger, fear—flit across his face. Eyes narrowed, he looked again from her to the drama teacher who'd just entered the room. She must have let down her guard, allowed her shock to show on her face—or maybe he'd been suspecting her for a while. Josh, despite his numerous faults, was not stupid.

Then he did what surgeons always do: he took control. He apparently reassured himself that he, Josh Edwards, M.D., could handle this. *Bad decision, Josh.*

"I need to talk to you," he said.

"Sure. Just let me get another glass of wine first." She peered at his almost-empty plastic cup. "You look like you could use a refill too. What are you drinking?"

"Scotch on the rocks."

She smiled her flirtatious grin, noticing the pathetically weak smile he managed in return. *Might have benefited from some acting classes, Josh. Though I guess it's too late for that now.* "I'll be right back."

She left him talking to a group of old classmates. An overly tanned woman was carrying on about how shocked she was to hear about the tragedy of Megan's death.

When she returned, a good ten minutes later, with their drinks, the bitch was still going on about Megan, the poor motherless Edwards children, what was this violent world coming to, blah, blah, blah. Josh, his eyes flinty, practically yanked the drink from her hand and took a huge gulp.

"Nice seeing you again," he told the group and, taking her elbow, pulled her away.

"Let's go someplace more private to talk," he said, looking over her head, scanning the group for somebody.

Looking for Detective Sam? she wanted to ask him. *You know, the guy who's not supposed to look like a cop because he's wearing a suit and accompanying Dr. Kate to her reunion.*

Dr. Kate could benefit from some acting lessons too—to help her pretend she was having a good time tonight seeing all these people from her painful past. And at least *she* would be around to take advantage of the newly acquired acting skills.

Well, probably she would. It was hard to be mad at Dr. Kate when she too had been bullied by The Six. And while not exactly the warmest person on the planet, the woman was not an elitist snob or a mean-spirited, narcissistic bitch, like some other people in their class. It was even possible that Kate didn't realize that Sam Wolfe was using her as a cover.

Though perhaps Dr. Kate had chosen to align herself with the other side. Maybe with her new, pretty face and her medical degree, Kate Dalton now saw herself as one of the golden few. What was that called when victims suddenly identified with their persecutors—Stockholm syndrome?

But someone else was demanding her attention at the moment. "Who you looking for?" she asked Josh.

He shrugged. "Oh, I was wondering how Sam Wolfe is doing."

She tried to look surprised. "I thought you said he was rude and incompetent and a general pain in the ass." *You know, Josh, one of that whole category of people—idiots—who don't have M.D. after their names.*

He scowled. "I don't want him to become my new best friend.

I just need to ask him something."

"I think I heard him say he was going to be talking to people in the library. I can't imagine why he couldn't talk out here like everyone else, but maybe he needed more privacy."

"Yeah, it's awfully noisy out here." He steered her toward the hallway. "Come on, I'll give you a tour of the school."

"Okay." As she recalled, the library wasn't too far away. But far enough.

"God, I must have drunk more than I thought," Josh said as they reached the second floor.

She peered at him. "You're not looking too good. Maybe you should sit down."

"The library's just down there." He pointed. "Though it doesn't look like the lights are on. You sure that's where Wolfe said he was going?"

"That's what I *thought* he said. Maybe he got waylaid on the way here." She paused. "Or do you want to go back downstairs to look for him?"

Josh swayed, putting a hand on the wall to support himself. "Need to sit down. Now."

She hurried to the door he'd pointed to, went inside to turn on the light. "Let me help you," she told Josh, pulling out a chair for him as he staggered inside.

Oh, how she would have enjoyed truly discussing the whole situation with him. How satisfying it would be to tell Josh exactly how helpful he'd been to her: providing her with invaluable information on his friends—Todd's attendance at the sales conference and the hotel where he was staying, the time and location of Todd's funeral, Megan's work habits and schedule, the location where Lisa was having her liposuction (her one botched job—though at least she could claim credit for the breakup of the bitch's marriage). And she so wanted to tell him, "I couldn't have done it without you, Joshie. Good thing you're such a die-hard gossip."

She'd love to rub his face in the irony of it all: *And you thought you were using me, Josh? Think again, bozo.*

But Dr. Edwards was in no condition to hear any of it now. He slumped forward in his chair, as if barely able to stay on the seat. Glancing around the empty library, he said, "Detective?"

Did he expect Sam Wolfe to leap out from behind the library stacks, charge in to rescue Josh Edwards, the way Josh had always been rescued throughout his short, charmed life?

Well tonight the cavalry was not on the way. And Josh Edwards's string of good luck was about to run out. Walking behind his chair, she pulled the gloves and plastic coverall from her tote bag.

Josh was out cold by the time she took out the scalpel. Probably just as well, she told herself. Men were always so disappointing when they tried to discuss their feelings.

"Bye, Josh," she said as she slashed his throat. "It's been fun."

Forty-Seven

"I don't know," the former drama teacher said, shaking her head, her elegant white pageboy swinging. "I'm afraid my memory isn't what it used to be."

Sam tried to ignore his surge of disappointment. Had he really expected Ms. Harrison to survey the room, then point a finger exclaiming, "There she is! There's Maria!" Such things occasionally did happen, he guessed, but never on his watch.

"Maybe you just haven't seen her yet," he suggested. Or maybe Maria wasn't here at all. Maybe the killer was smart enough to realize they'd be expecting her to show up tonight. She clearly didn't like being predictable.

"Maybe," the teacher said, not sounding convinced.

From the corner of his eye Sam saw Kate walk up to the makeshift bar set up near the front of the gym. Despite the smile she'd pasted on her face, he suspected she was not having a good time. Although Kate had been cordial to everyone she encountered and had seemed to genuinely appreciate Matt Phillips's apology, there was something about her posture that reminded him of someone bracing for a root canal.

He motioned for Kate to join them. When she did, he started to introduce the drama teacher.

"Oh, I know Miss Harrison," Kate said with a warm smile. "You probably don't remember me—I was Jane Murphy then. I worked on the stage crew in lots of school plays."

Miss Harrison smiled uncertainly. "I'm sorry, but my memory

seems to have slipped quite a bit during the last several years. But it's nice to see you again, uh, Jane. What have you been doing since you graduated?"

Just how bad *was* her memory? Sam wondered as Kate gave a modest account of her post–high school life. Of course it was also possible that Kate, one of many stage hands, had had less contact with the teacher than Maria, a conspicuously talented actress.

At least Miss Harrison was sharp enough to ask Kate intelligent questions about her work, and when another teacher stopped to talk to her, Miss Harrison seemed to recognize him. Before moving on to another group, she assured Sam that she'd "keep my eyes open."

He scanned the room, seeing Officer Bill Morris near the sign-in desk looking in Matt Phillips's direction. Lisa Smythe's bodyguard was standing right next to her, scanning the crowd, while Lisa talked animatedly to several couples. The other detective, Mark Hernandez, was stationed near the entrance, looking bored. Sam wondered if anyone suspected he was a police officer rather than a standoffish guest or neglected spouse.

So where was Josh Edwards? The last time Sam looked, Edwards had been in the middle of a largish group that included his office receptionist Mandy and her sister and his girlfriend Annette. But right now the only one of that group Sam saw was Mandy's loud-mouthed sister who, predictably enough, was getting herself another drink.

Then he saw Annette hurrying toward him. "Have you seen Josh?" she asked, her voice high-pitched and frightened. "When I came back from the restroom, he was gone, and no one seems to know where he is."

"Oh, he's probably around here somewhere," Sam said, motioning to Hernandez.

Officer Hernandez didn't know where Edwards was either.

"I'll go check the men's room."

Annette sighed, visibly worried. "Someone I asked said they seen him go off with a cute redhead with curly hair—I assume that's Mandy."

Was she worried about Edwards's safety or the fact that he was alone with a cute redhead? Sam wondered if Hernandez might be looking for a man who'd rather not be found at the moment, a man who, at the first opportunity, had whisked Mandy to some private corner. Considering Edwards's previous behavior, it wouldn't surprise him if the surgeon would endanger his life just for a little illicit sex. Now that Josh no longer had a wife to cheat on, he probably had to ratchet up the danger element of his erotic life in some new way. Or maybe he just got off on cheating.

Hernandez was walking toward them—from his expression, not bringing back good news. "Edwards is not in the men's room or in the hallway. I'll go look—"

A woman's scream stopped him, a bone-chilling sound that seemed to be coming from the stairwell.

Sam's eyes met Hernandez's. He had a very bad feeling that Josh Edwards had just been located.

Forty-Eight

Kate watched the blood drain from Annette's already pale face. She turned in time to see the grim look that passed between Sam and the dark-haired officer before the man headed out the door.

Another officer, a pock-marked young man with curly brown hair, hurried over. "Keep everybody in this room, Morris," Sam told him. "Don't let anybody leave." He scanned the room until he located Matt Phillips and Lisa Smythe, standing in separate groups on the opposite side of the room. "And for God's sake, stay close to both of them."

Stay close? Kate's stomach lurched. Surely Sam didn't think that someone had attacked Josh. Not here, surrounded by people, surrounded by police officers! Maybe somebody had had an accident. Or perhaps two former classmates, fueled by alcohol, had started to fight.

She glanced toward the open door, trying to glimpse what was going on. Mandy talked to the young policeman for a minute, then, looking worried, walked over to Kate. "Have you seen my sister?"

"I saw her a few minutes ago, getting a drink." Kate glanced at several groups clustered near the makeshift bar. Meredith didn't seem to be among them.

Mandy frowned. "I wonder where she could have gone. A girl in the hallway just told me someone was hurt in the library. She and some guy went up to the library to, uh, be alone, and they found a man lying on the floor."

"What man?" Annette demanded.

"I don't know. Somebody from the reunion, she said. Maybe he fell. She said there was blood."

Annette's eyes narrowed as she scrutinized the receptionist's face. "Where's Josh?"

Mandy shrugged. "How would I know?"

"Weren't you with him?"

"No!" Mandy blinked. "Why would I be with Josh?"

"When I got back from the ladies' room, both of you were gone," Annette said. "I assumed—"

"I was with one of my sister's friends. She pulled me out into the hall to tell me I needed to take Meredith home before we have to carry her out." She shook her head. "As if I can convince Meredith to do anything when she's drinking. She didn't use to be this way. It's the divorce."

Annette grabbed Mandy's arm. "Where is this woman you were talking to, the one who found the man in the library?"

Mandy scanned the room, then nodded toward a visibly shaken woman talking to a balding man. "The blonde in the blue dress."

Annette headed toward her.

Surely Annette was overreacting, Kate told herself. The man in the library couldn't be Josh. Sam had warned him not to wander off where the police couldn't keep an eye on him.

But he might have slipped out with a willing woman. That, clearly, was what Annette suspected. And it was in character for Josh, whose favorite risk-taking behavior seemed to be illicit sex. Could he possibly have gone off with Mandy's sister? Both of them seemed to be missing in action, and Mandy had said that her sister had had a crush on Josh in high school. Was the man so amoral that he'd take advantage of a drunken, emotionally fragile woman, while his own date searched for him?

From the worried look on Annette's face, she didn't seem to be getting much information from the distraught blonde.

"Mandy, isn't that Meredith over there?" Kate pointed to two women who were moving slowly toward them. The other woman had her arm around Meredith, who was visibly staggering.

Mandy hurried toward her sister.

They stopped near enough for Kate to hear the conversation. "I want to go home," Meredith was saying. "I feel sick."

"She wanted to go into the girls' locker room to take a nap," the other woman told Mandy. "I thought it might do her good to get away for a little while, but then she started throwing up."

Mandy draped one arm around Meredith's shoulder. "Come on, sweetie. Let's go home." Her eyes met Kate's, answering her unspoken question. "We're just going to have to convince the cop to let us leave."

"Cop?" Meredith said. "What cop?"

Annette marched over, looking furious. "That asshole policeman won't let me leave the room. Even though the woman who saw the guy in the library said he was dark-haired and wearing a navy blazer, just like Josh."

Or any of two dozen other dark-haired men who'd come to the reunion in navy blazers, Kate thought.

Annette's face was growing alarmingly red. "I told the schmuck that it might be my boyfriend in the library, but he says he has his orders. God forbid that any officer ever thinks for himself!"

"I don't care what he says. We have to leave," Mandy said. "Unless he wants Meredith puking on the floor."

The officer in question chose this moment to make his announcement. Speaking into a microphone, his deep voice blared, "Ladies and gentleman, can I have your attention?" He waited for the noise level to decline before continuing. "I'm sorry to interrupt your party. Unfortunately, a violent crime has occurred on the premises, and no one will be allowed to leave this room without police permission. We'll want to question everybody."

Mandy's mouth set in a tight line. "We'll see about that. Come on, Meredith, let's go get the officer's *permission.*"

Annette looked dazed. "Violent crime? What crime?"

She stared at the young officer, her expression changing from shock to anger. "I'm not going to just stand here, waiting." Looking determined, she followed Mandy and Meredith.

The noise in the room was so loud that at first Kate wasn't sure that she'd heard correctly. But when she turned around, Miss Harrison was standing directly behind her.

The drama teacher was staring at the backs of the three women striding toward the policeman. "Maria!" she said. "I think that's Maria Vorgan!"

Forty-Nine

"Maria!" the drama teacher called.

All three of the women who she might have been summoning kept walking. Kate wasn't surprised. If one of them, in fact, was a serial killer, she wasn't likely to be easily tricked into revealing herself.

Probably Miss Harrison was only imagining that she recognized Maria Vorgan. The teacher admitted her memory wasn't good, and she clearly hadn't remembered Kate.

"Are you sure it's Maria?" Kate asked.

Miss Harrison nodded. "I wasn't certain until a few minutes ago. She looks so different. But Maria always overplayed the big dramatic scenes. She still does."

Kate stared at the three women. Mandy seemed to be arguing with the police officer by the door, gesturing repeatedly at her sister. Behind them, Annette appeared to be waiting her turn to talk to him. Then she seemed to change her mind, turning suddenly and darting toward the back of the room.

Kate followed the teacher's gaze. "We've got to stop her!" Miss Harrison said.

Where was Sam? "Go get that officer," Kate said, "and I'll go after her." *And just hope that if she is Maria, she doesn't have her scalpel.*

Kate moved past clusters of people. "Annette!" she called, trying not to sound alarmed. Hoping to sound normal.

Annette stopped and glanced back at her, her expression

curious. She did not look like a crazed killer; she looked like a rather ordinary, almost-middle-aged woman who was worried about her boyfriend.

What if Miss Harrison was wrong about her? What if she was, in fact, only Annette Williams, an office manager from Boston, whose only serious psychological flaw was her questionable taste in men. Maybe she only resembled Maria Vorgan—or the way Maria looked fifteen years ago, when the teacher had last seen her.

Kate was abreast of Annette now. "I, uh, wanted to know if you learned anything about Josh," she improvised. "If he was the guy who was hurt in the library."

"I didn't get a chance to talk to the officer." She started to move away.

"So where are you going?"

Annette's eyes narrowed. "I'm not feeling well. I'm sort of woozy. I was thinking maybe Meredith had the right idea about going to the girls' locker room to take a nap."

Or to look for another route out of the building. A door from the locker room led outside to the track and playing fields. Granted, it was a circuitous route, but it had the major advantage of containing no police officers to block the exit.

"If you're not feeling well, maybe I should come with you," Kate said.

"That's sweet of you, but not necessary. I won't faint." Annette bit her quivering bottom lip as she looked at her feet. "And I'd really like to be alone for a while."

No, she wasn't a subtle actress. Miss Harrison had been right about that. Kate wondered, idiotically, if, even in their private lives, professional actresses always seemed to be playing a part. Were they all congenitally hammy?

Annette started walking. To the locker room to take her nap.

Kate followed. "Did Josh figure out it was you, Annette?"

The woman reeled around. For a split second her mask dropped. The once-friendly brown eyes now looked hard as flint, her lips clamped together. An intensity that minutes before hadn't been there seemed to sharpen her features.

For the first time Kate was frightened. *What the hell am I doing? Trying to get myself added to her list of classmate-victims?* She'd been wrong about this woman's acting talents. Annette was a very fine actress. She'd managed to hide from everyone the monster inside her.

Then, so quickly that Kate wasn't sure if she'd only imagined the change, the old Annette was back. "Did Josh figure out what?" she asked, looking only curious.

Kate glanced back, searching for Sam or the pock-marked policeman. For *somebody.* Hadn't Miss Harrison told the officer that the situation was urgent?

Only an idiot, she reminded herself, would try to stop a violent psychopath by herself. A rational person would protect herself and let the police—professionals trained to deal with dangerous criminals—handle the situation.

Except the killer would get away, free to murder more people, if Kate didn't do *something.*

Annette was reaching for the door that led to the locker room.

Stall. Don't let her leave. Keep her talking. "Did Josh figure out that you think he's having an affair with Mandy?" Kate asked.

Annette turned. She blinked, obviously trying to decide if Kate was tricking her or if she really was still buying Annette's worried-girlfriend act. She smiled ruefully, though her eyes still looked wary. "Oh, Josh knows I'm aware of his tendency to flirt with any attractive woman who crosses his path."

Then Annette shifted to her concerned look. "At this point I'm just hoping that's all that happened to him: he followed some babe to the library and, when he got a little too frisky, she slugged him. But right now I need to lie down for a while."

Annette opened the door and hurried in.

Following this woman into a deserted locker room was too much like strolling, unarmed, into a lion-filled Coliseum. Kate glanced behind her. Ms. Harrison was waving her arms as she talked to the pock-marked officer, pointing to the back of the room. Why didn't he *do* something?

Kate took a deep breath and opened the door. "Annette?"

She'd taken her first tentative step into the hallway when somebody grabbed her from behind. "I'm very disappointed in you, Jane," a familiar voice said.

FIFTY

Kate had walked right into it. Clever Dr. Dalton was tracking a vicious serial killer when—surprise!—the homicidal maniac caught her instead.

From behind her, Annette yanked Kate's arm behind her back. "I tried to tell you this was a mistake, Jane, but you wouldn't listen. So you get your wish: you're coming with me." The woman's breath felt hot on Kate's ear, but her words, thick with menace, made Kate shiver.

"Move!" The hand on her throbbing arm pushed her forward. "If you try anything funny, I'll break your arm."

Kate stumbled forward. She could hear the crazy, manic edge in the woman's voice, could even smell her fear, a rancid, sweaty odor beneath her spicy perfume.

Which of them, Kate wondered, was crazier? Granted, she didn't murder people she disliked. But, on the other hand, how deluded was it, how grandiose, to think that she could outwit a woman who'd eluded the police for months? What had she been thinking—that this was a test of their comparative IQs? That her medical training had somehow equipped her to disarm a dangerous psychotic? Too bad she hadn't done a rotation at a hospital for the criminally insane. That at least might have proved helpful.

They moved together like some wounded, four-legged creature, their breath sounding loud in her ears, their steps halting. Kate could feel Annette glance back to check if someone was coming after them.

No one was following them! Had anyone even noticed them leave the gym?

They were at the door to the girls' locker room now. "Open it!" Annette barked, pushing Kate's right arm higher.

Kate moaned, but she managed to open the door with her left hand. Annette shoved her inside.

The room looked the way it had fifteen years ago—rows of lockers with wooden benches in between, curtained showers in the back. "Sit on that bench and keep your mouth shut!" Annette ordered.

Kate did as she was told, gingerly moving the arm that had been pinned behind her back. Annette sat on the bench across from her, breathing rapidly while she scanned the place.

"Anybody here?" Annette called out in a friendly voice.

To Kate's dismay, only silence followed the question. "I don't understand why you're doing this, Annette," she said quietly, sounding to her ears more scared than curious.

The brown eyes that studied her were too bright, not quite matching the sneer of her face. "Cut the bullshit, Jane. I *know* that you know."

Kate swallowed. "So you *are* Maria Vorgan?"

"I *was* Maria. Before they derailed my life, before they turned everything to shit."

Kate fought a wave of nausea, taking a deep breath. "What—what are you going to do with me?"

Annette smiled. "It depends a lot on how cooperative you are. If you are very good, maybe I'll keep you as my hostage."

And then, when Kate was no longer of any use to her, Annette would kill her.

"Detective Sam wouldn't want me to slash his pretty little girlfriend's throat."

So she'd managed to bungle this so badly that she was even

assisting this monster in getting away, Kate thought. If the police didn't have to be concerned about her welfare, they might be able to force their way into the locker room, shooting Annette if she resisted. But with Kate as Annette's human shield, they couldn't even risk that.

Stupid, stupid, stupid! Kate remembered overhearing two nurses talking in the hospital once about the disproportionate number of physician/pilots who died in plane crashes. "They're so damned arrogant they believe that doctor-as-god hype and think they can do anything—until they crash." Laughing, one nurse had spotted Kate. "You, Kate, of course are the exception."

Apparently not. Today her arrogant assumption that she could handle anything was very likely going to get her killed.

Annette was studying her, looking puzzled. "You know I thought you, of all people, would understand, Jane," she said, as if they were two friends chatting. "After all, you were a victim of those adolescent sadists too."

She frowned at Kate. "But maybe they didn't wound you the way they did me. Or maybe you wanted so much to be just like them that you never even acknowledged what they did to you. What do they call that identifying with your persecutors, Stockholm syndrome? Maybe you just dismissed their humiliating you as a harmless teenage prank."

Kate stared at her, feeling sudden heat surge through her body. "I didn't *suffer?* You know *nothing* about it! You have no idea all the damage they did to me."

She could see the surprise on Annette's face, the renewed wariness. She was yelling at a woman who any fool would know not to provoke, but Kate didn't care. Rage seemed to have taken over her brain.

"Let me tell you, Maria, about that 'harmless teenage prank.' Yes, they also spread vicious rumors about me. Apparently I'd smiled at Lisa's boyfriend when he smiled at me, and that was unforgivable. But, in addition to telling everyone in the school I was so pathetic that I actually believed Todd Lawson wanted to go out with me, Lisa convinced Todd to get me drunk and have sex with me. Essentially it was date rape. Perhaps if I'd fought him, really screamed my head off rather than just telling him no, he might have stopped. After all, he could have lied, telling everyone that Plain Jane Got Laid, and I still would have been humiliated every time I walked into a classroom. But I wouldn't have gotten pregnant."

"Pregnant?" Annette frowned. "You had an abortion?"

"No, I wanted to keep the baby. I gave birth the summer after I graduated, but my baby died." Kate swallowed, commanding herself not to think about that beautiful infant, but to focus on this woman who believed that she'd cornered the market on suffering. "Her lungs were underdeveloped. If we'd been at a more sophisticated hospital with a good neonatal unit, instead of a primitive rural hospital, she might have survived, been a teenager now. And when I started hemorrhaging after the birth, I might not have had a hysterectomy the day after my eighteenth birthday." Kate glared at the crazy, violent, self-pitying woman sitting across from her on the wood bench. "So don't tell *me* those people had no impact on my life!"

After all these years, Kate realized, she'd never told anyone about her baby. Of course her parents and the hospital staff involved in the birth knew, but she'd never confided the whole story to anyone. Sam was aware of the rape, but only her mother and this mad woman, who probably couldn't care less, knew about her daughter.

For a moment Annette looked uncertain how to respond. "You should be happy they're dead," she finally said. "They *deserved* to die. Todd was still as disgusting as he was in high school; he would have forced himself on me if I hadn't killed him." Her momentary uncertainty was replaced by narrow-eyed, focused rage.

"And as for Lisa," she said, her voice hard, "I botched my first attempt, but I'm not giving up on that bitch. Some of the others of The Six were just self-centered opportunists, but Lisa was different; she *enjoyed* inflicting pain. So don't worry, Kate. I promise you, Lisa will get hers."

Did she want Lisa to die, Kate wondered. She certainly had not been sad when she'd heard that Todd Lawson had been killed, but had she been pleased? Right now though was not the time to think about her reaction. "What about Josh?" she asked instead. "What did he ever do to you? I thought you even liked him."

Annette's incredulous look was almost laughable. "*Liked* him? I was only using him, the same way he was using me. Josh was invaluable as a source of information about his friends—the convention his buddy Todd was attending in Houston, the time and place of Todd's funeral, where Megan worked and where she parked her car, the hospital where Lisa was getting her lipo. It's a very good thing that Josh was such a Chatty Kathy, because I didn't see too many other redeeming traits in him. He wasn't even good in the sack, despite all his practice."

Annette glanced to the back of the room, to the door that led outside to the track. "Get up! We're getting out of here."

Kate stood. Had that been a noise in the hallway? "Fine," she said a little more loudly than was necessary. "You're right about one thing, by the way. The deaths of Todd, Allison, Megan, and Josh were no great loss to the world."

Annette's eyes narrowed, as if she was trying to decide whether to believe Kate. She nodded. "I couldn't let them get away with their crimes. Someone had to stop them from victimizing others."

"I can see that," Kate said.

For a moment Annette looked as if she desperately wanted to trust Kate. Her expression changed as they both heard the undeniable sound of footsteps in the hallway. “Move!” she screamed, grabbing for Kate’s arm.

But this time Kate was prepared. She pushed Annette as hard as she could into a locker. Then she turned and ran.

She was almost at the door to the hall when Annette tackled her. Kate tried to shove her off, but the woman was too strong.

Something sharp and metallic jabbed into Kate’s throat.

“Come any further, detective,” Annette yelled, “and your Doctor Kate is dead.”

Fifty-One

Outside the door to the girls' locker room, Sam's fists clenched. The woman on the other side of the door—a probable psychotic killer—sounded on the edge of hysteria.

"We're not coming inside," he called. "Not unless you invite us, Annette."

"Smart move, detective. Particularly if you were hoping for a goodnight kiss tonight from your date." She laughed, a manic, out-of-control sound that made Sam want to break down the door *NOW!*

What if this mad woman had already hurt Kate? What if right now Kate was lying on the floor, unconscious or bleeding? Or worse.

"What proof do I have that she's not already dead?"

Silence was the only answer to his question. Standing next to Sam, Officer Bill Morris raised his eyebrows, seeking orders.

Then a familiar voice called out. "I'm all right, Sam. Annette hasn't hurt me. She doesn't hurt innocent people."

Sam closed his eyes for a second. He glanced away from Morris, blinking rapidly, trying to focus. Was Kate really safe from Annette or was she just trying to reason with a murderer? Were the "innocent people" former classmates who hadn't been bullies? Or were they fellow victims, other targets of The Six's abuse? He wondered if Annette even knew about Kate's high school misery. Had Kate told her?

"What do you want, Annette?" he called. *What do we have to do so you don't slit Kate's throat?*

"To get out of here. I'm going out the back door. Your girlfriend is coming with me. If you try to stop me, she dies. If you let me go, then I'll let *her go.* Now doesn't that sound fair, detective?" She laughed gaily.

Sam felt a sudden clamminess in his palms. He tried to recall everything the police psychologist had told him. Paranoid schizophrenics felt they were being victimized or plotted against. They had auditory hallucinations and delusions of persecution or personal grandeur. The first signs of the disease usually showed up between the ages of fifteen and thirty-four. Maria, in fact, had had her first breakdown at seventeen—after Lisa and Allison had humiliated her and Allison assumed Maria's role in *Romeo and Juliet.*

What else had the psychologist said? Paranoid schizophrenics could be intellectually responsive, alert, and even quite friendly, but if pushed, they were much more likely than other types of schizophrenics to respond with aggression.

Sam had to make sure not to push this woman. He wouldn't antagonize her, giving her one more enemy to destroy. But, most importantly, he couldn't let her leave the school with Kate.

He shook his head at Morris, mouthing one word: wait.

"Sounds fair, Annette. But why not leave Kate behind? She didn't do anything to you. In fact, she was victimized in high school, just like you were. The same people who hurt you hurt her too."

"I know all that. I know about Todd raping her, the whole school hearing about their date, her pregnancy, and the dead baby. I've heard it."

Pregnancy? Dead baby? Was Kate making this up to establish rapport with Annette? Or was it true?

If Kate had intended to forge a bond with Annette, it didn't seem to be working. If anything, Annette sounded annoyed.

Probably she didn't want to acknowledge that anyone had suffered more than she had. She had to be the Queen of Pain, come to avenge the teenage cruelty that had sent her into madness.

"Come out here into the hallway, Annette, and I'll make sure you're not harmed," he said, trying to make his voice sound gentle, caring. "I promise you I'll see that you get help. You're ill; you aren't responsible for what you did."

"Help?" She laughed that shrill, unamused bark. "You mean therapy? Locked up in a mental institution like an animal in the zoo? Oh, no, I don't think so. Been there, done that, detective. Thorazine and those other drugs put me to sleep, and those helpful therapists would have fit in well with the Gestapo."

He could *not* let this woman hurt Kate! "You know Kate is one of the innocent ones," Sam said, feeling desperate. "There's no reason to take her with you. You don't want to be like The Six, preying on the vulnerable."

The shrill laughter sounded again. "Oh, there's a very good reason. Because her innocence is going to be my shield. If that is, she *is* innocent. Sometimes wolves hide beneath sheep's clothing."

Her voice was less loud, as if she'd turned away from the door when she said, "Are you really a wolf, Jane? Have you decided it's more fun to have the power, to be the victimizer rather than the victim?"

Sam heard Kate's voice, but couldn't distinguish her words.

"Yes, the blood of the lamb will protect me," Annette called out.

Who was she talking to? Sam wondered if she was hearing voices. Didn't the blood of the lamb come from a slaughtered animal? Was this madwoman planning on turning Kate into a sacrificial offering?

Fifty-Two

Kate could feel a trickle of blood running down her neck, but she didn't dare reach up to touch it. Probably it was only a nick.

"Jane, are you really a wolf?" Annette asked her. "An evil wolf in sheep's clothing?"

Was Kate supposed to answer that? If she shook her head vigorously, she'd push the blade further into her skin.

"Well, Jane?" The pressure of the scalpel on her throat seemed to lessen slightly. "Have you decided it's more fun to have the power, to be the victimizer rather than the victim?"

"No." Kate's voice was barely louder than a whisper. "I don't hurt other people." At least not intentionally, she mentally amended, thinking of her mother. Who would look after her mother if Annette killed her?

The woman was yelling something now about the "blood of the lamb." Had she even heard Kate's response? Did it—did anything Kate had said or possibly could say—make any difference? Was *she* the lamb whose blood was going to be shed?

Annette was calling out to Sam again. "We're leaving now, detective. Don't follow me if you want to see your girlfriend alive. Understand?"

"Let Dr. Dalton go," Sam said. "I won't stop you if you leave her here unharmed. There's no benefit to kidnapping her. If you take her hostage, we'll have to come after you. If you leave her, you can get away."

Surely he was lying. Letting serial killers escape was not what the police did. And while Annette might be psychotic, she surely wasn't gullible enough to believe she could get a free ride out of there.

Unless Sam actually intended to let *this* murderer go in order to save Kate. Would he allow Kate's reckless arrogance to dictate police procedure and undoubtedly destroy his own career?

Annette grabbed her arm with a vice-like grip. "Move!"

At least she'd taken the scalpel from Kate's throat. She still clutched it in her right hand, but moving with Kate pinioned in front of her was obviously too slow and unwieldy for making a quick getaway.

She was pulling Kate to the door that led to the playing fields.

"Officer Wolfe really would get you help, you know," Kate said in her doctor voice: pleasant, caring, authoritative. "There have been a lot of improvements in the last fifteen years in mental health treatment."

Annette glared at her. "Do you know what electric shock treatments are like? I'll tell you. Like frying your brain and then, afterward, you feel like a zombie. They'd call it torture if it wasn't already named therapy."

"There are other treatments now," Kate said. "Better drugs with fewer side effects." She made herself meet the woman's eyes. "It's a lot better than life in prison."

For a moment it looked as if Annette intended to end the discussion right there, destroying the messenger along with the unwelcome message. Instead, she stopped abruptly. Her too-bright, too-intense eyes seemed to bore into Kate.

"This is what will cure me, the *only* thing. Not doctors or therapy or drugs. I have to remove the source of the poison that's killing me."

Kate didn't know what to say. How could she reason with someone who thought the solution to her suffering was eliminating all the people who'd ever hurt her? The only sensible course now was to keep her mouth shut so that Annette didn't decide to add her name to the hit list.

But if she'd been a cautious or sensible person, Kate would be in the gym with the rest of her classmates. "So is your plan working?" she asked Annette. "Has removing the source of the poison made you feel better?"

Annette's eyes narrowed. "They ruined everything in my life, and there were no consequences, no payback. They were powerful and popular so everyone looked the other way and said, 'Oh, that's teenagers for you.' No one held them accountable for what they did; instead, everyone blamed me, my mental instability, my weakness, as if normal people would just shrug off the abuse and pretend nothing happened."

The words seemed to be gushing out of her. Undoubtedly it was good that Annette was confiding in her; at the very least she was giving the police some extra time. But Kate could barely stand to listen. She wished she could clap her hands over her ears or run away; she couldn't ever remember feeling so repelled.

Is the crazy woman hitting too close to home, Kate? the omnipresent critic in her head asked mockingly. *Is this the way you wished you'd reacted to Lisa's and Todd's bullying, instead of burying the pain so deep inside that you and everyone else could pretend it didn't even exist?*

But Annette apparently wasn't finished with her reminiscences. "Until Allison decided she had to have my part in the school play, I was doing okay, hanging in there, getting used to my new school, taking care of my mother, who was coming apart after her divorce, telling Mom over and over again that everything would be fine. And then Allison and Lisa took away the one thing that I enjoyed, that I was actually good at."

Her acting, Kate thought. Allison and Lisa had created their venomous lies because Maria Vorgan *was* a talented actress, and

Allison couldn't bear the competition.

Annette/Maria's voice broke as she added, "They told the whole school I was an untalented dyke who had to sleep with the teacher to get a part. From that point on, my life was shit. Their poison ate away at me."

And now, mixed up with her guilt, fear, and repulsion, Kate was feeling one more unwelcome emotion: pity for this woman, or at least for the vulnerable teenage girl she'd once been. "They were terrible, selfish people, who never thought about anyone except themselves," Kate said. "Believe me, I know that."

Annette nodded eagerly. "But their toxins stayed in my system. Maybe when you had the baby and your surgery, Jane, you got rid of the poison. That's why you could start over, be healthy and independent. But nothing worked for me. The drugs, the shock treatments couldn't neutralize it. Their poison was too strong."

Abruptly Annette started moving again, dragging Kate with her. They were almost at the door. Wasn't Sam going to come after them? Or were the police waiting outside, ready to pounce?

Keep her talking, Kate told herself. Try to distract her. "How did you know where everyone was? I didn't keep track of any of those people after high school."

"You didn't read all those notices for our high school reunion? They were sent to my mother's address and she forwarded them to me. Apparently she thought I'd like to find out what happened to my old buddies."

Actually her *own* mother had sent Kate similar reunion information: the invitations, schedule of activities, news of classmates who would be attending. Except Kate had only glanced at the papers before ripping them up. "Nope. All I wanted to do about high school was forget it."

Annette stopped in front of the door. "I read about The Six's happy, successful lives in the reunion news and I thought, Why should they get away with it? Why should I be the only one suffering for *their* sins? So I applied for a job in the cosmetic surgery practice that Josh bragged about in his classmate news. The first day I came to work there he came on to me. And I knew I could lead him by the cock and he'd take me to the others."

Without warning, she shoved Kate in front of her. The blade was once more at Kate's throat.

"Open the door," Annette ordered. "You're going out first."

Fifty-Three

Kate stepped out the door, Annette's scalpel at her throat.

No police seemed to be waiting outside for them. She could hear Annette's rapid breathing as she too scanned the area.

"We're turning left," Annette said.

Left? The obvious way off the school grounds was to the right: across the playing fields to the street and school parking lot.

They turned. Annette's arm around her neck pinned the two of them together, making Kate feel like part of a four-legged beast lumbering forward.

Were the police out there somewhere, perhaps watching them through the scope of a rifle? If a police sniper shot Annette in the back, would the bullet pass through her body and enter Kate's?

After half a dozen steps and several backward glances, Annette seemed to relax a bit. She lowered the blade from Kate's throat. "We're going to that side entrance," she said. "Hurry up!"

They were returning to the school? It seemed risky, even irrational. Wouldn't Annette want to go to her car to escape the police?

Kate's throat felt strangely exposed, naked, without the hot arm pinioning her and the metal blade no longer pressing into her skin. Annette was pulling her as they practically jogged the last 100 feet to the door.

"What are you doing?" Kate gasped.

Annette's mocking smile resembled a grimace. "Change of plans. We're going back to the festivities."

Why? Kate wanted to ask, but she doubted Annette would tell. She, brainy Dr. Dalton, had been useless—less than useless, a hindrance—in helping to apprehend this killer. Instead, she'd managed to turn herself into a hostage, a pawn in Annette's deadly game.

Fifteen years ago Kate had promised herself that she would never ever again be a passive participant in her own life. When her baby had died, quiet, obedient, scared Jane Murphy had died too. The person she became made her own decisions—and sometimes had to suffer the consequences for the bad ones. But she had never again felt like a victim. Until now.

They were almost at the school door. Kate turned to Annette, taking a deep breath before she spoke. "I thought you only punished people who'd hurt you. You said you were holding them responsible for their cruelty. I thought you were vengeful but just."

"I am." Annette scowled at her.

"But I never hurt you," Kate pointed out.

"And you're not dead either, are you?"

"Yet," Kate said. She wondered if she were making an irreversible mistake. "My mother is very ill, terminally ill. She needs me to take care of her."

She expected Annette to say, "Too bad you didn't think of that earlier." But instead the woman's expression softened. "Ovarian cancer, right? I remember Josh told me that. My mother died a few months ago."

"I—I'm sorry."

"Me too. Her death made me realize it was finally time to tie up loose ends. There doesn't seem a lot of point to going on any longer."

Oh, God. Kate wasn't sure what Annette was planning, but it didn't sound good. Did the police even know where the two of them were?

"Open the door, Jane."

Kate clutched the handle, hoping the entrance was locked. It wasn't.

When they stepped inside, the hallway seemed deserted.

How many more people would this woman kill? The thought tormented Kate, like a hair shirt she couldn't remove. "Why don't you get out of here, Annette? Now, while you still have a chance to get away?" *Go now and leave me here. Let me take care of my mother and live my life.*

Annette chuckled. "Is that what you think I want—to get away?"

"Isn't it?"

"Oh, no. I want—I need—to finish my task. After that . . ." She paused. "After that I have no plans."

Annette's voice seemed friendly now: just two girlfriends chatting. "Of course that isn't how I originally intended to do this," she told Kate as they walked. "Coming to the reunion was probably too risky, cocky even. But I just loved the symbolism, ending the drama in the same place where it started. Such nice symmetry, don't you think? Coming around full circle."

Kate could feel her stomach lurch. She could see the entrance to the gym now, at the end of the hall. "What do you intend to do?"

"You'll see." Annette's eyes were no longer friendly. "If you really want to go home to your mom tonight, you'd better play along. I don't want to kill you, but I will."

One door of the gym was open. Kate frantically scanned the crowd inside, looking for Sam. Everyone from the reunion still seemed to be there—except the one person she wanted to see. Where *was* he?

The pock-marked policeman was near the entrance, surrounded by a lot of people asking angry questions. Surely he'd notice when the person his colleagues were searching for walked into the room.

But the man seemed oblivious to everything except her classmates shouting questions. He probably figured he was posted there to keep people from going out, not bothering with anyone walking in.

Annette pasted a big smile on her face. "Show time!" she whispered, clutching Kate's arm. "Think of Mama!" To reinforce the advice, she gave Kate a glimpse of the scalpel she still held in her right hand.

Fifty-Four

Annette was propelling them toward a small group in the corner of the room. One of the men, his back to them, glanced up as they approached. Matt Phillips saw Kate and smiled at her.

Matt! Certainly Annette had nothing against Matt, the least Six-like of the group? He had disassociated himself from the rest of his clique years ago. But did Annette know that? Did she care?

Remember your mama, Kate reminded herself. But instead all she could think about was this mad woman's scalpel slashing across Matt's throat.

Matt didn't deserve to die! But neither did she. "I don't want to kill you, Jane, but I will," Annette had said.

Annette's grip on her arm was so tight it was cutting off circulation. Her smile, to Kate's eyes, looked positively feral.

Kate met Matt's gaze, trying to telepathically transmit her message: *Danger! Run for your life!*

Apparently one of them wasn't telepathic. Matt was still smiling. "Where did you go, Kate?" he asked. "Sam was looking for you."

She could feel Annette's searing gaze on her, the vise tightening further on her arm. She tried to smile. "Oh, I went to the girls' locker room for a break. By the way, Matt, have you met my colleague, Annette Williams?" *You know, Matt, Annette-the-Psychopath. Surely Sam mentioned her to you the last time you chatted.*

Still smiling, Matt turned to Annette. "Oh, sure, we've already met. You're here with J.R. Edwards, right?"

Annette beamed at him. "That's right. You and Josh were discussing the joys of coaching a kids' soccer team, if I remember correctly."

And now Josh is dead. No more soccer games for Josh. Kate wanted to shriek it into the polite cocktail chatter.

Annette's death grip on her arm loosened. Once again the woman was relaxed, friendly. Acting.

Maybe this was a good sign; for the moment, Annette didn't feel threatened. Surely she wouldn't do anything to Matt out here, where he was surrounded by classmates. Always before Annette had approached her victims when they were alone—in hotel rooms, a church bathroom, a parking garage. When they were in a group, like Josh at this reunion, Annette seemed to lure them to an isolated area.

Certainly Kate could manage—somehow—to stop Matt from walking off with Annette. She might even be able to convince Annette that Matt was not like the other members of The Six, that he didn't deserve to be killed.

Kate turned to Annette. "Matt and Lauren were telling me how distressing it was for them to see their daughter being bullied in middle school."

Annette looked at the couple. "That *is* upsetting, isn't it?"

"Oh, do you have children too?" Lauren asked.

Annette shook her head. "Unfortunately I don't, though I've always felt very attuned to kids."

Lauren sent Annette her nurturing earth-mother look. "Well, there's still time to have them."

"I doubt it," Annette said.

"Speaking of time," a familiar, shrill voice from behind them said, "where the hell is your boyfriend, Kate? Thanks to his incompetence, we're stuck in this damn gym until God knows when. I would have had more fun staying home."

Could things possibly get any worse? Kate turned to see the scowling face of Lisa Smythe, accompanied by her muscular and very bored-looking escort.

"I don't know where Sam is," she told Lisa, noticing that Annette suddenly had the look of a kid with a pile of unopened Christmas presents. Lisa had no idea how much she was about to wish she'd stayed home.

Annette was edging closer to Lisa.

Kate took a deep breath. "What's the matter, Lisa, haven't people noticed your new butt?" Her voice sounded, to her ears, as if she was practically yelling.

Lisa looked as if her quiet, mousy maid had suddenly attacked her with the mop. For a second she stood there, mouth open, while Annette chuckled and both Matt and the stud-muffin bodyguard grinned.

Lisa's eyes narrowed. "Make yourself useful and go get me another drink," she told the bodyguard, who seemed only too happy to leave.

"I guess everyone was too busy noticing *your* astonishing new face to notice my little improvement," she told Kate. "You're the talk of the reunion. The Ugly Duckling gets a nose job. And a chin implant. And loses the love handles. Everyone is saying, 'God, if a plastic surgeon can make Plain Jane look like that, where do *I* sign up?' "

You deserve to die, Lisa. The thought astonished Kate, the feeling rapidly replaced by intense shame. Yes, the woman was vile, but what about the oath Kate had taken: First, do no harm?

"I guess I should start passing out my cards then," she managed to say. "Maybe I can drum up some new business." She had more important things to worry about now than what her former classmates were saying about her.

"Lisa, I know this is probably going to shock you, but quite a few of us have actually grown up in the last fifteen years." The previously laid-back, affable Matt Phillips had been replaced by a steely voiced man glaring at his former high school girlfriend. "Although you seem not to be aware of it, most adults don't give a damn about who someone was in high school. I for one wouldn't want to have anything to do with the insensitive, self-absorbed jock I was then."

Only the redness creeping up Lisa's pale face indicated that she'd heard him. She craned her neck as she scanned the room, probably looking for allies.

But the members of her high school clique who might have helped her were all dead. And her paid protector, Kate saw, was chatting up a buxom redhead while they waited in line at the bar.

Kate caught sight of Miss Harrison, the drama teacher, pushing through the crowd of people around the pock-marked police officer. Could he get over here in time to stop Annette?

Anyone else would have turned on her heel and stalked away. But Lisa had never gone in for compromise or retreat. "You sanctimonious bastard!" she yelled at Matt. "How dare you talk to me that way—after everything I did for you. Do you really think you would have been captain of the football team without a little arm-twisting from your friends?"

Matt shook his head in disgust. "I never asked for your help and I didn't want it."

"Well, you sure didn't turn it down!" Lisa said.

Annette was no longer smiling. In a voice that could have projected to the back of a theater, she said, "You loved being able to twist arms, spread lies, and get other people kicked out of the roles they'd earned by their own merit, didn't you, Lisa? Some people might say it was because you had no talent of your own, but I always thought that you just enjoyed making other people suffer. You got off on that."

Lisa's face got even redder, her hand balled into a fist. "You stupid bitch, you don't know what you're talking about. Is that what your boyfriend Josh told you? Or should I say *former* boyfriend since he seems to have ditched you at the party. As Megan used to say, Josh runs through sluts rather quickly."

"Oh, Lisa, I've known you for years," Annette said. "I'm hurt you don't remember. Let me give you a clue."

Before their eyes, Annette seemed to change into someone much younger, wide-eyed, and passionate. Gazing into the distance, as if searching for someone, she implored, "Oh, Romeo, Romeo, wherefore art thou, Romeo? Deny thy father and refuse thy name. Or if thou wilt not, be but sworn my love, and I'll no longer be a Capulet."

Lisa gasped, her face suddenly ashen. "You! *You're* Maria Vorgan?"

Frantically Kate scanned the room. Where was Sam? Why didn't the police officer Miss Harrison was so urgently talking to do something?

Annette was no longer the romantic Juliet. She glared at Lisa. "I am."

No more time. Kate knew it the second Annette moved toward Lisa. Her right hand—the hand with the scalpel—was raising.

"Stop!" Kate screamed. She launched herself at Annette, knocking both of them to the floor.

For a moment she was on top of the woman. "Traitor!" Annette screamed, shoving her aside.

Kate felt a sudden sharp pain in her side. She watched in horror as Matt rushed toward them. Annette was pushing herself to her feet.

No!" Kate grabbed for her ankles.

But Annette spotted the movement and sidestepped. "Not yet!" She stared at Kate, her face contorted with rage.

From the corner of her eye, Kate saw the kick coming. Then

a sudden, intense pain in her head commandeered all her attention.

Was that a gunshot? Everything went dark.

Fifty-Five

Kate opened her eyes to see Sam was sitting in the chair next to her hospital bed.

"How you feeling?" he asked in a soft voice.

Like hell. The pain medication was obviously wearing off. "A little sore," she lied.

He smiled. "A little?"

"A lot then." Her mother had been in earlier, accompanied by Betty Sue, and Kate had tried hard to minimize her discomfort, for her mother's sake. Betty Sue had told her not to worry about her mom. "She even seems to be getting some of her energy back because she says you'll need her to take care of you."

Kate attempted a smile. "I guess then we'll just have to take care of each other."

It was a relief not to have to pretend to feel okay in front of Sam. "Though I guess I'm lucky that Annette didn't hit any major organs." The wound to her side was painful, but she'd live.

She met his eyes. "I think Annette wanted to die, Sam. After she got rid of the rest of The Six, she said, she had no plans. That's why she was willing to risk going back to the gym—she didn't care if she was killed. She couldn't tolerate another mental hospital, and after her mother died, she felt as if she had no reason to keep living."

"Suicide by cop," Sam said, his face grim. "The way Annette

staged this—coming back to the gym, marching past a police officer—ensured she'd be caught. And by making it look like she was on the brink of murdering you she made sure she'd be shot rather than taken into police custody."

Kate glared at him. "What do you mean 'making it look like' she was going to murder me? You think she was pretending? Because if you do, I'd like to point out this is *not* a little flesh wound here."

Sam held up his palm. "I'm not minimizing your injuries. But I think Annette didn't want you to die. After she slashed your side, she looked right at me, Kate, and raised her hand with the bloody scalpel, as if she was about to plunge it into you. She was showing me that she was going to finish you off if I didn't kill her first. And then I shot and killed her."

Granting Annette/Maria her last wish. Kate shook her head. "Her whole life—it was so sad."

"We learned her mother was also schizophrenic, in and out of mental hospitals all her life," Sam said. "That's why her father abandoned them; he couldn't cope with his wife's mental illness any longer. He just left the house one morning and never came back."

"Leaving his teenage daughter to cope with it alone," Kate said, her voice hard. "And then when the two of them moved to Houston, Annette also had to deal with an unfamiliar town and a new school with bullying classmates who took away the one thing she enjoyed: her acting. Allison and Lisa's insistence on grabbing Annette's part in the school play just pushed her over the edge. And after that she blamed The Six for everything that went wrong in her life."

Sam nodded. "But the thing I don't get is why now? Why did she wait all these years to seek retribution?"

"I can only guess about that," Kate said, "but I think some of it might have been due to her mother dying. Annette was close to her and probably wouldn't have done anything to endanger her own life while her mother still needed her. If Annette really did hesitate to kill me, I bet it's because I told her my mother was ill and I had to take care of her. It was just after her mother died when Annette read all of The Six's accounts of their perfect lives in the high school reunion newsletter and their bragging infuriated her. Everybody sounded wealthy, successful, happily married—the opposite of her own life. She was convinced they'd all stepped on a lot of other people to get where they were. And now, finally, it was the right time in her life when she could finally get her revenge for what they'd done to her."

"The irony," Sam said, "is that a lot of them *weren't* particularly successful or happy. They just wanted their classmates to think they were. And Annette apparently believed their self-aggrandizing B.S."

And due to their careless adolescent cruelty and their more recent need to impress their old high school classmates, four people, in the prime of their lives, had died.

Sam studied her face for a long moment. "Uh, I meant to ask you, Kate. About what Annette said about you having lost a baby."

Kate closed her eyes. "It's true. I gave birth the summer after my high school graduation. She—my daughter—died a few days later."

"I'm sorry," he said. She saw the glint of tears in his eyes as he glanced away. "I'm truly sorry."

"Me too. And until last night I never realized just how sorry—and how angry—I still am."

She slumped back on her pillow, exhausted, the wound in her side throbbing. There would be time later for introspection. Probably quite a lot of time would be needed to excavate the painful feelings she'd kept buried for so long.

Annette/Maria had turned her own rage outward, striking

back at her high school tormentors. Kate, on the other hand, had ignored her hurt and anger, telling herself the past didn't matter, she could leave it behind, alter it in the same way she'd changed her looks, her name, her old Plain Jane life. While Kate's coping method had not harmed other people, it had harmed herself.

She realized now that an essential part of her had been grievously injured by Todd's assault, Lisa's vicious rumor campaign, by her parents sending her away to give birth in secret at the horrible unwed mothers' home. Worst of all had been the death of her beautiful baby and the accompanying dream of having more children.

She'd told herself that the terrible losses had fueled her ambition, made her even more determined to build a successful career. And perhaps that was true. But the costs had been so high. While Dr. Kate Dalton was pretty, accomplished, and successful, she was also achingly lonely, afraid to trust others or show them the vulnerable person behind her shiny professional mask. And only now was Kate realizing it.

"Yet you saved the life of the person who initiated those attacks on you," Sam said.

Kate shrugged. "Lisa is a selfish jerk—she was in high school and she still is. But we can't choose who lives or dies based on how worthy we think they are."

"Matt and his wife believe that you probably saved his life too. Neither of them expected Annette to be dangerous. They just thought of her as Josh's date."

Kate glanced at the huge arrangement of flowers that Matt and Lauren had brought that morning, along with their heartfelt thanks. She suspected she was blushing as she said, "Well, they're generous people. They stopped in today to say goodbye before they drove back to Oklahoma." Lisa Smythe, too, had sent flowers with a message to "GET WELL SOON." Kate hoped that would be the last time she heard from Lisa.

Sam cleared his throat, looking uncharacteristically flustered. "Now that we're no longer professionally involved—except, of course, for Carly's future rhinoplasty—I was hoping we could spend more time together. If that's okay with you."

Kate started to say she wasn't sure about her plans for the future—how long she'd be in Houston, how much attention her mother was going to require. In fact, right now she didn't feel certain about much of anything.

But instead she took a deep breath and smiled. "I think that can be arranged."

ABOUT THE AUTHOR

Karen Hanson Stuyck is the author of five previous mystery novels: *A Novel Way to Die, Fit to Die, Cry for Help, Held Accountable,* and *Lethal Lessons.* She has worked as a newspaper reporter, an editor, and a public relations writer for hospitals and a mental health institution. Her short stories have been published in *Redbook, Cosmopolitan, Woman's World,* and other magazines. She lives in Houston.